Barking for Business

A Sharp Investigations Novel

Book One

BY: E. N. CRANE

EDITED BY: A. O. NEAL

Dedication

Thank you to my dogs: Perry and Padfoot.
Their shenanigans, antics and behavior are the model for all things Winnie.
Thank you to my husband, because he knows how many "people" live in my head and he's never had me committed. He also keeps me in coffee and snacks when I start yelling at imaginary people.
Special thanks to Jeff Neal for lending me his military knowledge. Most of this is made up, but I strive for imaginative accuracy.

Chapter One: The Cookie Caper

"Don't you dare hit my dog, Private!" I shouted through the open passenger side window of my MP vehicle. The lights and sirens were going, and we were causing quite a scene flying through the base. The car chase had started after Winnie jumped into the suspect's vehicle just outside the mess hall and we were now at least a mile away. I could barely make out the triangles of Winnie's ears, jumping on the Private's lap when his hand dropped toward his hip.

Gun! I thought.

I dropped my cookie and jerked the wheel of my car toward the fleeing suspect. He jumped and jerked his wheel, but I still couldn't see his hand.

"Your hand!" I shouted and he held them above his head, the car hit a bump and... crashed through a wall. The Jeep hit, bounced back, and then the bricks crumbled in a light rain around the car. I hit the brakes and climbed out, desperate to rescue my partner, Sgt. Winnifred Pupperson, K-9.

The subject ran screaming from the car, Winnie following behind him and nipping at his heels. Her tail wagging and leash dragging behind her, it was all a game to her. She came when I whistled and took her place beside me, a German Shepherd Malinois statue with food crumbs on her face. The wall had a vehicle sized gap, small bricks crumbling from the parts still standing. The Jeep he drove was demolished, accordion style. Its front bumper now beneath the steering wheel, front wheels facing opposite directions and vital fluids pooling beneath it.

"Gas! There's gas!" he shouted when I ordered him on the ground. His uniform said his name was Young.

I took two steps, sidearm drawn, to see that the brick wall his truck now sat in surrounded a fuel yard. Common sense said to put the gun away, so I grudgingly holstered the Sig Sauer after verifying the subject wasn't armed. I stared through the hole, wondering where everyone was. There were four pumps, the Jeep crashing nearest the first one from the left. The same pump where my commander stood, holding the nozzle and obscured by smoke. The man had nearly been obliterated, but he dared not move until someone confirmed he could. Crews rushed forward, someone pressed the e-stop for the fuel pumps and another soldier took the pump from his hand and hung it back up.

"Sir?" I called out. The figure didn't move.

I waited for a beat. Then another, but still nothing. Maybe it was an optical illusion. I took hold of my suspect walking him out of the immediate danger area, Winnie right beside me. Hoping to finally have the answer to his mysterious flight from the mess hall, I patted his pocket. In it, I found what the other soldier had handed him and pulled it out. It was a key. I stared at Private Young and watched his eyes dart to the rear of the vehicle, back to me. Not subtle in the least.

"Sit! Stay!" I ordered him, waiting for him to kneel before turning my attention to the smashed truck.

The rear of the vehicle looked safe enough to investigate, not on fire. Taking Winnie's leash, we approached slowly, not wanting to limit our ability to run if it caught suddenly. I had her scent the area and she alerted to the odor on a footlocker built into the rear compartment. Inserting the key, I popped open the lid and looked inside.

"Sharp!"

Seriously? He ran and fought my dog... over this?

"Sir?" I replied, but I couldn't see him.

A loud pop came from the engine compartment and Winnie and I retreated. Back at the subject, I hooked him up and frog-marched him to the MP truck. Once he was secured to the seat with the doors locked, I turned to the front seat and downed my iced coffee. The next few hours were going to suck, might as well motivate myself with the elixir of the gods. Standing away from both the scene and the suspect, I had a moment of regret that I hadn't gotten more coffee while in the mess hall. Note to self, always get more coffee.

Then, I waited for the commander to rise from the smoke and start yelling, my K-9 by my side.

"This is gonna suck, girl," I said, and she bumped her head against my hand in agreement.

It's hard to believe I made it this many years in the Army. Between my WNBA height and my Three Stooge's levels of coordination, the name Cynthia Sharp will never be in the books for winning a Medal of Honor. Maybe a Purple Heart, but it would be hard to prove my injuries were from the enemy. With lavender eyes and dishwater blonde hair, I was an anomaly on every continent. With the fur missile beside me, I was a natural disaster brass dubbed "Hurricane Cyn" when they were feeling kind.

"Why the hell is there a Jeep in the side of the fuel yard, Sharp?!?"

Sharp, said with such hatred and frustration I tried to shrink myself and look innocent. If I had a dollar for every time my name had been yelled in that tone, we'd have retired three days after MP school. Standing amid the chaos and swiftly arriving emergency vehicles, I could only imagine the legacy we'd leave on this base. Legacy being the kindest way to phrase it. Realistically, our names would live on in infamy for decades. To command staff, we were a menace. To our fellow soldiers, we were a joke.

To each other, we were everything.

Commander Allen, in charge of all military law enforcement personnel on base. His promotion had been hard-earned seven years ago, the hardest being the two and a half since I arrived. The trim, athletic man, stood over six feet tall. He had enough muscles to fill out the T-shirt he wore with the Digi-camo BDUs and his hair topped with a veteran hat he'd inherited from his father. I'd heard a rumor that he used to smile and be relatively jolly, but that was not the case since I arrived. I'd never seen so much as a lip twitch upward on that man's face, but I liked to pretend it was because of the location and not the company.

Florida, like always, was hot, humid and miserable. Also, on fire as the engine compartment of the crashed Jeep erupted in flames. The fire crews took a couple of steps back while another crew arrived. This crew had a new way of extinguishing flames that was messier but effective. The rig had caught quickly and burned hot, but it was out just as fast. Everyone still stayed clear as a few random pops erupted from the now burned and crushed vehicle.

I hate Florida, I thought as a bead of sweat tickled its way down my back. The chaos in front of me raged on, but it was the same thing on a different day. We hadn't had one day without something being completely destroyed, usually in the pursuit of trivial justice. Florida, designed to make you hate life, was never anything but hot and humid. Standing in the open on base was bad enough, standing in the open here was a form of torture that should be reserved for child molesters and people who smoke weed in traffic.

"Are you listening to me, soldier!" Commander Allen shouted and I snapped back to his eyes. His light grey eyes were so angry. His face dark red, and his eyeballs were abnormally large. Fairly certain it is unhealthy for him to be this angry in Florida. Maybe not this angry in general, but especially in Florida.

"Yes, sir!" I answered him automatically, glancing down at my partner.

Sgt. Winifred Pupperson, Sgt. Winnie for short, had her tongue lolling out of the side of her mouth. As the smoldering remains of the vehicle let out a cloud of jet-black smoke behind our commander, she looked not the least bit concerned over the disaster. Her weight leaned on her left leg, her right stuck out in a devil-may-care jaunt and her face registered exactly zero fluffs.

A long awkward pause followed, but I stared straight ahead. More awkward silence. I glanced down at Winnie. She looked back at me, nothing. My eyes went back to the commander. I blinked at him twice. He stared at me. Winnie let out a yawn.

He remained silent.

How long has he been silent? I thought. Still nothing.

"Sir?" I asked and his face transitioned from red to an almost purple. This man had been in the Army for more decades than I'd been alive and if he died tomorrow, it would probably be my fault. Well, it would probably be Winnie's fault, but no one distinguished between the K-9 and the handler. At least they hadn't in my career, but there was always room for a first.

"I asked you to explain!" he shouted again, gesturing behind him. The ground around us is now completely covered in foam and a dry extinguishing agent while a group of men try to clear the area to get a tow truck in. Three men stacked bricks while two more stood by to assist with a sudden combustion.

At least it is no longer on fire, I thought, just as an ember shot up to prove me wrong.

In my four years with the Army, I had admittedly caused a few international incidents. There was the demolished marketplace in Afghanistan, the destroyed cheese wheel in Germany, the cow in Sweden who I still insist died of a heart attack unrelated to us. This though, was by far our biggest and most spectacular stunt for something trivially illegal.

"Theft of personal snackage and toiletries," I chose my words carefully. His experience kept his face steady, but even I struggled to believe it and I was there for the whole thing. Why was it never drugs or bombs that started these things? Why was I never the national hero who thwarted a terrorist? At the end of the day, I'd never once solved a crime that mattered on a national scale. Maybe I would never save the world, but I never thought I would destroy so many things in so many parts of it over freaking cookies.

"Explain, soldier!" He shouted again through gritted teeth. I stared straight ahead, mind over-analyzing and curiously blank. There simply were no words. It was too long a silence after my first failure to pay attention.

"On the ground, soldier!"

Resisting the urge to sigh, I assumed a push-up position. Sgt. Winnie, assuming this meant playtime, jumped on my back and covered my already sweat sticky face with slobber. The ground was melting your flesh warm and somehow also damp. Everything in Florida was always damp. *I hate Florida, I hate Florida,*

I thought, each word marking another push-up. I was not built to live in the humidity. I was not built to conduct high speed chases. I was not built for the Army. My lack of finesse, grace and physical agility made me stand out from most of my unit. I couldn't blend, I couldn't conform, and most importantly: I couldn't go a single day without destroying government property.

I push-up *hate* push-up *Florida* push-up.

"On your feet, soldier!" My commander commanded and I popped tall. At some point during my fitness motivated attitude assistance, Winnie had grown bored and flopped on her side. She now had four paws stretched out, her elongated neck emphasizing the constantly working nose. I tried to discreetly nudge her with the toe of my boot, but she refused to take this moment seriously. Winnie refused to take anything in life seriously and it was part of the reason we made a great team.

"Now, explain this!" he commanded, and I once again took in the carnage behind him.

"Sir, Sgt. Winnie and I were conducting surveillance in the mess hall at the request of Captain Jacks," I began. "He came to the guard shack repeatedly, reporting that he thought there was a thief on base. He had no evidence, suspects, or suggested course of action so everyone could decline to investigate. Everyone except me, because he knows my record is... spotty."

"What did he say went missing, Specialist?" he asked, his face returning to a slightly more normal color. We'd reached the tricky part, because he was starting to look borderline healthy, and had even called me by my proper title and rank. As soon as I explained the definition of "personal snackage", it would all go south. Captain Jacks remained poorly regarded, both on base or off of it. He had a slight frame, thin hair, and beady eyes that made him look both terrifying and suspicious. His rank was earned with education, granting him the ability to by-pass grunt work and go straight to... whatever he did. No one had ever actually explained what Capt. Jacks' function on the base was, and it didn't seem like a good time to ask.

He was a commanding officer with rank, shiny shoes, and inflated ego. Three things I avoided whenever possible. While avoiding the commander was problematic, harder to avoid is the visual of an Army base on fire. I let out a small sigh. I needed an out and I had no options.

"Sir..." I started as another cloud of smoke shot out of the engine block and drifted lazily toward the sky. I stayed ramrod straight, Winnie lifted a single eyelid, and we watched for another catastrophe.

Nothing happened.

"I want the full report, Sharp," he advised. I nodded and watched the smoldering remains of a military Jeep. Hard to decide if I'd rather give this report or be on fire.

Probably being on fire would end quicker.

"He said the thief was stealing his cookies, sir. Cookies and clean towels, but he was especially concerned about the cookies," I answered. It was one thing to investigate stolen cookies to make the brass happy and quite another to have to explain how you set fire to government property doing it.

"He said that every day at lunch he would go into the mess hall, order his food, and while he filled his drink cup, his cookies would always go missing. Right from his tray, while he stood

9

there. Seemed like a straightforward observe and report, I just had to stand kind of out of the way and watch. Winnie had been banned from the motor pool after the... incident with the wheel grease. So I brought her in with me while the car underwent routine maintenance. It turned out that his cookies were falling off his tray because he was trying to balance the cup with his teeth and tilted the tray 45-degrees, which he didn't notice. Then he'd slam his hand on the tray and send the cookies flying, kicking them under the counter shuffling to the right back to his tray. There was like... three dozen cookies under there."

"So you told him his cookies were under the counter?" Commander Allen asked skeptically and I bit my lip.

"No, sir. First I needed to compose myself. While I was taking a moment, I saw the soldier operating that Jeep, Young according to his uniform approach another. The meeting looked pre-planned. Both were sweating and constantly looking around so I dropped into a chair to watch. They talked for a minute maybe, Young handing the second soldier a folded stack of money. In exchange, Young received something small that he stuffed into his cargo pocket."

"Who was the other soldier, Specialist?" Commander Allen interrupted and I was relieved to hear that I was still "specialist" and not back to soldier.

"Garcia, sir. So casually, I strolled past Private Young and had Winnie check his pocket. She alerted and I ordered him to empty his pockets. Then... it kind of went wrong," I said and dropped my gaze. I could barely get the words out anymore without laughing. Not a laugh of amusement, but the desperate laugh of the mad trying to understand how it all went so wrong.

Winnie chose that moment to let out an incredibly loud fart with a smell that had even the seasoned commander taking a step back and I had to choke back a giggle fit with a cough.

"Both men panicked. Garcia took off toward Captain Jacks and knocked him over. Private Young went toward the chow line. Young had whatever it was in his pocket and Winnie took off after him. Sadly, it *is* the chow line. As you know, she is mostly motivated by snacks and a chow line is... is a chow line. Young barreled through the line, Winnie pursued stealing food and gaining ground fast. Honestly if I could run and eat at the same time like that, I might run more. Anyway, Young dove out of a back door and... tactically acquired a military jeep. At least, that's what I thought at first but it must have been left for him. Winnie jumped through the unzipped back window just as he gunned the engine and I had to drop the leash."

"You let your K-9 go rogue?" his eyes were bulging. My gaze dropped down lower, but I kept my chin parallel to the ground. It was one of the first things you learned at Lackland, you lead the K-9, they don't lead you. If they are in front of you it's because you allowed them to be. I essentially gave Sgt. Winnie free rein to... crash a military Jeep.

"Yes, sir. I recovered my vehicle and initiated a pursuit. I'm not wholly clear on all of the events, but it would seem Private Young ran through something... tasty... in his bid for freedom. From what I could see, she was trying to eat his pants and he thought she was attacking him. He started hitting her and I shouted at him to stop. He reached to his side and I thought he was armed, so I swerved toward his car, startling him. He jerked his steering wheel to the right and drove through the wall of the fuel yard. He exited the vehicle, I questioned him, and recovered the item from his person. Then... the fire started and... well... you were there."

A muscle in the commander's jaw was working. He was either considering his options, evaluating the story, or he found something in his teeth. The silence was deafening.

"What was in Private Young's pocket? Cocaine, Heroin, Weed?" Commander Allen asked. He was clearly angry at the events, but it was unclear who the anger was directed at. Me, Private Young, Winnie or the world in general. Likely, it was the first but I preferred to remain optimistic that it was someone else this time.

"No, sir. Winnie only does explosives detection. What was in his pocket was the keys to a locked trunk in the Jeep. The key must have smelled like residual explosives because when I opened the trunk, it was full of illegal fireworks," I answered and we both looked back at the Jeep. The firefighters, suited up for fuel fires, were still standing by. They were just watching the smoldering carcass of the Jeep's engine compartment. They had immediately shut off fuel to the pumps, but why hadn't they moved the car? It seemed like poor planning to not have moved the car.

"Where are the fireworks, Specialist?" he asked, looking at his shoes. He was either dumbstruck that I foiled an actual crime, or just tired of looking at me. Either way, he wasn't yelling.

"They are still in the back of the truck, sir," I answered.

We watched the Jeep, the firefighters standing next to it, and stared.

I should have removed the fireworks.

"You should have removed the fireworks," he confirmed my personal thought. He took a step forward, Winnie getting to her feet. "Let's get them before this gets any worse."

We took four steps toward the vehicle when an ember sparked from the engine. We stopped and watched, convinced there was no way it could... but it did. The ember floated through the open rear canvas of the Jeep and drifted to...

"We should run, sir," I shouted, and turned. Grabbing Winnie's leash, I made a dash for the nearest, non-flammable building. I could hear the commander running behind me, just as a whoosh sounded. It was followed by a crackle, two explosions and I turned just in time to see the sky light up with green circles... and everything caught fire.

The commander's personal vehicle, the Jeep full of fireworks, the fuel yard, and the firetruck were completely engulfed in flames. Despite the gear, the firefighters wisely chose flight over fight. Without access to the truck, there was no choice but to stand-by and watch it burn. Four more aerial fireworks burst into the air. They were red, white and blue and I mentally gave them a salute.

"That could have gone better," I muttered. Winnie grumbled in agreement and nudged my pocket. I handed her a dog cookie and popped an Oreo in my mouth. "Definitely could have gone better."

Chapter Two:
Court Martialed

"All rise for the Honorable Judge Pianka," a short, bald man older than my father announced. The room stood as one, wooden chairs scraping ancient floors in the echoing cavern of military court. I was in my dress greens, hat neatly set on the wooden defense table, medals and ribbons pinned to my button-down jacket and my shoes polished enough to be their own beacon during a full moon. My hair was in a bun that thanks to the air conditioning, only required a pound of hairspray and my shirt probably wouldn't be capable of sustaining life.

"You may be seated," the judge said and I sat. I was pushed back from the table, staring at my shoes. I'd been in court before. I'd met Judge Pianka before. I'd sat in the galley, in the witness box and at the prosecution table.

I had never been the defense.

Sgt. Winnifred Pupperson was on the ground beside me. She was wearing her vest, name stuck on the side with Velcro, her military collar, and a stupid expression that mocked me. Her tongue was hanging out the side of her mouth, her eyes were squinted and with every pant she was laughing.

Laughing.

My eyes shifted back to my shoes. Beside me was the court appointed attorney, but there wasn't much for him to do. Not after the news broadcast... and the memes... and the videos online from the chow hall... not to mention the mild wildfire the fireworks started.

Behind me, I could hear Captain Jacks breathing heavily. When Private Garcia ran into him, his lunch smashed all over his uniform, and thanks to Winnie, there wasn't replacement food. Hangry, he'd stormed back to his quarters to see he was trending. A few non-commissioned officers had been making a video of him losing the cookies every day and it was now a natural disaster remix set to an up-tempo beat. In the row behind him was Commander Allen, wearing the first smile I'd seen since the day I arrived. It was the day Winnie peed on the foot of a visiting colonel by way of introduction and both men decided we were rotten apples. In her defense, the colonel smelled like pine trees and we'd just spent three days camping on "mandatory reassignment leave". In my defense, I thought it was hilarious and couldn't stop laughing. OK, so that's not a defense and I still don't feel bad about it.

Or, I didn't until I looked up at the panel and saw Colonel Ross staring down his hooked nose at me. He had beady eyes and wiry glasses. His hair was long and dark and greasy... no, wait, that's Professor Snape. Colonel Ross was a white man, with white hair and white teeth and far too many visible nose hairs. I had been informed your nose and ear hair grows extra-long when you get older, but he still could have trimmed it for this hearing.

Just like I could have reprimanded Winnie for peeing on him.

The judge sat in the middle of the table, between the four members he'd filed in with. All of them were in uniform, and all of them were sporting rank I'd never see even if I wasn't about to be kicked out of the Army. Besides Colonel Ross and Judge Pianka, there was Winnie's trainer at Lackland, Sgt. Ian Cruz, beside him was a man I'd never seen before and a woman I knew very well. She was the most terrifying of all of them because she had in front of her a very thick file folder. Lt. Karina Suttles, Personnel and Records, and holder of the complete list of my military indiscretions. From tricking my recruiter into sending me to basic despite my weight all the way to the blown-up fuel yard. I'm not even sure that was all of the reports or just a summary list. One folder hardly seemed enough to cover my career... at least the indiscretions contained within it. The novel in front of Judge Pianka looked more on par with what I expected.

He flipped it open, confirming my suspicions.

"For the record," Judge Pianka began, shuffling the papers in front of him. "This hearing is a Fitness for Service review of Specialist Cynthia Sharp and her K-9, Sgt. Winnie."

He then read our service history into the record.

Our complete service record.

At the start of this hearing, I had two paper cups of coffee in front of me. My lawyer, Lt. Gunn, had mistakenly thought one of the cups was for him until I growled. The first cup was half empty when Judge Pianka started reading. I was a third of the way through the second when he stopped.

It would seem that when it came to military working dogs, not all were created equal. Sgt. Winnie was destined to be a house pet when someone came along and thought she would like a job. With her working line heritage of Belgian Malinois mother and German Shepherd father, the breeder expected great things from her. She learned her basic obedience faster than the rest of her litter mates, was at the peak of physical fitness, and was presented for duty at Lackland without the slightest reservation she'd be the first picked, first to pass and the first to be off saving the world with the next incoming class of MPs.

The same could not be said of me graduating Basic Training. I was able to get the MOS as military police not because I was the best, but because I refused to be anything else. When I'd signed up, I wanted to work with K-9s, and the only certain way to do that was to be an MP. My main qualifications were an ability to stay up for days on end and shoot with terrifying amounts of accuracy. The rest of my soldiering skills were average to lacking but I got by. Despite my outward plus-size appearance, I ran the mile in just the barely passing time frame, managed the minimum number of push-ups and sit-ups in the two-minute limit. I was chosen for the K-9 program because at the time of assignment, I was the only one who applied. I'm still not sure why none of my classmates requested the assignment, but I had a feeling they knew I would do whatever it took to go. So, they made it possible.

Winnie and I arrived at Lackland two months apart. Though she was top of her class, none of the previous groups had found a handler who would work with her. Words like *stubborn* and *disobedient* were thrown around. Along with words like *unmotivated* and *lacking in drive*, we were basically carbon copies on paper. It had been the hope of someone higher up to get rid of two problems by pairing us together, assuming I would quit when presented with such a dog and she could finally be washed out after the third handler failed.

Our first day together, we had the unfortunate privilege of being assigned night watch. While I thrived in the pitch-black night, Winnie was more suited to daytime sunbathing. A munitions vehicle was moving through the base but it was going the wrong way. Cautiously, we followed it and reported our suspicions to the base commander... Just in time for Winnie to smell the jerky one man had in his pocket. She attacked the masked, fake soldier and ripped open his pocket for the jerky. He surrendered quickly and we foiled a gun heist orchestrated by an inside man.

Unfortunately, we also sent four soldiers to the infirmary with gunshot wounds. Not from the suspects, nope. Those gunshots were from munitions that exploded in the fire Winnie started when she tackled the man with the jerky who was holding a Molotov cocktail. They outlined that incident in addition to our unfortunate destruction of a marketplace in Afghanistan and the destruction of a national treasure in Germany.

I stopped reminiscing when the unknown Captain began speaking.

"Specialist Sharp, Attorney Lt. Gunn, I am here to address the incident that occurred on November 13th at 1300 hours. Specialist Cynthia Sharp and Sgt. Winifred Pupperson," the man spoke before hesitating. He stared at the paper in front of him, looked at me, then looked at the dog in question.

"Sgt. Cruz?" Mystery captain asked the man at the end of the table.

"Yes, sir, that is her name," Cruz confirmed. Ian was a handsome man, dark hair with broad shoulders and a complexion that would probably do better in Miami than San Antonio. He was six-foot something and his eyes were the same color as Crater Lake on a stormy day. He gave me a smirk before answering and my heart stuttered, just a single beat. It had been a while since we'd been in the same room and we had an almost history.

Winnie sat up at the sound of his voice and let out a low whimper.

"Her breeder's daughter named her, sir," Sgt. Cruz added, but the Captain still wasn't satisfied. Ian and I had spent a fair amount of time together during training and of all the people at the table, he was probably the only one who knew me well enough to hate me. The fact that he didn't hate me said more about his character than mine, because I'm not exactly delightful when asked to let 90-pound dogs jump on and bite me repeatedly. Day after day, week after week, bruise after bruise. When he'd disappeared in Afghanistan, only to reappear in my quarters the day I was leaving, I'd given Winnie a lot of treats

19

for the headbutt to the family jewels she'd offered. I snapped out of my bitter reverie when he answered a second question for Mystery Captain. "She really loved Hocus Pocus, sir."

Mystery Captain nodded, I assume to keep things moving, because he didn't so much as smile. Probably he had no idea who the Sanderson Sisters were. The military had tried to change Winnie's name when she got to Lackland, but she remained Winnifred Pupperson. There are rumors and folklore surrounding such things, but the fact remains the score is: Army zero, stubborn K-9 one.

"Alright, the investigation conducted by my staff found that you violated three very serious policies in the apprehending of the suspect, Derrick Young. While the crime was actionable, you allowed your K-9 to operate independently, you purposefully drove toward another soldier's vehicle while both were in motion, and you failed to secure evidence that turned out to be combustible from the scene of an incident. Is there anything not included in this overview?"

"No, sir," I answered. It was technically a fib, since I'm pretty sure having Winnie in the Chow Hall was a violation of health codes of some kind, my socks were not black like they were supposed to be and I had been eating Oreos while in pursuit of Private Young.

None of that seemed especially important, though.

"The review of your service record shows that you spent six months in Afghanistan, after which you spent eight months in Germany before you arrived here in Florida. There is a note here that says you are not allowed back in either of those countries as an agent of American defense. Is that correct?"

"Yes, sir," I answered, and he stared at me with a slightly open-mouthed look of awe. Apparently, the brief summary of both incidents as "destruction of public property" hadn't quite landed with him. Sgt. Cruz, however, was wearing an ear-to-ear grin and Lt. Suttles was masking a laugh as a cough.

Beside me, I felt my attorney shaking very subtly. I spared him a glance out of the corner of my eye and saw that he was also laughing. My own attorney, laughing. With a sense of petty vengeance, I stretched my leg out and lifted it. With a casual cough, I dropped it down and ground the heel of my dress shoe into his foot. He choked mid-laugh, upending his water cup. The sound of the glass hitting the table startled Winnie and she jumped up on full alert. Landing on the defense table, she growled at the now soaking wet notebook.

"It's OK, girl," I said, pressing my hand gently along the length of her back. She settled, for a moment, before placing her head down on the table.

"Specialist Sharp, why aren't you allowed in Germany?" Mystery Captain said, pretending not to notice the 90-pound dog on the table in front of me. She was licking at the spilled water with her tongue. As she cleared an area, she crawled farther along the table, nudging the legal pad in front of Lt. Gunn. Every nudge of the legal pad sent it closer to the edge of the table. Mesmerized, I forgot to answer.

"Sharp?" Pianka prompted and I shook off the trance.

"Technically, sir, I'm allowed in Germany. Just not with Sgt. Pupperson," I said and continued to watch the notebook move closer and closer to the edge. Without warning, Winnie's head shot up, ears and nose toward the galley. I tightened my grip on her leash, "Winnie, no."

Too late.

She launched herself off the table and over the railing behind me. I held firm on her leash, issuing corrections and orders, but it meant nothing. Captain Jacks had NutterButters and he decided that moment was a great time to open them. Winnie's paws hit him square in the chest and the whole bench rocked. He screamed, not at all manly, and tried to shove Winnie off. She slobbered on his face, stole the cookies, and effortlessly scaled the railing to resume her seat beside the defense table. Silently shaking my head, I removed the remainder of the wrapper from the cookies and placed it in the trash bin under the table.

"Specialist Sharp," Colonel Ross said, his voice sounding harsh.

"Yes, sir?" I asked, forcing my gaze onto his.

"Do you have any control over that dog?" he seethed, and my hackles went up. It was one thing to call me a catastrophe but treating Winnie and I as less than a single unit was going too far. This dog and I had been to war together, scrubbed barrack bathrooms together, and once we accidentally detained a US Marshall who was undercover and made him lose track of his suspect.

But we'd done it together.

"I do, sir. There is a sign in front of this courtroom forbidding food and drinks beyond water in the proceedings. Winnie was enforcing the law we swore to uphold, as she has done countless times before in the past four years. She then rewarded herself with the confiscated item," I said and watched Sgt. Cruz's eyes fill with amusement. Judge Pianka had a massive grin, and Lt. Suttles was trying to mask her laughter with yet another dignified cough. Crappy record or not, I was very entertaining for those who stayed on Winnie's good side.

"I hold your future in my hand, Sharp, and you want to talk back to me?" the colonel said with indignation. I rose to my feet, Winnie taking hers as well. We were prepared to fight, and my attorney decided that was a good time to do his job.

"Objection, your honor. While Colonel Ross sits on the board, he does not solely hold the decision of Specialist Sharp's continued service in his hand. Additionally, Winnie is trained to obey and enforce all rules and regulations. It was a statement of fact."

"Sustained," Judge Pianka said and the colonel went red in the face. Mystery Captain was still staring open-mouthed. No one was inclined to speak, least of all me. I had some choice words, a few hand gestures and a bag of Winnie poop for the colonel, but none of that would be especially helpful just this moment.

"Specialist, in the interest of my happiness, why is Sgt. Winifred Pupperson no longer allowed in Germany?" Judge Pianka said and Sgt. Cruz sat up straighter. I stared at my thumbs, painted in their boring beige nail polish and the omnipresent dirt under them. It was ridiculous that I even stayed in the Army, I might as well go out on a high note.

"Cheese, sir. Cheese and sausage. We were patrolling Oktoberfest and a rather rude man tried to taunt Winnie with a sausage. He then tried to steal sausages and claim they were his right as leader of the festival. Winnie endeavored to uphold that law as well by retrieving the stolen merchandise. In the process, she knocked over a hundred-pound cheese wheel and crushed a national treasure," I said, smiling at the memory of the squished statue.

"Did they survive?" he asked, flipping through his notes on my military record.

"What? The sausage man? Yes, though he no longer taunts police dogs," I answered, but he was still staring.

"The national treasure, did they survive?" he asked again, and I shook my head.

"No, once it was crushed, I think the birds ate it," I answered and noticed a few members of the panel go pale. For a group of seasoned military personnel, they were taking the death of pretzel sculpture very hard.

"Sgt. Winnie killed someone?" his voice was strangled, and he reached for his water. "Then the body was eaten by birds?"

"Well, it was made of pretzel dough, sir," I said and the alarm changed to confusion as everyone but Sgt. Cruz and Lt. Gunn tried to figure out what I was talking about.

"The national treasure wasn't alive, sir. It was a pretzel statue of a man who served as a government official. The same guy who was stealing sausages. He was presiding over the festival as some sort of chairman. He insisted his statue was a national treasure, though the people didn't look especially offended," I clarified and still, everyone was confused.

Everyone but Cruz, who had a smirk and was making the *keep going* gesture with his hand. I decided to pretend I was blind because the rest of the story was irrelevant. No one needed to know that the same man had grabbed my ass in a poorly judged drunken maneuver and taken a fist to the face.

"You were barred from a country for crushing a pretzel statue?" Judge Pianka asked, and I crossed my fingers behind my back.

"Yes, sir. Though the man was fired. I think if I asked nicely, the German people would allow me back in their country," I answered. Now it was Lt. Gunn's turn to dig his heel into my shoes, but I pretended not to feel that. He had wimpy heels and I'd been bitten repeatedly by the aforementioned K-9's.

"Are there any more questions from the panel?" Judge Pianka asked, looking up and down at his fellow members. I hesitated as they shook their heads and then spoke.

"Sir, before this concludes, can I make a request?"

"You can make a request Sharp; I cannot guarantee you it will be granted," Judge Pianka said. His face showed curiosity and humor. He had laugh lines in the corners of his eyes, his forehead creased from years of brow raises, and I realized how much this job had aged him. He couldn't have been more than 40 years old, but he looked older than Ross. Ross looked like a butter-bar through and through. Lt. Suttles face held apology and Cruz... well, he just looked perfect.

"Sir, Sgt. Winnie... what will happen to her?" I asked, looking down at the dog in question. Her face was rested on crossed paws, body at rest, eyebrows moving. She was the picture of innocence, adorable and guilt free. "We are a team, whatever else has happened over the years, we're a team. She's my best friend and she doesn't listen to anyone else."

"That's a question, Cynthia, not a request," the Judge said and my eyes went to him. The professionalism had faded and he was looking at us with kindness and gratitude. "You and Winnie are officially civilians as of four days ago. Administrative error with your contract, you were honorably discharged. There's a C-130 flight to Ohio in three days and you're on the list. Thank you for your service, Sharp. You are going to be a legend on this base for a long time to come."

Chapter Three:
Like Mother, Like Daughter

"Ma, you don't have to shout. That's not how phones work," I said, rubbing my temples.

"When are you getting here?" she shouted again and I clawed my fingers down my face. "When does your plane leave?"

"It leaves an hour ago," I said, flopping back against the bench. It's 80 degrees, I'd already sweat through my jeans and T-shirt, and my water bottle was dangerously close to empty. The plane had arrived on time, but no one had been allowed to board until it was loaded... or unloaded. Just another day of hurry up and wait... and melting.

"What?" she shouted, and I saw Sgt. Cruz moving across the tarmac. "I can't hear you. I'm in the car!"

"Ma, call me later!" I shouted into the phone.

"You don't need to shout, Cyn," she scolded me and I banged my head against the wall behind the bench. If I had anywhere else to go, literally anywhere, I wouldn't go home. I was a late in life baby, my siblings were all well into their 40s and popping out babies like it was going out of style. My parents were retired, staying employed just long enough for me to get my own health insurance. All my siblings were at the top of their field. Heidi is a doctor, Seth is a structural engineer, and Molly... Molly did something philanthropic that kept her in third-world countries. She said they needed her skills more than Americans did.

I think she just wanted a break from the delights of family.

"Bye, ma!" I said and hung up with my eyes closed. Three weeks. I'd be in that town, in that house, for three weeks and then I'd... I'd suck it up because there was nowhere else to go, but I'd have my own place in that stupid town.

Hopefully.

"Being kind of rude, aren't you?" said a soft male voice next to me and I rolled my eyes behind my lids.

"Thumper rules, dude. If you can't say something nice, hang up before you get in trouble," I answered and I felt him shift closer.

"Or punch them in the face?" he said, the Cuban coming through subtly and my eyes snapped open.

"Shut up, Cruz," I hissed and looked around. No one else was nearby, but the last thing I needed was the "honorable" taken out of my discharge.

"He deserved it," Ian Cruz- avenger of ladies. He passed me an ice-cold water bottle. "You should have mentioned it at your hearing. If a prime minister had grabbed my ass, I'd have done more than punch him in the face and crush his statue with a cheese wheel."

"It was a formality. I was already not in the military anymore, and I'm guessing it would have done nothing but further prove Winnie and I have no control," I said, gratefully cracking the seal and taking a long drink. I looked down and saw Winnie had emptied another water bowl, so I gave her the rest of mine. She sniffed it once, pawed at the edge and dumped the whole thing on the ground where she proceeded to lick at the puddle like an ASPCA commercial. "You're an asshole."

"But I'm a cute asshole, right?"

"Not you, fool," I said and shoved him in the arm. "But... maybe."

"Fool? College educated and 'fool' is the best you can do? You disappoint me, Sharp," he said and my face burned.

"Who told you I went to college?" I checked the area for witnesses, again. I needed to murder him for knowing too much, but no weapons were nearby. Such a shame to get my hands dirty, but some things weren't meant for everyone to know. My education, punching a foreign diplomat, and kissing my training sergeant in an alley in Afghanistan.

"I have sources, chica. Don't question that I know more about you than anyone else in this place," he said and wiggled his brow. I gave him another eye roll. "We got interrupted overseas, maybe we can try again."

"What are you doing out here?" I asked, changing the subject again.

I looked at him properly and saw he wore jeans and an olive drab tee topped with a lightweight flannel. He looked comfortable and casual, while I had pit stains and under-boob sweat. The sound of a suitcase rolling on the ground made its way to us and we watched Captain Jacks wheel his bag toward the plane. It hit a rock, tipped to the side, and burst open. Towels, socks and T-shirts took off across the tarmac and he tried to run after them as the wind whipped his underwear out of the case. His face was creased with worry and concern.

"Waiting for my flight," he answered. His gaze was not on the captain and I turned to see a half-dozen airmen walking from the C-130. Three of the Air Force females stared at Sgt. Cruz and started giggling, turning red and offering him a mock salute.

"Don't let me keep you from your ride," I muttered. A twinge went through my stomach. Definitely not jealousy... Nope. Afghanistan was so long ago, why would I be jealous of members of the Chair Force? It's not like he'd called or emailed... or visited. I shook it off and stroked Winnie's head. Her fur sticky and gross, just like me, and there was still no sign the plane would board soon.

"Green is not a good color on you, Cyn," he said with a nudge on my shoulder. "I haven't forgotten Afghanistan and I certainly haven't forgotten-"

"Shows what you know, I joined the Army because I look *fantastic* in green," I said, side-stepping the accusation. I was definitely not jealous.

"Liar, liar," he whispered right against my ear and I shuddered despite the heat. Bumps ran down my arm and I caught the scent of something warm, masculine, but sweet. He laughed softly and I moved away from him. The man messed with my mind and it was way too hot and humid to think clearly.

"Headed back to San Antonio?" I asked and he shook his head, putting his hand next to mine on the bench. Not that I noticed... or wanted it closer. Nope, just the heat and boredom... maybe.

"No, I am working out of Wright-Patterson for the time-being. Just a half hour or so away from you in... what is it? Yellow Springs?" he said casually, but my pulse quickened. This man who had tortured me and given me my best friend was going to be my geographic neighbor. The man I'd thought would be my last kiss before I blew up... who'd.... Winnie let out a whimper and I tried not to answer with one of my own. "Will I be seeing you, Sgt. Pupperson?"

He extended his hand to Winnie and gave her a rub behind the ears. She melted like chocolate in the desert and I found myself judging her. She gave in so quickly for a little affection and she was the one who'd head-butted his man parts and ended what promised to be a fulfilling encounter. He turned his eyes full on me and I swallowed hard. Probably just the heat. I definitely didn't salivate for anything... except chocolate.

"I like the going home outfit," he said, eyes in line with my chest. He extended his hand and I felt my cheeks flush as his hand skimmed my shoulders, sliding down my back and going for... my cell phone. It had been on the bench next to me and he took a finger to unlock my phone, making very deliberate eye contact while I worked my mouth like a hooked fish.

I shuddered.

"Yeah, they asked me to go home in civvies," I said without thinking.

"Don't want you representing the Army in public?" he asked with a wide smile. He typed something into my phone and handed it back just as his phone alerted. It was a happy chirp of some sort, it suited him only in that I'd never heard it before. He pulled it out and started working the keys while I registered my mistake. Never give information to the enemy.

"Shut up, Cruz," I muttered and crossed my arms defiantly. He laughed and slid his phone back in his pocket.

"I suppose I should go help the Captain reclaim his skivvies," Ian said, standing up. He raised his hands over his head and his shirt rose, just a little, giving a glimpse of muscle and smooth skin. I involuntarily licked my lips and he chuckled. "I'll be in touch, Cyn."

He tugged my ponytail, turning my face up and brushing a kiss across my temple. Just as quick, he went to help Captain Jacks at a light jog. I looked down at my phone and saw he had sent himself a text message. We had exchanged numbers... just numbers, I reminded myself. Afghanistan was a long time ago and he hadn't kept in touch then. This wouldn't be any different. Nope, exactly the same. Stop pounding stupid heart.

"So..." I said, watching his jeans hug his butt as he crossed the field. "That... happened."

Winnie wiggled her eyebrows at me and I nodded.

"Yeah... not that weird... but the view was nice."

She let out a grumble.

"What do you think?"

Winnie dropped her head into the puddle she'd made spilling her water dish. She grumbled again, let out a wide yawn, and farted. I stared at her and smiled. My mom was going to hate Winnie and I was suddenly very excited to go home.

Six hours later, we landed at Wright-Patterson and I decided murdering the president to never get on a plane again, is a brilliant solution to a new problem. Sure, that was an extreme response, but honestly, it's the risk you take with the job and I'm not a fan of bureaucrats. Really, anyone who could run for office had never experienced life from the perspective of the governed. They were all men of means who made policies affecting people that never touched them personally. Nope, I was willing to give up my freedom if it meant never doing this again and getting rid of one less privileged pompous... I stuffed a cookie in my mouth wishing it were coffee. I hadn't had a day this long since 48 hours of physical exertion in Basic. In the mud and the rain. Yet even sleep deprived jumping jacks would have been better than the hours I spent in Florida, ready and waiting to leave on the hot and humid tarmac.

I really hate Florida.

It had been another hour after Sgt. Cruz walked away before the powers that be let us aboard. We'd been out of water for 45 minutes, the sweat stains had turned into a wet T-Shirt contest, and Winnie had declared my duffel her personal shelter. Once onboard, the seats were net and every sweat soaked inch of me chafed on the straps. Winnie had to be attached to me by regulation, and there was no good place to attach her to me in my jeans and T-shirt so I wrapped a belt around my thigh and clipped her to it. At the time it seemed genius, but the idiot next to me had a pocket full of snacks and despite being four feet away, I could identify every one. She'd started crawling toward them at take-off and by the end of the six-hour flight, my inner thigh muscles on my right leg could crush a man's skull... Right after they stopped twitching.

The aircraft hadn't been any less hot and humid than the base, until we were at altitude. My sweat dried and the clothing was now a crunching mass of cotton that had started to bring new meaning to abrasive. Limping and maneuvering my way toward the exit while maintaining safe distancing, I tripped on Winnie. She let out a howl, we crashed to the floor and my leg started twitching from the incomprehensible amount of stretching and strength training it had just endured. Winnie followed her howls with barking and we were given a wide berth as her teeth gnashed at the air. At least a dozen boots shuffled past us while I gripped her leash with white knuckles. It was the perfect end to a perfect day and still it had the nerve to drag on. By the time we were upright and the coast was clear for us to leave, only the flight crew remained onboard.

Solo, and with a new pain on my left elbow, I braced myself for the horrors I would meet outside. Would someone be delivering dog kibble or potato chips? No way to know except get off the plane. I stepped off the aircraft, and was met with a brisk wind that made me smile. I closed my eyes and took a long inhale after verifying no such lures were present. The air was crisp and smelled like fall. Just beyond the fence were hills coated in a soft white blanket, trees with leaves of a million colors and the scent of fireplaces drifted lazily through the air. Ohio in November has snow, cold weather, and hot coffee. I couldn't help feeling grateful that this was home. Bliss at the idea I'd never again live in Florida.

My second thought was holy hell why don't I have a hoodie.

Teeth chattering, I shouldered my duffle and held tight to Winnie's leash. Head down, I started toward the nearest building and prayed it would lead to the outside world. Winnie looked around elated, and started immediately dragging me toward an open area for a well-deserved break. Her tail was wagging at an alarming rate, her mouth spread open in a smile. Cold and near death or not, she just looked too happy to refuse. Arms crossed, head bent, I prepared for the bitter cold while she had her fill of fresh air. I braced myself for death when something warm wrapped itself around my shoulders.

"Oh god, thank you," I said and turned to see a smiling Sgt. Cruz.

"Not God, but close depending on who you ask," he said with a wink and I rolled my eyes.

"If it's the airmen brigade, I doubt they have much experience to compare you too," I smirked back at him. "But if it makes you feel like a man, knock yourself out."

"Speaking of feeling like a man, you weren't really ready for home, were you?" he asked and my eyes narrowed as he scanned my body up and down. Reflexively I crossed my arms under his gaze and felt the jacket slip.

"I was in the Army, not the Coast Guard. I'm not 'semper paratus'," I mimed, mocking their Latin slogan of "always pre-pared" while stuffing my arms in the jacket Cruz had given me. "Also, I'm keeping your jacket."

"It's not my jacket," he gave me a wink. "But you can have anything else of mine you like."

"Promises, promises, Cruz."

"Anything," his breath tickled my neck and I shivered, but not from the cold.

Suddenly, he disappeared to join the throng of people headed toward indoors and warmth. I looked down at the left breast and wouldn't you know, it said Sharp. The bastard had managed to find and give me my own damn jacket. I stuck my tongue at his retreating backside and let Winnie lead the way toward a patch of grass near the fence.

We stood for a moment, taking in the cool air and having a bit of peace. It was quiet, even for a military base. There was no hum of motors, no crashing waves, no smell of sulfur permeating every breath. It was beautiful and in that moment, it was magical to be home again. That moment being right before a shrill voice carried to me from the guard shack.

"I need to get my daughter, young man! How dare you stand between a mother and her child! Isn't it bad enough you send our children off to die, now you won't even let them see their mothers when they get home?" I shrank into myself and hurried Winnie for cover before she could spot us. Too late. "She's right there! Cynthia! Cynthia! Tell this man to let me in!"

Her voice, already at volume 8 had reached 12 and even the jet engines were quieter. I stared at my mom, all 5 foot something of her and 180 pounds of pure maternal guilt. She had shoulder length grey hair, a sharp jawline and a voice only a daughter could love. Could love if she was very, very far away. Beside my mother stood the youngest person I'd ever seen working a gate. If he was 18, he hadn't been there long. His hat emphasized ears he hadn't yet grown into, and I bet up close he still showed signs of a breakout. He was maybe 5 inches taller than my mom, but you couldn't tell from here. My shoulders hunched in defeat, I held up a finger toward my mom indicating I would be just a second and trooped toward the same building I'd seen everyone else headed to.

"Don't walk away from me, young man! I am not done!" I heard her shouting in her mid-Western accent and I started running with Winnie in tow. She resisted at first but picked up speed quickly as my mother's voice carried and went from stern to threatening. From threatening to... Crap. My mom was going to jail. I was out of breath before I made it to the door and Winnie kept gaining speed. We pushed through the crowds of people, milling and waiting for further instruction. Winnie channeled her Shepherd side and started nipping ankles to clear a path, but we weren't fast enough.

I burst through the doors on the street side of the hanger, my screaming mother just out of earshot. The guard had his hand on his taser and spoke rapidly into the radio microphone clipped at his shirt. It was impossible to hear him over my own mother though. She released a string of obscenities so creatively assembled, I was in awe for a moment. Just a moment though, as I saw the young soldier's thumb release the restraint on his taser and slowly inch it out of his holster. In the background I heard sirens, back up enroute, and I still had three yards to run. Winnie and I were about to be notorious on yet another base. This one wasn't even an Army base and they would remember us forever.

"Wait! Please, ma! I'm here!" I shouted, my own Midwest accent coming in thick with frustration and worry. Neither the guard nor my mother looked at me and I cringed. I was breathing heavily, but I couldn't get any air. Tired, I power walked to the shack, coming in line with her ancient Subaru hatchback and working my way around shouting for calm and patience. Just as I reached between the pair, my mom reached out to shove the guard.

Welcome home, I thought and begged the guard not to send ten thousand volts through my mom.

Chapter Four:
The Welcoming
Committee

Yellow Springs, OH sits about 45 minutes outside of Dayton where Wright-Patterson sits. I didn't live in Yellow Springs, however. Yellow Springs was considered the "city" where I live. Sweet Pea, Ohio, the original middle of nowhere. Afghanistan had felt like a metropolis compared to the seventeen light poles and four pastures we passed that marked the start of Sweet Pea. Two more rights and a left, we pulled up in front of my parents' house and on the stoop sat a woman.

"Oh no, not this again," I heard my mom mutter, just as I opened the door.

"Cynthia! Thank goodness you're home!" A small woman with grey hair and oversized spectacles exclaimed from the porch. I had a single foot out of the car, but I hastened to remove the rest of my person. Anything worth sitting on this stoop for had to be more interesting than my mom's car.

"Mrs. Margot, how are you?" I said, going over to help her stand. She was 100 when I was ten, so she was probably a thousand-years-old now. Glen Margot was a friend of my mother's mother, and she managed to move around stooped over in ankle length skirts faster than both sets of my grandparents... mostly because they'd passed before I was born.

"Did you tell her, Lynn?" Mrs. Margot said, looking at my mother. She was leaning on her walker and I eyed the tennis balls on the feet carefully. My eyes were darting back to the car where Winnie was going nuts at the sight of a stranger. Lynn Sharp, though much like my nickname was Cyn, hers was Lynn from something no one would tell me. I'd tried to use my police investigative resources to find her legal name, but it only got me 200 push-ups and a week of bathroom cleaning duty.

"She just got here, Mrs. Margot," my mom said, absently reaching for the back door of the car. "Can't this wait?"

"Ma, no!" I shouted, but not fast enough. Winnie flew out of the car and went straight for the tennis balls on the bottom of Mrs. Margot's walker. I grabbed her collar just as she took hold of a tennis ball with her teeth. We tugged and the walker moved with us, Mrs. Margot falling forward into a sixty-degree angle as Winnie shook the tennis ball and I tried to get it out of her mouth.

"I'm so sorry, Mrs. Margot! I'm so sorry!" I cried out, finally getting the ball out of Winnie's mouth and placing her in a down stay in the center of the lawn.

"What is that?" she exclaimed, out of breath and shaking.

"Sgt. Winifred Pupperson, Winnie for short," I answered, giving the dog my best death glare. "We are... I mean we were partners in the Army. We... were discharged together."

"She's a menace!" Mrs. Margot exclaimed, raising a finger to point accusingly.

"I'm so sorry," I replied, not daring to defend Winnie. Mrs. Margot would probably outlive all of us, but there was no need to test the theory with ball retrieval. An awkward silence stretched on and I shifted uncomfortably before I caved.

"You... wanted to ask me something?" I said, not moving closer. My mom had come up to the stoop and was righting Mrs. Margot. My mom had Mrs. Margot and her floral bag returned to the upright position, and both women were staring at Winnie like she could, at any moment, attack again. They weren't the first to do so, but it felt like a snap judgement they had no right to make. Whatever the reason, I needed coffee and cookies. So they needed to get moving on the chit chat or get moving out of the way.

"I did ... but..." the much older woman said, and I watched her brows furrow. She stared at us, assessing and indignant. We were not living up to the expectation. Her mouth emitted a soft clicking sound and when she opened it, I realized she was playing with her dentures.

"Well, if you don't need us, we should probably..." I gestured at the house behind her and she stared at me. Her jaw worked faster, the dentures moving more rapidly away and back against her gums. Her eyes took on a look of mild desperation and I decided whatever trauma Winnie had caused was not enough

41

to get me out of this. Unfortunate really, we had zero skills with real world applications.

Unless she needed something demoed.

"I need your help. Someone is stealing the church Bingo money," she said, settling back in on the stoop. Carefully, she moved the walker to the side and gestured for me to come toward her. My mom shot me a warning look, but I had no idea what I was being warned of so I sat. Winnie came over and bumped Mrs. Margot's hand in apology and she offered her an ear scrunch of acceptance. Winnie flopped over, putting her full weight across both of our feet and dropped her head to the ground with her tongue lolling out.

"Sounds like something the police should be helping with," I said, patting Winnie on her butt.

"Those ninnies!" she snapped, and I winced. "They couldn't investigate a book out of the library. They said our bookkeeping doesn't lend itself to a proper investigation. We list the buy-ins as donations and we can't report a mandatory donation amount. We don't give receipts so it's not possible to prove it's missing. That young man is as bright as his uncle and that is saying something awful."

"What would you like us to do?" I asked, mentally trying to figure out if she thought I had any financial prowess. I would log in to my banking app right now to clear up that misconception. For once, my $200 monthly Starbucks purchases would be to my benefit. As far as investigative skills, most of our success could be attributed to being in the right place at the right time. Even those were poorly coordinated successes. Maybe if I gave her my service record that would be evident.

Giving her the side eye, I decided against it. The file would crush her.

"I want you to find who's stealing the money!" she spat and I shrank in on myself. At twice the size of this woman, I should be well-equipped for this, but she terrified me.

"I meant..." but I had no idea what I meant.

"Weren't you the police?" she asked, and I hung my head.

"Kind of," I answered, looking at my tennis shoes.

"That is a yes or no question, Cynthia. Were you the police?" her voice commanded an immediate and simple answer.

"Yes," but I crossed my fingers behind my back just in case God was listening. Commonly, people compared me to armed security with a dog and I reminded them that the *armed* didn't just include my gun. As long as I had Winnie, though, being a security guard was fine... as long as I never had to admit it.

"So, you have investigative skills, don't you?" she asked, with a healthy helping of side-eye.

"Kind- yes," I answered, knowing that "kind of" would only get me another glare. Given that my last "investigation" had been missing cookies and I'd blown up a lot of military vehicles. Yes felt excessive, and I still hadn't gotten the smoke smell out of my hair. Winnie and I were, at best, skilled observers. An honest review of our work would be competently destructive. We got answers, but usually at a much higher cost than they were worth.

"We can hire you," she said, still clicking her dentures but slowly. "It wouldn't be much, but..."

"I appreciate the offer Mrs. Margot, but if the police can't help..." I started and she started clicking faster. My mom, looking from Mrs. Margot back to me, shook her head and squeezed between us. She opened the front door and went inside, Winnie scenting the air that escaped.

"I didn't say they couldn't help, I said they wouldn't," her voice was clipped.

"I... maybe start from the beginning. I'll see what I can do," I said, sighing internally as I watched Winnie dart through the open door after my mom.

Traitor, I thought at her retreating tail.

When I opened the door twenty minutes later, there was absolute silence inside.

Very, very quiet and I panicked. Taking the hallway at sprint pace, I stuck my head in the living room, dining room and the opened door to the basement before running into the kitchen. My mouth fell open and I stared at Winnie, sprawled on her back, legs in the air while my mom gave her belly rubs and...

"Bologna?" I asked in astonishment. I had never been allowed bologna the whole 18 years I lived here.

"No, dear, it's a ham steak," my mom said scornfully, and I relaxed. At least she was consistent. "Mrs. Margot told you about the funds Mrs. Elenaire swears she can verify are gone based on a mental tally?"

"Yeah..." I said, opening the fridge door. I stuck my head inside and inhaled the scent of garlic. My mom's fridge always smelled like garlic. Another constant.

"Well?" she prompted and I pulled out a container of pasta. Not bothering with the microwave, I pulled a fork from the drawer and speared some pieces into my mouth.

"Well what, ma?"

"Well, what did you tell her?" my mom answered with exasperation. Winnie cocked her head to the side at me in disapproval.

"That I needed to go to bed and I'd get back to her tomorrow," I answered. Satisfied, I stuck the top back on the container and returned it to the fridge. I washed my fork with soap and water, dried it with the towel hanging from the handle of the oven, and placed it back in the drawer. Everything precise, routine and clean, just as I'd found it. I turned around to face my mom after folding the towel into precise thirds and hanging it in the exact center of the stove handle.

"What, Ma?" I asked, walking back to the dining room and shouldering my duffle bag.

"I've never seen you clean before," I rolled my eyes. "*That* I have seen."

"Night, ma," I said and headed toward the staircase. Our house is a two-story, four-bedroom house with a basement. The second floor had a master and the three bedrooms, mine having belonged to Heidi before she moved out. At some point, it had been a storage room, but then I was born. It was the last door on the left, just across from my parent's bedroom, and I made my

45

way there without any thought to the sudden scuffling sounds behind me.

"Cynthia, wait!" I heard my mom call, but I decided the jet engines had damaged my hearing and I kept going to my room. Waiting would probably mean a lecture of some sort... or worse, more questions. If Mrs. Margot thought "kind of" was an inappropriate answer, my mom considered it the same as punching her in the face.

"Cynthia!" my mom called again, and I opened the door just as she reached the second floor landing.

"What, ma?" I said, pushing in the door.

She paled and I cocked my head to the side. I turned back to the room and flipped up the light switch, preparing to throw my duffle on the bed.

Only there wasn't a bed.

In the center of the room was what appeared to be a weight bench. It was dimly lit, even with the light on, and everything was cast in ominous red shadows. A chest of drawers was on the left side of the room, straps hung from the ceiling on the right.

"Did you guys take up murdering people when you retired?" I asked, walking in and taking hold of a strap. It was made of silk and I wrapped it around my hand twice, looking around. "Though why would you need a swing for... oh, God!"

I yanked my hand back as I spotted the assortment of vibrators.

"Cynthia, it is perfectly healthy for two people..."

"Ma, what are the vibrators for?"

"Don't be a prude, Cynthia. Your father and I wanted to mix things up. Your sister recommended those Grey books, Fifty whatever, and we decided we should..."

I gagged on my spit and took a step back, just as Winnie took a step in.

"Really, it's only natural... put that down, Winnifred!"

I turned just in time to see something bright red with straps hanging out of her mouth. My mom made a grab for Winnie, but she took that as an invitation to play and gave chase. She sped around the room, tail flying through the air, and my mom stumbled after her, knocking over a chest that held an assortment of padded and metal handcuffs.

"Oh my..." I began.

"Cynthia, get your dog!" my mom shouted at the same time.

Winnie dashed past me, bounding down the stairs and making a dash for the kitchen. Relieved to escape the little shop of horrors, I sprinted after her. Once in the kitchen, we played ring-around-the-Rosie at the kitchen island and she took off toward the dining room. I made it into the room just in time to see two chairs topple and her tail disappearing into the living room. Something crashed to the floor and the front door opened.

"Honey... I... What the hell?" I heard a man's voice. Then there was a grunt and the sound of the door crashing into the wall behind it. I dashed around the corner and saw a tan tail, held high in the air, disappear out of the front door and into the night.

"Hi, dad!" I said racing toward the front door.

"Hi, Cyn," he said and righted himself. His grey hair had the disheveled look of running his fingers through it repeatedly.

His tweed coat and slacks were just as I remembered- faded and wrinkled. He was roughly six feet two inches and when he wanted to kiss my mom he had to hunch. I tried to not picture the last part at the moment.

I paused a beat when I was in line with him to check that he was okay before continuing my pursuit of Winnie. My dad, however, could not have predicted his poor timing with the next sentence.

"Why is there a dog running away with your mother's ball gag?" he asked, just as my toe was going over the threshold. It caught, I tumbled down the two-step stoop and landed on my arm.

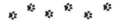

Four hours later, I was drugged and in the basement guest room with a neon pink cast on my arm. Urgent Care had been chaos and once again, it was no one's fault but mine. Not only was my thumb held stable in a permanent thumbs-up until the hairline fracture in my radius healed, I was the only one who thought it was hilarious. I used the new position of my hand to tell all the people who passed they were doing a great job. Including my mother, who was bright red and a little flustered. Her response was to kindly inform me that I owed her $65 for the damaged item and I was expected to be out looking for a job in the morning.

I gave her a thumbs up.

She smacked the back of my head.

Rather than risk another tumble, my dad helpfully escorted me down into the basement. He then politely informed me that it was not recommended I come back upstairs. Apparently, he and my mom had a standing date. When I suggested they try laying down like normal people, there was a very stern look. I was the only one who thought that was funny as well. Hard to say if it was the drugs or he'd lost his sense of humor when Winnie gave the ball gag to the neighbors to throw.

They did not throw it and declined an invitation to my mom's potluck.

Either way, it was nearly midnight when I was clean, tucked in and finally able to go to sleep. All the day's disasters aside, I was glad to be home with Winnie on the bed beside me.

Chapter Five: Help Wanted

"Good morning, I'm here about your vehicle recovery position," I said and waited. I had a steaming travel cup of coffee in one hand, and Winnie's leash hanging off the casted, upright thumb of the other. In front of me was an overweight, under-height man with greasy, mostly gone brown hair. He had on a bowling shirt and khakis, looking like the Goblin King if he ever gave up on life and his health. His shirt had the name *Keith* stitched into it, but the business cards on the counter said Petros and the face said RUN!

"It ain' fer you," he said to the knife in his hand. He had an apple that he was meticulously whittling down to the core, keeping the ribbons on a plate. "Don' need no blondie Godz'a in my office."

Winnie growled and I tugged on her leash in correction. A bit of coffee sloshed onto my hand and I said a silent apology to the gods of caffeine. It was for a good cause: money to purchase more caffeine.

"Sir, your ad on Indeed encouraged former military members to apply. I was military police. Is there not a position available?" I asked, professionally bitchy.

"What's that?" he pointed the knife at Winnie and I growled. Winnie licked my hand. Right, we needed a job.

"She's a retired military K-9," I answered through teeth gritted in a fake smile.

"Huh, it's cute."

Winnie and I both growled. The man went back to knifing his apple.

"Vehicle recovery?" I prompted and he let out a loud sigh.

"Look, ya don' really fit the image we're goin' fer. But, ya bring in this and we'll talk," he said, tossing a file at me.

"How much?" I asked and he looked at me properly for the first time.

"How much what?" he answered dismissively.

"How much do I get if I bring this car in?"

"Ya get a job," he was showing too many teeth.

"Pass," I said, pushing the folder back to him. "I don't work for free."

I turned and Winnie stood to follow.

"Ya get the recovery fee," he said to my back and I turned. "Ya can have the recovery fee if ya bring the car in, an' you can have the job."

I nodded and took the file back. Petros/Keith had more than a few teeth missing and yet somehow gave the eerie impression of a full mouth. The look in his eyes was like Winnie in the chow hall. He was ready for a snack and a disaster.

Well, he isn't getting either, I thought and squared my shoulders. We walked out of the door and climbed into my 15-year-old Jeep. My love of the faded grey Wrangler probably explained my willingness to join the Army as much as anything else. This Jeep had taken me to college in Colorado and the base on my first day of basic. It was reliable, trustworthy and consistent.

Just about the only thing in my life that was besides Winnie and my mom's kitchen.

Behind the wheel, I grabbed my third coffee for the day and chugged while reading. The file said we were after a cherry red Firebird. The delinquent owner was Roger Ritter, and I did a double take. The man in the picture could be the twin of Petros/Keith inside the creatively named Joe's Towing Agency. His height was the same, his address was off the beaten path in a section of town dedicated to farms and survivalists. Google maps said chicken farm, and I hoped for the best.

I backed the well-traveled Jeep out of the lot and turned right. Technically, I should have demanded a towing capable vehicle, but the Jeep had a winch, and I was fairly certain everything that man touched was coated in sleazy man-grime.

Two more right turns and thirty minutes later, I was in front of a six-foot-high fence of aged wood plank. Winnie and I got out and I peeked over the top while Winnie flattened her tummy to the ground and sniffed at the gap underneath. On the other side was dirt, debris of failed construction projects, and car parts.

There was not, however, a red Firebird.

We followed the fence to the end where it turned from wood plank to chain-link. The interior view didn't change, but I didn't have to stand on tiptoes. The links were filled with plastic slats and each glimpse showed more rubbish and garbage. At the last corner, I heard a new sound besides the creaking of wood and ancient metal.

Winnie cocked her head to the side, and I stared at her. I was trying to place the sound; she tilted her head the other way. Suddenly, she was digging under the fence, but I still didn't... I grabbed for her leash as the sound registered. My hand flailed through the air, finding nothing to hold onto.

I had forgotten her leash.

My hand grabbed at fur, scruff and whatever part of her I could find as she burrowed. I got her collar just as she slid under the fence, leaving me holding a pink camo collar while the owner ran toward the sound of two-dozen chickens. Without regard for stealth, I just started shouting.

"Winnie! Winnie! Get back here!"

Then a plume of feathers erupted everywhere. Terrified, I launched myself over the fence with my non-broken right hand and touched down into absolute chaos, Winnie at the center. She had immediately barged into the chicken coop. All 90-pounds of her in a coop designed for a dozen hens of no more than 5 pounds. Birds were squawking, things were moving in all directions making a cloud of dust and feathers that closed my airways as I struggled to choke out commands.

"Winnie!" I shouted again. The chickens were kicking up dirt and my eyes were shut tight but I kept my hands outstretched, hoping a dog would run into the empty collar at the end. "Winnie!"

The next sound was the ratchet of a shotgun, chambering a round.

"What er you doin' on ma' property?"

"Trying to recover a Firebird, but I can see this was a mistake. We'll be going now," I answered, groping around for Winnie's neck scruff. My hand closed around something soft and I tugged. It squawked, pecked my hand and I let go. "Damn-it, Winnie! Leave the freaking chickens alone!"

Something trampled my foot and I grabbed it. A yelp confirmed I had a dog this time and not a chicken. With my hands, I inspected the dog, found its head, and slipped the collar back on, cinching it tight. She grumbled, but I didn't give an inch.

"That lil shi' sent you to get the car? Wha' he thinks you'd be able to do, gir'y?" the man bellowed with a full-bodied laugh. I snapped my eyes open and trained them on his mirth-filled form. He was wearing overalls with nothing underneath; his fuzzy chest and fuzzier arms showcased a ponchy gut and a lack of dental and personal hygiene.

And still, he was laughing at me.

The gun was hanging haphazardly at his side and he wasn't paying much attention to it. When the laughter turned into choking and he doubled over, I considered helping... except then he said something about little blonde girls and I... threw a chicken at him. The chicken only went two feet, then flapped its wings and went to the ground. It carried on clucking and pecking, not caring in the least that it had briefly been flying.

Chickens were terrible weapons.

"M' brother thought that you, giant woman, wo'd get the car back?" the man hacked out with spittle and phlegm.

"Keep your damn car!" I shouted and started leading Winnie toward the front yard. No way was I jumping that stupid fence again. As the squawking behind me quieted, I looked down and saw something sticky smeared on my partner's face. It was also on her paws and little white granules stuck to her snout.

"Is that…" I started just as a shotgun exploded behind us.

"You'll pay for ruin'n 'em eggs!" he hollered.

"Run!" I shouted. Winnie took off for the gate and I scrambled to keep up. Another blast rang out and I ducked. After a third, I flattened myself to the ground and pulled Winnie down with me, belly crawling forward. My cast followed me through a mud puddle, adding wet and muddy to my list of reasons to hate both this man and his brother. At the fourth blast I was nearly out of the man's yard. With relief, I heard the chirp of a siren and I let out a long exhale. I could see red and blue lights through the gaps in the fence and a voice echoed from the bullhorn.

"Gun down, Roger," the officer said, and my hand kept a firm grip on the dog ready to charge.

"Wrecked ma eggs!" he shouted from behind me.

"Gun down!" came back from the bull horn. Something heavy clattered to the ground and I got to my feet, slowly. The fence slid forward and there, in the Village of Sweet Pea Uniform, was Daniel Kirby. The hottest kid in high school. He'd been two grades ahead of me and light-years out of reach, but there wasn't a Double-X chromosome, and a fair amount of XY, who weren't well aware of his existence. Even those not interested in dating men admired his eyelashes, style and his excellent choice in gym shorts.

"Well if it isn't Cyn the Determined," he chuckled and I gave him a death glare. "S'pose I should have expected to see you sooner rather than later. I heard you were at the hospital last night."

"From who?" I demanded. I pushed myself to my feet and brushed myself off. I looked down and now the mud was streaked with pink dye from the cast. Great, an even bigger mess.

"Sister-in-law," he answered, and I grimaced.

"That man tried to kill me and you want to talk about my cast?" I said, waving the soaked, mud and dirt covered fiberglass in the air.

"Can't kill you," Daniel drawled, eyes looking around the yard. "Won't let him buy rounds with actual bullets. It's basically just a flash bang."

My eyes scanned the yard. No holes in the fence. No indentations in the dirt. No indication that actual projectiles had appeared anywhere. So now I was just a wuss. Winnie wagged her tail, her stomach, paws and nose caked with the same mud.

My mom was going to kill me.

"That man is a menace," I muttered, crossing my arms and smearing mud and wet fiberglass down the front of my shirt. The once white shirt was now brown, filthy and see-through. Just what I wanted to be wearing in front of the hottest guy in my high school.

Except you're not in high school, I reminded myself with a face palm. Wet fiberglass smushed against my face and pain shot through my arm. I started wrestling the stupid cast off before I grew mildew.

"Of course, he is, why do you think we don't sell him real bullets?" he said, eyes on my chest.

"Someone should stop letting *you* fire real bullets, Daniel. If your wife pops out another kid, half the incoming kindergartners will have the same last name," I was walking toward the now open gate, still fighting the wet cast and sharp pains.

"I thought you'd be down at the dairy, what with your field of study," he said, and I shot him a dark look.

"You thought wrong," I said, body checking his shoulder and leaving a smear of mud on his pressed and pristine uniform. The jolt of impact sent another wave of agony through my arm and I bit back bile. Being childish was costing me more than I was getting out of it. He didn't care that he was muddy. He didn't care that he was standing in chicken poop. He just wanted to point and laugh. So I flung the cast I'd finally gotten off at his head, but it fell short and just lay there like a sad pink beacon of failure.

I turned over the engine, blasted some Taylor Swift and left a trail of dust behind me. In the rearview mirror, I could swear that man was laughing, waving my dead cast carcass at my vehicle.

Forty minutes later, I was clean and sitting in urgent care waiting for my arm to get a new cast. It had been 20 minutes back into Yellow Springs to get to the facility and I hadn't taken any pain pills. It was not yet 10AM and already there were a half dozen people seated beside me. Grouchy and in pain, I looked around for a place to sit where no one would talk to me. No one was coughing, so I took that as a good sign they weren't there for virus related ailments. More than one person was bleeding, though, so I was happy to let them go first as I took a seat in the corner to watch the door. Armed with coffee and a newspaper, I started wondering where to apply next that wouldn't get me shot at. I also discovered that no one posted jobs in the newspaper and I discarded it on the chair next to me.

"Are you here about the job opening?" a man asked from my left. I turned to see a short, round, man with grey hair and a hangdog face in a security uniform. His eyebrows were twin caterpillars, his nose hair nearly an inch past needing a trim and his ear hair telling the same story.

"No, I need a new cast. What job?" I asked, trying to find enthusiasm. Security would be a step down from MP, but it would be easy enough. Plus, the hospital has coffee... and vending machines. Easy access to snacks and caffeine were a plus for any job, and the walls didn't look like anyone had shot up this place. It checked all my boxes so long as the old man's clothes weren't an indication of the appearance standard.

"Looking for a new guard to cover the evening shift," he said, sizing me up while seated. I stood up and extended a hand. His eyes went up and up to meet my gaze. "Geez, you're tall."

"Cyn Sharp," I said, taking the hand he hadn't offered. It felt like a crumpled napkin, but he held eye contact.

"Gerald Ford, no relation," he answered, and I nodded. We shook and he eyed the hand he was holding. "This the one that needs a cast?"

"No, this one," I said, holding up my other arm with an empty coffee cup. He nodded and seemed to ponder for a moment longer than I found comfortable. "You need a guard?"

"Yes... do you have any experience?" he said, still staring like a lost puppy. This was either his first time hiring a new person, or his first time interviewing a hospital patient for a job.

Maybe both.

"Yes, I was an MP in the Army for a few years. Canine handler. She retired with me. Would she be able to work with me?" I asked and his face took on a promising expression of approval. If Winnie could come with me, I was sold on the security gig.

"Can I meet this canine?" he asked and I nodded, heading for the door just before the nurse called my name.

"Sorry, can we meet you at your office?" I said, watching the nurse tap his foot impatiently. I couldn't be certain, but he looked like the same man who'd put the cast on my arm last night. Gerald nodded, gave me directions to the office and I promised to meet him there as soon as I was done.

I approached the male nurse with what I hoped was an unassuming smile.

"New cast?" I asked, holding up my arm.

"What happened to the one I put on yesterday?" he responded, not a trace of a smile. It was the same man and he was not happy.

"Mud and some chickens. Have you been here since last night?" I asked, hoping to distract him from the evident anger on his face. His shirt said Sean without any indicator of first or last name.

"How do mud and chickens remove a cast?" he asked, arms still crossed. He wouldn't budge on the angry annoyed thing.

"Technically, I removed the cast but it wasn't wearable because of the mud," I said. My coffee cup had been empty for some time, but I still lifted it to my face, just in case I missed some. As I rotated my arm, agony shot through the limb and I let out a muffled scream.

"And the chickens?" he pretended not to notice my agony and I nodded. The cup was still empty so I tossed it.

"Cyn the Determined, still one step behind a disaster," he said and rolled his eyes.

My mouth opened to ask how he knew that stupid nickname but the sound of something crashing caught my attention. It was followed by a scream, two short barks and an overhead page for security.

"Please, no," I muttered and took off toward the sound. Behind me, I could hear what sounded like a slow moving stampede of hospital employees, but I was faster. I dashed up the hall, around the corner and came to a halt at the sight. Winnie had a man with a hand truck full of meat products and meat substitutes pinned to the ground. He was holding a bag of peanut butter cookies and from what I could tell, Winnie didn't know which to "tactically acquire" first.

"Winnie, leave it!" I commanded and she turned to stare at me. Then she looked back at the man below her. "Winnie, come. Now!"

I ordered and she flattened her ears to come stand beside me.

"Are you alright, sir?" I asked, not moving closer in case he was inclined to seek revenge.

"I'm layin' on the floor with toppled product. No I ain't alright!" he responded. The man had light skin, a face pock-marked with acne scarring. His uniform said EM Foods and it looked two sizes too big for his barely-there frame. "Just walking through the lot doing my job, when I see a dog. I go to say hi like I do and it attacked me! Chased me into the building, tackled me onto the floor."

"Were you saying hi or taunting her?" I asked, crossing my arms under my chest, which caused another jolt of pain and my eyes to water but I managed to stifle the scream. His eyes shifted and I had my answer. "You taunted her with cookies, thinking she wouldn't be able to get out of the car. You walked away and she came after you. This is what you deserve!"

I stretched my arms out to indicate the mess and my arm crashed into a wall. It was too much and this time I screamed, falling to my knees with my arm cradled against my chest. The mud-covered Winnie placing her head on my lap.

"Probably we should put that cast back on," came the laughing voice of the male nurse behind me. He slid his hands under my arms and hauled me to standing while Winnie tried to lick my face.

"I think maybe we'll pursue other candidates," Gerald said from my left-hand side. At a loss for a good counter point, I nodded.

"Thank you for the consideration," I said and followed the nurse back to Urgent Care, my demon dog in tow.

Chapter Six: The Farm

"Oh good, Cynthia, you're home," my mom said from the entryway to the house. She was bustling around with a scarf and wool coat, digging through her oversized purse for something. "I just got off the phone with Joseph, over at the dairy. They need a new Animal Technician to help with breeding and I told him you'd be down there by noon."

She looked up, hand wrapped around keys and looked me over.

"Why is your cast black?" she asked, and I shrugged.

"It matches my soul."

"Why are you wearing different clothes than this morning?" she kept going and I resisted the urge to bang my head on the wall.

"There was an incident with mud and chickens. I need more coffee. Ma, why did you tell Joseph I'd be down at the farm? I don't..."

"You have the degree," she said.

"Yeah, but..."

"You have the necessary certifications," she continued.

"Yeah, but..."

"You need a job?" she asked, brow raised.

"Yeah, but..."

"Then you'll work on the farm. They are not that formal there. He recommended old jeans, boots and a hoodie. That coat will get destroyed. I've got to go, dear," she said, giving me a kiss on the cheek and walking out of the front door. It closed sharply behind her and I heard the lock tumble into place.

"What just happened?" I asked, looking down at Winnie.

She let out a wide yawn and led the way to the kitchen, flopping under the table. At a loss, I followed her. Coffee started brewing, and I ran through the day's list of disasters. Not my finest hours, I decided as I doctored the life-giving bean water. We devoured all of the snacks in the kitchen before trekking down to the basement to prepare for our first day on the farm.

At twelve-thirty, I was staring at a balding man with a large belly. He had on a green flannel shirt, faded jeans and cowboy boots that looked a little too clean for a man on a dairy farm. Joseph

Stafford had been the ranch manager of the dairy since I had first come for ice cream at five-years-old. I'd always been fascinated by animals, animal science and everything that involved avoiding human interaction. When I'd gone to school in Colorado, I'd majored in animal science with the hope of creating a super species capable of mass destruction. In actuality, I learned how to care for and maintain animals and their outputs for production purposes.

I also got a lot of weird looks for hoping to create a werewolf spider monkey and that's when I learned to truly appreciate the phrase "talk less, smile more".

"So, you're in charge of measuring the output and maintaining the supply at the recommended storage conditions. You'll have to check out the animals and submit any health requests or concerns to me and I can decide if we should contact the vet," Joe said, and I nodded along. For two months after college, I'd done this. For two months I'd mucked stalls, maintained hormone levels and assisted in the birth of cows.

Which is why I joined the Army.

Winnie was following behind me, sniffing the cattle pens and looking bewildered. She'd never been to the country, or a farm. She'd been bred and trained in a suburb and then served in desert and city environments. The closest she'd come to a larger animal was an unfortunate incident where we happened upon a gator in Florida. We were trying to outrun a swarm of bees Winnie upset by jumping up and taking down their hive. Running from the gator, there was a massive spider web and the biggest spider I had ever seen.

Have I mentioned that I hate Florida?

"Now your job is to watch them while the morning tech closes out and get them tucked into bed for the night," he said, affectionately rubbing a dairy cow. "You have any questions?"

"No, sir," I said, having already visited the human resources trailer and learned my pay, hours and expectations.

"Good," he said and a man in a lab coat came out of one of the stalls.

"Looks like Betty just had a clogged duct. We cleaned and cleared it. Week off the rotation wouldn't hurt her, either," lab coat man said and my mouth dropped open. "Might want to keep that mouth closed around here, Cyn. We have a *lot* of flies."

The man in the lab coat was my height, maybe an inch taller. He'd filled out his wiry, lithe frame into a muscular trim one. His hair was dark, his eyes were bright and for just a moment I forgot we were standing in cow poop.

"You two know each other, then?" Joseph asked and the lab coat man shot me a wink before answering.

"Yeah, Cyn and I went to high school together. New cast?" he asked, and I nodded.

"What do you mean by *new*, Larry?" Joseph asked, eyes narrowed at my black wrapped thumbs up, now imprisoned in a sling due to my "inability to be trusted with it free".

He let out a laugh and my eyes kept darting between the eyes and the name stitched on the lab coat. Dr. Lawrence Kirby, DVM was standing in front of me and he was nothing like the scrawny kid from high school. He was mouth-wateringly hot and I couldn't find words... or stop staring.

"My brother called. Said Pete found a new sucker to go after Roger and I'd never guess who it was," he was all smiles. "Cyn the Determined, soaking wet and covered in mud, crawling on the ground away from a man shooting blanks. I'd have paid to be there. Will you re-enact it?"

"He'll be shooting blanks if he doesn't stop running his mouth," I grumbled.

Joseph started to laugh but quickly changed it into a cough when I growled. Winnie perked her head up and moved a little closer, giving Larry a cursory sniff. He patiently kept his hand lowered, giving her the option of making the first move. She went closer, he ruffled her ears, and she... peed on his work boots.

Joseph took a sharp inhale, looking between the two of us, but I just smirked.

"This your revenge for the Cyn the Determined comment?" he asked, smiling wide and still giving Winnie the love.

"Is there going to be a problem with your dog and our vet, Cynthia?" Joseph asked and I shook my head no.

"That wasn't a hatred peeing, she was marking him. He's hers now," I said and shrugged. Larry laughed and Joseph paled. In the interest of full disclosure, I went on without prompting. "We've spent four years together; she has different pees. There's the hatred, I think you are weak peeing. Her territorial peeing, urination peeing and once fear peeing. It was only once though."

"Was that for the explosion in Florida or the one in Afghanistan?" Larry asked and I stared at him open mouthed.

"Neither. Stalker much, Scary Larry?" I bit back with his own embarrassing childhood nickname.

"Yeah, plus most of your exploits make the major media broadcasts. Only a couple phone calls to find out you were behind them. What made her fear pee?" he asked, and I could feel Joseph shifting beside us. Larry had gotten the nickname Scary Larry because of an unfortunate brace's incident with a spinach puff, but apparently with his flawless smile, he was no longer interested in childhood taunts.

Must be nice to be a real adult.

"Another story for another day. I have animals to technician," I said and gestured toward Joseph to continue his tour.

"Right, well, tonight you'll get Betty settled. Get her acclimated in the solo stall, then you can do the culture rounds and finish with the horse pens," he said. He was uncertain leading me past Larry, keeping an eye on Winnie, both of whom followed us into the stall. Inside was a Jersey cow, white with black spots, and she was laying with her feet tucked under, head resting on a haunch, her calf lying beside her. Winnie walked in, took one look at her and walked back out to sit guard at the pen door.

"She has this for her udders," Larry said, passing me a small jar. "And she'll need a blanket. Without the rest of the herd, the frost point is beneath her comfort level."

I nodded and reached down to pet Betty. Unwittingly, I started singing.

"Betty, I won't make assumptions about why you switched your homeroom, but I think it's cuz of me," and she leaned into my touch. I rubbed her ears and continued. "Betty I was riding on my skateboard past your house and I almost couldn't breathe."

It was quiet and her eyes dropped shut. I dropped her blanket on her and turned to leave the stall and found two dumb-founded men.

"What?" I asked, back stiffening under their gaze. If I split my pants open, I was going to quit life and live under a bridge. A woman can only take so many blows to her pride.

"Didn't have you pegged for a Swiftie," Larry said with a shrug and I looked daggers at him. He smiled a lopsided grin and a mouth full of teeth that proved he'd kept wearing his retainer like a good orthodontic patient.

"Erherm," Joseph said, clearing his throat. I realized Larry and I were staring at each other just a little too long, and now I couldn't look at either of them. "Dr. Kirby, if that'll be all, Cyn has to get to work. Even with the cast, there's still a lot for her to do."

Larry nodded and walked away, Joseph following behind him so I could get to work without being distracted by the view.

Five hours later, everything hurt and I was ready to quit. Winnie had been recruited to round up sheep and she failed miserably. Out of embarrassment, I grabbed an ATV and drove into the field to round them up myself. We then had an incident where she caused a prized horse to run away, which I lured back with an apple. After that, she stretched out in the barn and took a nap, thankfully allowing me to do the job I was actually being paid for. My sling was somewhere in the back 40 and I doubted it was suitable for medical use after it landed in a cow pie.

"Need a drink?" A friendly voice said behind me. I turned to see Larry holding a jug of water so cold the outside was completely covered in condensation. I nodded and he passed it over. Gratefully, I gulped half before handing it back to him and taking him in. He was wearing jeans and a faded band T-shirt, his tennis shoes well-worn and filthy. He had an unzipped hooded sweatshirt over the whole thing, and I found myself wiping more than just left-over water off of my mouth. "Where's your shadow?"

"Uhhh..." I said and blinked at him.

"Winnie?" he clarified, the crooked smile coming back.

"Oh, sleeping, I hope. They might not let her back after today and she's not allowed back at the house," I said, watching a bus pull up in front of the ice cream parlor. Larry followed my gaze and a troop of seniors disembarked, Mrs. Margot among them. They formed a neat line outside the shop and went in one at a time, coming back out with cones and cups of different colors. Mrs. Margot came out with a double scoop of something pink and her eyes immediately zeroed in on me. She waved me over and I tried to look like I hadn't seen, but there was no fooling her and I couldn't put this off forever. Resigning, I let out a long exhale and slipped my jacket back on over my sweat stained shirt.

"Where are you going?" he asked.

"To disappoint an old lady," I answered and walked to Mrs. Margot.

"Cynthia, good to see you're using your education and not wasting time and money. Have you considered my offer? It wouldn't take you away from this," she said, eyeing the barn behind me, my cast and finally the unknown feces caked to my boots.

"Mrs. Margot, I..." I started and stopped. Behind her was a man in a baseball cap with a moustache and a much too familiar frame. I watched him move, ordering his own ice cream at the counter and then looking around while they scooped. Shifty, nervous and definitely out of place. "Who's that?"

Mrs. Margot followed my gaze and scoffed.

"Brother of the preacher. Just got into town yesterday, a bit of a dip," she said, taking a bite of her chocolate cherry. "He and Reverend Tim have been having private counsel since he arrived but neither seem too concerned with the bingo money. Though it's been awhile since we've seen Reverend Tim, he got the 'rona and hasn't been out for weeks."

I watched another man, bigger and more exotic, walk up beside the skinny man with the moustache. Even from here, the smaller man was obviously sweating bullets. The bigger man was joined by an even bigger man and they escorted the little moustache man to a corner. Their conversation was quick, body language intimidating, and the man looked to be struggling to remain upright.

"What's his name?" I asked, watching his hand tremble as the server handed him his cone, plain vanilla.

"Don't know, but you can come to bingo with me and find out," she said and I looked back at her. "It's tonight in the church community room."

"I'm not done here until 1930," I said and she kept eating her ice cream.

"Perfect, Bingo starts at 8PM. You'll meet us there," she said and walked away while I watched the reverend's brother.

"What's wrong?" said a voice right next to my ear and I jumped.

"Nothing," I answered, reflexively reaching down and petting Winnie who had appeared at the same time. "Just, I thought I recognized a man."

"From?" Larry prompted, following my gaze to where the two larger men had spoken to the smaller one. His eyes looked at the bus and Mrs. Margot gave him a wave.

"My last job, but... that wouldn't make sense," I said shaking my head and checking my watch. "Guess I better get back to work if I'm going to make bingo."

Chapter Seven:
The Reverend's
Brother

I t had been over ten years since I stepped foot in a church. At a young age, I had decided that the idea of bribing people to be decent wasn't for me. My mom and dad hadn't liked it, but they were too old and tired to fight a teenager over philosophical opinions on life. I walked into the community room prepared for the dusty smell of old bibles, extinguished matches and melting wax.

This room held no semblance to a church.

The walls were cushioned, and long cafeteria style tables lined up in rows before an elevated platform. A Bingo number wheel sat in the center of the table, two women seated at it like Roman sentries at the gate. They had severe noses, wrinkled skin, and artificially colored hair. The room was loud, nearly every seat occupied. It smelled like muscle rub, stale cigarette smoke, and even more stale coffee. At the front table was Mrs. Margot and my kindergarten teacher Mrs. Zuber. She'd been like Mrs. Margot's older sister, which make her like a million-years-old. Yet, with her artificially red hair and zest for life, she managed to look healthier and have more energy than I did.

I walked to the table, reaching into my pocket for a ten-dollar bill. Mrs. Margot took my cash, Mrs. Zuber handed me two tickets, 5 cards and a dotter.

"What do I do with this?" I asked, looking at the items.

Mrs. Margot let out a disapproving tut and started pointing.

"Those are your game cards, you use that to mark them and those are drink tickets," she said and I nodded.

"Drinks?" I asked, scanning the room for a bar.

"There is a bowl of punch on the back table. If you want a hit of something stronger, you have to bring it yourself and sneak it in," Mrs. Zuber advised me and then slid me a small bottle of Tito's vodka. "Since you're helping us, I'll help you."

She winked and my mouth fell open. My kindergarten teacher gave me alcohol. I opened my mouth, closed it again and a cane banged my calves.

"Out of the way, girl. Some of us need to get to our lucky seats!" a wizened old man said from behind me and I looked down at his shrunken frame and red, white and blue cane topped with an American eagle. He was sporting a hat that said Navy Veteran and I decided that I'd better get out of the way before he came at me with something worse than a cane.

Like the Navy song. Maybe even Row, Row, Row Your Boat, or white cracker jack pants.

The room was growing steadily louder, and I scouted for a seat in the back so I could watch the room. After a quick stop at the punch table, I spiked my drink to help with the pain I hadn't taken pills for and stood against the back wall. From this angle, I could see everything. The good news about a room full of seniors, I could see over the heads of all of them. The bad news, they were not above kicking, punching or whacking you out of their way and my already abused body was not in the mood.

"What are you looking for, chica?" came the sensual voice next to me and I turned to see Ian Cruz leaning against the wall beside me.

"Shouldn't you be... somewhere else?" I asked, downing my vodka punch in a single drink and taking a sharp exhale. "Sweet baby Jesus."

He sniffed my empty cup and gave me a bright eyed smile.

"Enjoying your retirement?" he gave another sniff at my neck and his smile got wider. "Or helping out farm animals?"

"I'm going to need another drink to talk to you," I said, turning my attention back to the room. At 815 on the dot, the room became perfectly silent and still. A projector flicked on and without preamble, the ladies at the front started spinning the basket and calling numbers to the rapt attention of the room.

"How did you get the cast?" he whispered into my ear and I fought a shiver.

"Ball gag incident," I didn't take my eyes off the room, he didn't take his eyes off of me.

"Is it as good as that leave you were on in Canada?" he asked, eyes sparkling.

I bit the inside of my cheek and didn't answer.

"What's the prize?" I wondered out loud and got a dark look from a man in an electric scooter.

"Fifty dollars. Each round is a fifty-dollar prize, four rounds and then a bonus black-out round. Shouldn't you be looking at your cards?" Ian answered, but I'd stopped listening to him. The moustache man had just entered the room from the left and was walking slowly and nervously toward the table Mrs. Margot and Mrs. Zuber had occupied. On the top was the cash box, the roll of tickets and a few empty miniature bottles of liquor.

I tracked him with my eyes, moving slowly along the back wall. Without looking, I could feel Ian behind me and he had seen exactly what I had. We moved in silence, the entire rest of the room focused on the front and the women at the wheel. Absently, I dropped my cards on the table beside a man in a floral Hawaiian shirt, but that was a mistake.

"Cheater!" a blue haired woman with yellowed dentures shouted. The entire room turned to us and the reverend's brother froze. "He can't play those cards; he didn't pay for them!"

The man was quickly stamping my game one card, a greedy look in his eyes. Mere seconds after the cards touched the table, he heaved to his feet and shouted...

"Bingo!"

"Cheater!" the woman countered and then everything went downhill quickly.

The man, offended by her accusation, threw the cap of his dotter at her head. In retaliation, she pulled a four-footed cane from under the table and whacked him on the arm. I tried to move away but my foot caught on lord knows what. I fell backward, landing on top of Ian. Hawaiian shirt man shoved up from the table, sending bingo cards fluttering to the floor and an uncapped dotter fell down. An electric scooter zoomed by, ran over the dotter and shot ink the length of the table. I scrambled to get back up, elbowing Ian in the gut and gaining my feet just in time to see the heel of a black sneaker disappearing through the open door.

Ignoring the death threats, I ran to the door and shoved it open. The steady rhythm of footsteps running came from the left and I took off in that direction. They were even and measured, a person comfortable running and confident doing it long term. There was no way for me to sustain that pace, and I knew I was at a disadvantage. Instinctively, I started shouting.

"Winnie! Winnie, come!" as we ran past the parking lot. A sleepy, mud-coated and disheveled dog jumped from the back of my wrangler and trotted beside us. "Seek!"

She put her nose to the ground, keeping pace but without much enthusiasm. A breeze came by and her head lifted. She froze, scented the air twice, and darted to the left. I followed and Sgt. Cruz followed close behind us. Winnie led us down an alley and stopped in front of an oversized blue dumpster. She scrambled onto the lid, jumping wildly. I scanned both directions, but there wasn't a ladder.

"Give me a boost!" I said and Ian lifted me up with the skill of a cheerleader. Winnie jumped forward as the dumpster lid crashed open and the man with the moustache popped out. He shoved Winnie, who toppled into us and we crashed to the ground, my left arm landing in a puddle of melted snow, rainwater and animal urine. We got to our feet, my pants somehow ripped at the knee and Cruz's entire outfit was spotless.

I kicked garbage juice at him and he dodged.

We watched the retreating figure run, both arms pumping at his sides and I knew the run. I knew the run like I knew the walk and the posture. He glanced back, for only a moment, but I knew the eyes. It was just like watching him cross the runway and chase after his underwear.

"Does he remind you of..." I started, and I felt Cruz nod beside me.

"Doesn't make sense though, does it?" Ian asked and I shrugged. "I mean, he's a Captain."

"Where do you think he went?" I wondered, but I never heard an answer. A shriek rang out from inside the bingo room.

My first reaction was to grab Winnie's leash, but sadly Sgt. Winnifred Pupperson was gone.

"Crap," I swore, and ran full speed back to the church community room.

We raced back in, expecting to see a dead body or a steaming pile of poop. Instead, the hundred plus people filling the room had gone silent at the sight of the spilled bingo numbers. Hundreds of them, rolling along the floor and under the tables. People ran after them, trying to set the game right, but it was in vain. Winnie was standing on the table chewing on B32.

Never again would there be a B32.

Behind her, the room was a wreck. Every person had ink, torn paper and walking aids scattered everywhere. Most looked like victims of a newspaper printing explosion. Some had remained clear of the chaos, only to find themselves on the floor when an angry player shoved a bench and managed to release the brake. A bench full of senior citizens took off toward the back table and Winnie took off after it, giving it one good extra shove and it collided with the punch bowl table in the back.

Collided and completely up ended it.

"Winnie, no!" I shouted. Too late. She'd taken off after a new toy, dropping B32 to seize a tennis ball. More specifically, the tennis ball capped end of the blue-haired woman's cane. Unfortunately, the woman was balancing her rather impressive bodyweight on the device and when my dog plays tug, she plays to win. Winnie pulled a ball off one of the four ends of the cane, and the woman toppled over. She landed in the middle of the spilled punch and plastic cups just as the man in the Hawaiian shirt came to congratulate Winnie and went down himself.

"The cash box!" Mrs. Margot cried, and silence fell over the struggling seniors.

"Wha-" I started, but it was obvious.

The table where they had carefully sat guard had tickets, bingo cards and dotters.

There was no cash box.

"But... his hands were empty!" I said looking to Ian for confirmation.

"Not entirely," he said and lifted his palm. Stuck to the center was the fake brush comb moustache that hadn't looked right on the man's face. "He lost this when he left the trash can."

"I knew it was fake, but then... is it really Captain Jacks?" I asked, watching the seniors work to collect their belongings and Mrs. Margot taking a stiff drink from another of Mrs. Zuber's secret bottles of hooch.

"Only one way to know," he said, dusting his jacket sleeves and going to the door. "Let's go find Captain Jacks and see if he's missing a fake moustache."

"Cool, I guess," I muttered, staring at what I would most likely have to pay to fix. I looked down at my arm and sighed. "Let me know what you find out."

"You don't want to come with me?" he asked, perplexed and a little disappointed.

I held up my left arm, cast now dripping slowly toward my elbow.

"Oh, I do, but I have to go back to the hospital," I answered.

Chapter Eight: Mysterious Captain

"Grow mold overnight?" came from Betty's pen as I passed, and I swallowed a yawn.

"Huh?" I asked, gulping coffee like it held the cure to life.

Larry popped his head out and gave a lopsided grin. He inclined his head toward the neon green cast on my arm and I stared down at the monstrosity. The same nurse had been on, the exact same nurse. He took one look at my sopping wet cast and laughed for 45 minutes before applying the heinous color to my body.

"Another tale of Cyn the Determined on the record?" he asked with a smirk and I shook my head.

"If you don't stop with that damn nickname… It was ten years ago, get a new one!" I tried to be outraged, but I hadn't had enough coffee.

"Why do they call you Cyn the Determined?" came the smooth voice of Ian Cruz and I flinched.

"Sweet Pea secret," I answered, but Larry just answered over me.

"In every grade she was in, Cyn was always the tallest. Not just the tallest girl, but the tallest everything. Naturally, she was sought out to join the lady's basketball team," Larry said and I could feel Cruz smile.

"Yeah, yeah, I suck at sports. He knows!" I said, hoping to stop the story.

"She didn't just suck; she was a disaster. She bounced the ball on her foot, completely missed the backboard and to add insult to it all, she could touch the hoop and still miss when dunking," Dr. Kirby, the future murder victim, said. "She never stopped trying though. Every school year she would show up to try-outs and every coach would be ecstatic to see her… until she started playing. In desperation, her sophomore year, the coach asked her to join the team when half of them got sick with mono."

"Dirty mouthed athletes," I muttered and shuddered. "Bet half of them got it from your brother."

"Most likely," Larry said with a smile, but kept going with the story. "So she's on the team, goes to practice for a week, and then the last game of the season arrives. Our team wasn't great. We were three out of five. Cyn, though, Cyn was determined to make us number 2. She stole the ball from her own teammates, double dribbled and traveled all up and down that court for an hour and you know what?"

"She didn't score a single shot?" Ian said and I decided a double homicide was probably just as much jail time as a single homicide. Much like shoes, puppies and guns, I was always down for a good buy one, get one special.

"Not only did she not score a single shot, but she also broke the school auditorium," Larry Kirby said and I rolled my eyes.

"I didn't break it!" I said, trying not to hear the sound of 60 people running from a steadily collapsing set of bleachers. "I mean, what are the chances a wayward ball would hit the release on the spectator stands and force an evacuation?"

"You're leaving out the part where your solution to the collapsing bleachers was to try and prop them open with the mascot's water bottle, which didn't have any water in it," Larry interrupted, and I shook my head.

"Fine, the water bottle had vodka which caught fire when the electrical mechanism sparked trying to close on the bottle. There, are you happy?" I said, dropping to a hay bale and closing my mouth on the coffee opening. I drank coffee while they laughed... and laughed. Orange was an OK color once you got used to it. Maybe prison would let me embroider my name on the front, so it feels like being back in the Army.

"So, you have a history of starting fires and minor explosions that predates your military service?" Ian asked, eyes dancing wickedly.

"Yeah, yeah, laugh now, Cruz. I know about more than one of your *predates*, and let's just say the Army and the men of Taiwan..."

"Where's Winnie?" Larry interrupted and I turned to see his face red with embarrassment. He either felt guilty about sharing my secret, or he was concerned the Taiwanese men would come for their long-lost brother.

"She refused to get out of bed today. Apparently, her royal highness does not believe in mud and animal poop that isn't her own," I answered and went back to drinking coffee. "She's also in a massive amount of trouble for destroying the bingo hall and making it so I owe the church twenty-five hundred dollars and a new B32."

"It seemed the B32 was the most upsetting part to them," Ian added, and Larry grinned like a fool.

"You don't mess with bingo in these parts," Larry confirmed.

"Did you find out anything?" I asked, looking at Ian. He was still in just jeans and a T-Shirt. Today his shirt and boots were black. Next to Larry in his lab coat, I was having seriously wicked fantasies. Standing between the two of them, touching their chests, having them pour coffee in my mouth. I looked down at my empty cup and sighed.

There was no energy for such things without more coffee.

"Yes, this is Captain Jacks," Ian said, turning his phone toward me. On the screen was a round faced man with a red nose, red cheeks, two chins and watery eyes. He had on Army greens, but the roundness of his face obscured his tie and it was hard to notice his rank next to his ears. It's possible the song "Do Your Ears Hang Low?" was written about him.

"Alive?" I asked skeptically. He looked a little too involved in his alcohol once you got past the ears.

"Yes, last seen fishing with two six-packs off the coast of Mexico," Ian answered, and I nodded. Some people with vices live forever, I guess. "Though that has been a bit, given that no one has tried to look for Stew Smith. The time he became Stew Smith seems to coincide with Captain Jacks reappearing for duty..."

"The guy we knew as Captain Jacks? Does he know the actual Captain Jacks?" I asked, leaning against the wooden rail of the pen. I popped the lid off my coffee cup and tipped it, hoping for more.

There was none.

"I haven't seen a look of longing like that since I wouldn't let Winnie eat the contents of a trash can outside of mess, Cyn," Ian said, and I met his gaze with effort. His eyes were so bright and happy, and he didn't have a coffee cup in his hand. He probably sold his soul to the devil for the looks, the lips and the lack of caffeine addiction that cursed me. "Do I need to dress like the Starbucks mermaid for you to listen to me?"

"I was listening! You said Winnie wanted to eat trash. That's not really new. Who's the fake Captain and does he know the real one?" I asked and saw Larry walk away toward the other end of the barn. I ignored Ian again to watch the good doctor from behind.

"We don't know," Ian said and I looked back at him. He was masking his face. "Either, but we are trying to find the newly named Stew Smith to ask. Also, the man who is not Captain Jacks, but currently known only as Captain Jacks."

"This is giving me a headache."

"That would be the vodka," he countered, and I threw my empty paper cup at him. He flicked it out of the way and shot me a wink.

"We're the government, or I guess you are, how do 'we' not know who he is?" I asked. "I get that Stew was last in Mexico, so maybe he's a little out of touch… but that guy? He's an idiot. He's an idiot pretending to be an old dude. How hard could it be to find him?"

"Have you seen the movie Renaissance Man?" he asked, moving beside me to lean on the fence. This story looked rehearsed, he'd offered that picture a little too easily and had a few too many answers at his fingertips.

Probably another perk from selling his soul.

"With Danny DeVito?" I asked, conjuring up the shorter man with a distinct voice teaching Shakespeare. My dad had loved the movie as a college professor who saw promise in everybody. I mostly watched for the cadences to Shakespeare references. Then I made them dirty and used them on my High School English papers. Yet another reason I'd joined the Army.

"Yeah. There was a character who used a fake name to join the Army to hide his crimes," he said, and I nodded picturing the actor. He was hot. "It isn't just a movie thing. People really do join the Army under an assumed name and hide out. They don't usually get rank and draw attention to themselves, though."

"Or lose their underwear on the way to an airplane?" I asked and Ian smirked.

A paper cup appeared in front of my nose and I took a long inhale.

"I love you," I said, taking the cup and drinking.

"Me or the coffee?" Larry asked.

"Just this moment, both. Probably mostly the coffee," I said when I was willing to remove my mouth from the cup.

"Disappointing," Larry said, and I shrugged. I needed more coffee to lie.

"So, this man joins the Army, pretending to be an old man who retired. What was his explanation for Benjamin Buttoning it? Then what? Decides to blow his cover, play preacher's brother in a small town and steal bingo money?"

"Is this still about that massive destruction that happened down at the church yesterday?" Larry asked and I rolled my eyes. Ian grinned widely. "I heard you owed them money, but was your cast really covered in cat pee and spiked punch?"

"Shut up. What do you know about the church group ice cream and bingo crew?" I asked, remembering that he had probably seen the seniors stop by the dairy for their pre-bingo ice cream more than once.

"Not much," he said with a shrug. Still smiling, drinking his own coffee. He had circles under his eyes and licked the rim of his cup with dedication. He was human *and* still had his soul. "They stop by the dairy, buy way too much ice cream and then head over to the church where they drink, wreak havoc and cause a scene. Not apparently as big a one as you do."

"Do they always take a bus?" I ignored the jab.

"Yeah... most are no longer allowed to drive legally," Larry answered, and I drank more coffee.

"Does the reverend usually come with them to the ice cream part?" I thought aloud, remembering the oversized men backing the fake captain into the corner.

"Yeah, but I haven't seen him in a while," Larry answered, rubbing his jaw. His hand rubbed over stubble and the sound gave me goosebumps. Probably I needed to spend time with more two-legged people. Mostly males... a breeze came by with the scent of cow manure and killed that fantasy.

Cold water has nothing on cow dung.

"What's 'awhile'?" I was mentally cataloging the information with what Mrs. Margot had told me. She said bingo had been going on for decades and they had the money secured. In the last few weeks, the tally hadn't been adding up. Mrs. Elenaire was the number whiz who hadn't been wrong since I was in diapers, her words, and it doesn't make sense that a few hundred would go missing here and there. Especially not when she kept the money in her "unmentionables" drawer between games.

"A month maybe," Larry spoke as he was still thinking. "About the same time the shopkeepers started reporting thefts."

"What shopkeeper thefts?" I asked, looking at him. He had Ian's undivided interest as well.

"Little things, along Main Street, that were put out for display. The shopkeepers always put out a small table with a few of the items available for people to look at and then decide to come in. You remember when you broke that table full of..."

"Stop!" I said, turning red. Stupid porcelain cows and the man had made me purchase every last shattered heifer. "When?"

"For about a month. Mostly on the North end and it's always something weird. A silver bracelet, or a unicorn figurine... so far the weirdest was Mr. Ambrose's old pacifier," Larry continued. Ian's eyes held a great deal of merriment. Apparently our town shopkeepers were just as amusing as everything else he'd encountered.

"Is any of it valuable?" I asked, pulling out my phone and entering notes in an app. "The north end is near the church, but honestly most everything is near the church."

"Strangely, no. It's like whoever took it did it more out of habit or compulsion than actual gain. That pacifier was nasty," Larry said.

"So we have missing money, a fake Army captain, a missing reverend and missing nick knacks?" I asked the two men and they nodded. "Anyone have any ideas?"

"If I bring you more coffee, will you look at me like you looked at him?" Ian asked and I narrowed my eyes at him.

"Look here, Romeo, there is very little I would not do for a reasonably passable cup of coffee. Unfortunately, the very little includes you," I said, emphasizing the *little* just to be insulting. He smiled wider.

"You'll change your mind, chica."

"What about me?" Larry asked with an eyebrow wiggle and I face-palmed. Both seemed like a great idea... until they weren't. Like Rocky Road ice cream when you're allergic to nuts.

"Have either of you seen two gorillas in suits walking around?" I decided to get us back on track.

"Like Donkey Kong gorillas throwing barrels? Or Wise Guy gorillas?" Larry asked.

"The second one, but if you see the first, text me a pic," I answered.

"There were two guys who looked like muscle loitering on the edge of the church lot the other night," Ian said and I turned to him. "They were eyeballing people going in and out, and I thought the taller one had picked the pocket of an old lady and taken cat treats."

"Why cat treats?" I asked and he shrugged.

"Probably she has a cat," Ian teased, and I rolled my eyes at him. Larry let out a laugh and the two did a fist bump.

"Cynthia!" Joseph called out and I turned to see the older man bustling over. "One of my heifers is about to give birth. You need to get over there! I don't pay you to flirt."

"I wasn't..." I started but closed my mouth. Only a fool would argue a moot point. Larry and I stood, heading toward the main arena where I'd seen Juniper, the pregnant cow, resting yesterday. With a last thought, I turned over my shoulder to Ian.

"Find the reverend?" I asked and he nodded. I nodded back and followed Larry around the corner. A large female cow was laying on the ground, two ranch hands next to her. Juniper was a Jersey cow, just like Betty, with her tail swishing from side to side as the calf bubble got steadily bigger. She would occasionally convulse and shudder, drinking water from a little bucket, but largely she looked at peace.

At the sight of Larry, she gave a soft moo and the small protrusion beneath her tail inched forward. I reached over to check her water and birthing liquid squirted from around the calf. I grabbed a towel, massaged her stomach with my right hand and stared in horror at my left. The green cast was now gooey and covered in a mucus film.

"Damn," I swore and Larry looked over the cow at me.

"So much for number three," he said, and together we welcomed the new calf into the world.

Chapter Nine: Murder and Muffins

I let out a wide yawn and stared at the door of my exam room in Urgent Care.

I'd been sitting on the paper covered bed for an hour. My arm was still encased in neon green fiberglass with mucus, hay, a layer of dirt and something that smelled alarmingly like dog poop stuck to it. It had been a full day of caring for and logging the progress of animals. My brain was fuzzy, and my body ached, but in the quiet of the hospital I could admit that I loved every minute of it. I did not enjoy the dirty look my mom gave me when I went home to change before coming here.

My pocket buzzed and I reached in for my phone.

"Yeah?" I stifled another yawn as I answered Ian Cruz.

"Where are you?" he asked. I could hear a lot of buzz and chatter in the background. A police radio squawked and something beeped but hard to say if it was his end or mine.

"Hospital. My cast needed to be replaced," I answered and heard a dispatcher over the line. "Where are you? Have you been arrested?"

"No, I am at the reverend's house. Cyn, he's... not doing well. They don't think he'll make it," Ian answered as the wail of an ambulance passed on his end.

"Is he coming here?" I asked, looking around the exam room. The door wasn't locked but it would be a bit of a stretch to get to Emergency from here. I walked to the door and nearly collided with Nurse Nightingale, though technically his name wasn't Nightingale. I just started calling him that after he threatened to remove my arm rather than allow me into the hospital with this cast. I countered that he'd have to bring me in to get to the saw to take off my arm. He countered he had everything he needed in the trunk of his car.

Then I tried to run away, hit an ambulance with my face and ended up in this room anyway.

I was definitely sleeping with one eye open tonight.

"Hang up the phone," he said, taking it from my hand. He pressed the end call and dropped the device on the counter. He had two wax paper wrapped bundles and a wicked gleam in his eyes. When he held up scissors, I started wondering if maybe he was more aptly related to Donald Harvey.

"How far is this room from Emergency?" I asked, moving closer to the door. I seriously did not want to be the victim of an Angel of Death serial. "Someone is coming in and I want to talk to him."

"It's just up the hall," he answered, eyeing the disgusting lump on my arm the way I generally look at Winnie poop in the back seat of my car. "That… is not allowed to leave this room. One way or another, it stays here."

He powered up the fiberglass saw, and I jumped to my feet, deciding flight was a much better strategy when faced with a man holding a saw.

"This won't hurt," he spoke, taking slow steady steps forward and I took a long inhale to scream.

Then I choked on the stench coming off of my arm. My stomach rolled, and I decided having one arm was probably better than having two with one that smelled like this. So, I returned to my seat. Eyes closed, the saw revved up and… the cast was off. My arm had stayed attached.

Nurse Nightingale shut off the saw.

I was saved.

With new gloves, he opened the packages and started soaking them in water, while I tried in vain not to look at what new color was being attached to my arm. Neon green was pretty much the worst in my mind, but it's hard to say if they don't have colors I hadn't thought of yet.

"Do you, by any chance, know Nurse Sean?" I asked, trying to get a view into the sink. He shifted and completely blocked my view.

"Yeah, he's my husband," the man said and I shrank into myself. Nurse Sean had been a medium sized Latino man with strong biceps and tattoos of the cross. This man was

African-American, built like a tank and looked capable of crushing my arm into dust. Even without the saw, I could still lose an arm.

"Has he... mentioned me?" I asked, shrinking back further.

"He has," was the only response. I closed my eyes while he cleaned my arm and put antiseptic on the cuts. Next he applied the cotton sleeve and started rolling the wet fiberglass up my arm. It was a nondescript off-white color and I let out a sigh of relief. Nurse Denny, I read from his shirt, apparently wasn't as vindictive as his husband.

"Thanks," I said. He nodded and kept checking the fiberglass. He held it up to the light and examined his work, twisting until every angle was to his satisfaction. Nurse Denny nodded, gave me a grin and a sugar-free lollipop before walking out of the door. I cautiously followed and took a right through a door marked exit. Just outside were a series of colored lines with tiny arrows showing direction of travel. I followed the red one and was gratified to learn red lines meant emergency everywhere.

A stretcher was being pushed through the doors to the ER just as I arrived. Hesitating, I looked down to see a woman with four times the normal amount of stomach, red-faced and screaming while a man in glasses kept trying to hand her ice chips while clutching a blue blanket. She took the ice chips, threw them at his head, the EMTs, and the nurses when they appeared. I ducked one that came past me and took cover.

Probably not the reverend.

I stood by the doors, then I sat, then I leaned against the wall. People came in and left, but none of them looked near death. None of them looked like Reverend Tim, or at least what he'd

95

looked like the last time I saw him... When was the last time I saw him?

When the good reverend came in, however it was an unexpected unwell. While he was inflated to twice the size I think a human should be, he had a smile on his face and was tenting the sheet over his body. Reverend Tim, it would seem, had plans to leave this world with more than just a smile on his face.

"How's it hanging? It's not hanging! Would you look at that?" He said jovially, his red face apoplectic. He looked like a zit about to pop and the machine hooked to him was making sounds of distress. All he needed was a robot to start screaming about "Danger, Will Robinson" and it would be an old school Sci-Fi movie. His skin had red patches, his head was missing hair and he was covered in crumbs. "Magical muffins! Little Mary makes magic with the new delivery crew."

"Mary? Muffins? Reverend Tim, what do muffins have to do with your... condition?" I asked, but his body convulsed. The machine went nuts and suddenly a lot of people in scrubs were shoving me out of the way to rush him in. I stared on in open-mouthed silence. My phone buzzed and I answered.

"Hello?" I said, not looking at the display.

"Did you see him?" Cruz asked and I nodded but I wasn't comprehending.

I dropped my arm and stared at the door.

"Sharp!" My hand was screaming. Oh, right, phone.

"What, yeah. Drugs?" I asked, still pondering. Reverend Tim was old. Not biblical old, but old enough that his level of enthusiasm would require medicinal enhancement. Not just his below the waist excitement, either. He'd been a drab, dreary man my whole life. His sudden zest was unnerving.

"Cyn?" the voice floated back through my phone.

"Yeah?" I said, staring absently.

"Chica are you OK?" he said and I cocked my head to the side.

"Yeah."

"Can I ask you about something?"

"Yeah."

"Hang on," he said and I heard him moving around.

"What are Mary's Muffins," he said into the line and I stared at the phone.

"What are what?" I asked.

"Mary's Muffins and More. The Reverend had at least two dozen bags with the name and crumbs on every surface. He was shouting about Magic Mary. I thought it was a strip club thing, but these muffin bags... Is there a lady named Mary selling pot muffins?" I stared... did Sweet Pea have enough of a market for a specialty muffin shop?

"There used to be a Margret's Muffins on Main St, but there was never a Mary. Could it be like a church thing?"

"I don't know, chica. Something for you to look into. I gotta go," he said and hung up. Before I could put the phone away it buzzed with a text message from my mom.

Mom: Come get your dog, NOW!!

Me: I'm on my way, is she OK?

My mom replied with a picture and I stopped in a hallway to zoom in. My mom's phone wasn't ancient, but her camera could definitely use more pixels. There was something in Winnie's mouth that looked like a pink silicone branch.

"Excuse me?" I said to a young man walking past me. He stopped and his scrubs indicated he was an orderly, his ID tag reading "Robert". I passed him my phone with the picture zoomed in on Winnie's mouth.

"Can you tell what this is?" I asked. The young man looked at the phone, squinted his eyes and shoved it back against my chest.

"You're sick lady!" he said, and took off down the hall.

"What was that about?" a familiar voice asked, and I turned to see Nurse Denny.

"My mom sent me this picture, and I can't figure out why she's upset, so I asked that guy and..." I started, while Nurse Denny took my phone. His face went red, then he burst into laughter that shook the hallway.

"Your whole family is nuts," he said, handing back my phone mid-collapse into a fit.

"What the hell is it?" I asked as he gasped for air.

"A dildo, girl. Your dog took your mother's pink sparkly dildo," he said, and I dropped my phone.

Twenty minutes later, Winnie and I were in my Jeep slowly cruising Main Street. The shops were largely the same as they'd always been. Retro with a touch of country charm and inviting paths to stroll. Nothing new or trendy graced these storefronts, and I had the feeling nothing ever would.

On the seat beside me was my phone. The screen was cracked, and it was now the dirtiest thing in my life after my dog's mouth and anything I wore in Florida.

"My mom sent me a picture of a dildo, Winnie!" I said into my review mirror. She had her head out of the window and wasn't listening, so I rolled it up. "Winnie, it was a dildo, and it was in YOUR MOUTH!"

She wiggled her eyebrows and let out a whimper. Immediately upon entering the house, I'd grabbed Winnie and her care kit to do a very thorough tooth brushing. Her mouth was theoretically clean but it would be a long time before I'd believe it. My mom was in a state over the second item from her "playroom" Winnie had destroyed, claiming that it had just arrived that day and was brand new.

"No windows until you stop putting things in your mouth that don't belong there, Missy!" I said, watching her wiggle her eyebrows at me. She let out another whimper and flopped over on the seat with a huff.

"Don't give me attitude. I was working!" I said and she let out another grumble. "Where you should have been, you lazy working dog!"

A loud fart joined the next grumble.

"Fine, pout. I don't care," I said, staring out of my own, now slightly open window. To the left I saw a new storefront between the appliance repair shop and the coffee hut with a creepy name. It had stars circled around a baseball inspired script that proclaimed, "Mary's Muffins and More". It was in the same storefront that used to house "Margaret's Muffins" but whoever Mary was had given it a revamp and a coat of fresh energy.

Curious, I pulled into a parking slot directly out front and hopped out with Winnie right behind me.

"This is a bakery," I said to her in my best warning voice. She placed her ears back, tail down. Somber, good girl Winnie. "Behave."

I opened the door and the sound of sleigh bells announced my entrance. The air smelled of sugar, dough and cinnamon. Gone was the glass display case and the strangely old-fashioned diner vibe. The shop was now a pastry boutique, tables showcasing delectable works of art. It took Winnie four seconds to give up being a good girl and launch herself onto the counter where an assortment of miniature cupcakes were displayed.

"Winnie, NO!" I shouted, but it was too late. There were now four fewer of the tiny cupcakes and I picked her up off the floor to keep her from getting more. "Hello? Please help! My dog shoplifted and I need to know if there's chocolate in it and also to pay you, but mostly the first!"

A melodic laughter drifted in from the back room, followed by a red-haired woman. She wasn't short at five and a half feet, but I still towered over her. The wavy red hair swinging to her mid-back complemented the freckles in her alabaster skin perfectly. She'd upgraded her glasses frames from round to green plastic cat-eye, but other than that she looked the same, if not better, than the last time I'd seen her.

"Mo!" I cried out, setting Winnie down to give her a hug.

"Hi, Cyn!" she squealed, hugging me back. "When did you get home?"

"Day before yesterday. When did you get back from Teach for America?"

"A few months ago," she answered, behind us a loud crash sounded as a metal plate rolled around on the floor. I whipped my head around and stared.

"Oh my god, you didn't!" I said, running over.

But she had. Winnie had devoured all of the tiny cupcakes on the tray and looked more than a little pleased with herself.

I felt myself go pale.

"Please tell me-" I stared, and Mo walked around the counter, the picture of calm. She turned the display. A small sign in neat handwriting said:

Dog Cupcakes- Free to Good Boys and Girls

"Oh, thank dog," I said and relaxed my shoulders. "But you are definitely not a good girl! What is the cost for rotten, terrible dogs?"

Mo laughed, a sound like wind chimes in the woods. Peaceful and calming. She'd always been the calm one of my friends. The first to laugh off a bad day and offer a positive outlook.

"We don't discriminate here," she said, pulling more mini cupcakes from behind the counter and tossing one to Winnie. "If you have four legs and fur, you get a pass on all misdeeds."

"Is the owner going to be mad?" I asked looking around. "This used to be Margret's Muffins. Who the heck is Mary?"

Mo burst into a belly laugh and she doubled over.

"What? Are you OK?" I asked, rushing behind the counter to check on her.

"I'm fine. Fine-" she gasped. "Oh geez, Cyn, you know my real name isn't Mo, right?"

I screwed my face up and thought as hard as I could. No, they hadn't called her Mo in school. She was... my eyes went wide.

"Mary O'Connor! You're Mary? These are your muffins?" I asked, my mouth hanging open.

"Well... those are my muffins," she gestured to the display case on the left. "Also, my cupcakes, cakes and bread, but mostly they're for other people."

I laughed and looked around.

"That's so cool, congrats!"

She smiled.

"I heard you blew up Florida."

"Not all of it, just a fuel yard on an Army base," I said, trying not to look ashamed. It *was* only Florida.

"That's kind of disappointing. Aside from Disney World, why does Florida even exist?" Mo said, reaching down to hug Winnie. "How did you score this monster?"

"Mo, Mary, geez... This is Winnie. Formerly Sgt. Winnifred Pupperson, but now that she's retired maybe the rank and last name should be too," I said. Winnie extended a paw and Mo shook it.

"I think maybe she likes the rank," Mo said, laughing as Winnie licked her face and barreled her over onto the floor. Mary fell on her back laughing and hugging Winnie, who I'm fairly certain was trying to lick every residual dusting of flour and sugar off of the woman. "I'm much happier as Mo, but Mo's Muffins is a strip club in Dayton, so I had to diversify."

My mouth fell open and then I busted into a belly laugh of my own.

"Speaking of men who like muffins..." I said and she wiggled a brow. "Yeah... walked into that one."

"Sorry, I forget we're adults now," she said, getting off the floor and making a series of pops that sounded a little too familiar. "At least mentally, physically I'm well aware every time I spend more than five-minutes hunched over a cake. Whose muffins do you want to know about?"

"Reverend Tim," I said and she paled a little looking around. "Sorry, he's not..."

"I know, but still, if my mom heard me talking about muffins in that tone near the reverend, I'd be so grounded. She'd take away my phone and internet privileges, which is half my business. He's been getting a lemon poppy-seed and a blueberry every day for two years now, according to Margret who just rolled all her regulars to me and they seemed fine with it. When he got the virus, he'd order them to go. Recently though, these creepy men in suits have been coming in to pick up his muffins. They claimed to be Uber-eats, but I'm fairly certain they are bears dressed in monkey suits," Mo said, relaxing into her story. "Is he OK?"

"He's in the hospital and he's... uhm... very enthusiastic about your muffins," I said, gesturing to my pants and holding up a finger.

"Eww! Are you kidding?" she asked, somewhere between horror and laughter.

"No, but I think maybe the gorillas-" Winnie let out a bark staring out of the front window and we went over to look at what she'd seen.

She'd spotted two goons walking up the block. One was a tall white man with meaty fists and a look rivaling coma patients in awareness. Beside him was a bigger man, maybe Mediterranean. His suit could have been used to cover the touring Cirque company, but it looked painted on. They both had noses with a few too many bumps from past breaks.

"Are those the guys?" I asked, watching larger man swipe a small object off the table in front of the magic shop and put it in his pocket.

"Yeah, those are the guys. Did he just steal a plastic magic wand?" she asked, pressing her face next to mine on the glass.

"Maybe it turns into flowers and he has a date?" I said, watching them stroll down the street before making a right into the local movie theater. Strange destination for gorillas.

"And maybe I slipped the reverend Viagra," she said dryly, and I nodded.

"Can you watch Winnie, Mo?" She nodded as I rushed out of the door and tried to cross the street casually. Harder than anticipated when I walked behind a car in reverse and nearly got flattened.

"Sorry!" I called out as I ducked into the theater.

Sweet Pea Cineplex was a tribute to old western architecture with sweeping widow's walks and shuttered windows. Inside, it was an homage to the dusty past of cinema. There were velvet ropes in brass stands, an older style podium to tear tickets. A free-standing popcorn cart and a mannequin in a red hat were poised in surreal stillness.

"Here for the show?" he said and I leapt out of my skin. Not a mannequin. His face was grey, and it was impossible to tell if it was make-up or his actual skin. He was somewhere between 16 and 116, with ominous hair coloring and very wide eyes.

"Ye-es?" I stammered and he pointed to the board. They were showing Top Gun with Tom Cruise. "How much?"

"Five dollars please," he answered, and I would swear on my mother's dildo's he practiced being creepy. I forked over the money and he moved to the ticket stand, printing and then ripping my ticket.

"Popcorn?" I shook my head no.

With a sweeping gesture, he beckoned me toward the double doors to the building's single screening room.

"Thanks," I said, walking past him sideways. No way was I turning my back on creepy mannequin man. "Don't kill anyone."

I gave him the double guns with my temporarily permanent thumbs up and backed into the theater. Unlike modern movie theaters, this one was set similar to stage theaters. You entered the back of the house, and four aisles led you forward toward the screen on an elevated platform.

In the front row were the two men in suits, the fake Captain Jacks and a smallish man with his back turned toward me. I crept toward the seats, and strained my ears, trying to catch any sound they were making without making too much of my own. The entire rest of the theater was empty, not ideal spying conditions.

"I'm working on getting the money. I just need more time," the fake captain said. I rested my cast over a seat and tried to look discreetly down the aisle. The muscle stood facing the two seated men, who were one chair apart. "You didn't have to kill him!"

"We didn't kill him," the klepto gorilla said. "He just got a little too excited about the muffins."

"The hospital called, he's dead! You said you wouldn't hurt him!"

"You said you'd deliver my product, Mickey," the seated man said in an oily voice. Not Italian... but not wholly American and definitely not genuine. I missed what came next when the Mediterranean man laughed at a volume reserved for foghorns. "Shut up Henry, you should be seen and not heard."

"Yes, boss," he answered in a deep baritone and I watched him scoop a plastic toy off the ground and put it in his pocket. He had a flash bang laugh and a stealing problem. How was this man not arrested daily?

"You had weeks, Mickey. Weeks upon weeks, and then years. Years you spent hiding from me. There will be no more extensions, for either of us. Monday, I have the money and I have my product, or I have your thumbs," he said as the lights started to dim. I could hear the crackle of speakers and welcomed the sudden darkness to escape.

"What's that, boss?" the other gorilla said, and I looked up.

"Go get them!" he said, as I stared in horror at the cast on my arm.

Nurse Denny had given me a glow in the dark cast that was signaling the bad guys like a freakin' beacon.

"Crap!" I said, bolted up and ran as fast as I could out of the theater while the gorillas tripped over each other in the darkness.

Chapter Ten: Memories and Enemies

"**A**re they gone?" I whispered, sticking my head around the corner. Mo had just bagged a large ornate cake for two men in rainbow spandex, and she was smiling wide at their backs.

"Yeah, I don't see them out there anymore," Mo said, peeking around the corner. "So, Reverend Tim is dead?"

I nodded, showing her the messages from Ian confirming it. It was three lines, the text strangely broken for a man of his skills.

Ian Cruz: Confirmed O.D. Poss Viag.

Ian Cruz: Awaiting confirm, toxic technology.

"What is 'toxic technology'?" she asked, squinting at my phone.

"I think it's supposed to be toxicology, but I'll have to confirm that with him because this is weird enough that toxic technology might be real," I said, leaning against the wall. It was after 8, and all of the streetlights illuminated the walkways, but the twinkle lights crisscrossing the street was the real attraction. It was like being in a fairytale land set in reality.

"I forgot how pretty it is here at night," I said, staring out of the window.

"Yeah, I didn't realize I missed it until I came back," she said, coming up next to me to flip the open sign to closed. "You wanna grab an ice cream?"

I nodded and grabbed a broom.

"I'll help you clean," I said, and she smiled. "Just this once, though. Because my dog made most of this mess and she's never coming back."

Winnie was passed out next to a high-top table with her paws in the air, crumbs stuck to her chin fur. When I'd run back in, I'd dove for cover quickly. This wasn't the first place the muscle checked, and Mo's steady stream of customers was enough of a deterrent that they hadn't lingered long after they came in. Winnie, however, thought their entrance was an opportunity to steal every blueberry muffin on a foot-tall display. Somehow knowing I was hiding and couldn't yell at her, she managed to steal half of the banana nut as well before Mo could grab her and lock her in the back with me.

"Hey, saves me from having to toss them. She took out the day-old discount table," Mo laughed, and I smiled. "So... who's Ian Cruz?"

"He's the Sgt in charge of K-9 handler training for the Army at Lackland outside San Antonio," I answered with a shrug, starting my sweeping near Winnie. "Or at least he was... I'm not sure that's what he does anymore."

"What do you think he does?" she asked, packaging unsold pastries. Mary missed very little.

I shrugged again.

"I've been thinking he's with CIC, Army criminal investigations, since I was in Afghanistan," I said, and she raised a brow. "Yeah... I was stationed there. He just showed up and..."

My brain briefly flitted to the stolen kiss we'd shared. The kiss and the moment... before Winnie head-butted his nuts. Sometimes at night I dreamed about that kiss and all of the much more satisfying ways it could have ended.

"And what, Cyn?" she said, eyes wide and I realized thoughts must be flitting on my face. Thoughts I hadn't shared with anyone.

"We thought we were going to die. I'm not accountable for what happens when my life is in jeopardy," I said, trying not to look as flustered as I felt. Mo didn't buy it.

"Maybe we need more than ice cream for this chat. I have some French baking chocolate?" she offered, and I smiled.

"Trying to butter me up? Between me and the reverend..." I started to joke, but the front door crashed open and we both turned. "What the hell?"

Winnie was on her feet, growling.

Standing in short shorts, a halter top and two pounds of curly brown hair piled artfully on top of her head, was Amber Carter. It was 60 degrees outside, and she had no sweater or boots in deference to the strong wind that had picked up the chill.

"I need a cake," she said in a nasally voice that put Winnie's hackles up and made me wish I hadn't had to turn in *all* of my weapons when I retired. Weapons and hearing protection. "Eww, you let dogs in here?"

"I can't believe they let you in here," I said, trying not to gag on the scent of Moonlight Path that wafted in with her. She'd been drowning herself in body spray since high school, and not a single girl I knew hadn't choked on her chemtrails. "My dog is the less offensive smelling thing in here and she just farted."

"Ew," Amber said, and Mo gave me a fist bump. "Disappointing to see you, Cynthia. It's a shame you didn't die in war. Then our town would have a hero instead of a zero. Maybe you'll accidentally burn something down and we can ship your body overseas and pretend you died there."

"It's a good thing you chose not to wear a sweater in near winter. I'd hate for you to survive the cold," I said and Winnie wagged her tail, eyebrows wiggling in approval. Mo hid a smirk and stared at Amber. "But your body will make a fun ice pinata for people to smash at your funeral."

"We're closed," Mary said, gesturing to the door. Amber ignored her.

"I need a wedding cake," Amber said to Mo. "I need it tomorrow; it needs six tiers and I want it to be flavored with skittles. Each layer a different skittle flavor but with like... a different color so it's a surprise, you know? So like grape is yellow and orange is apple. Why aren't you writing this down?"

"Because you're nuts," she said, laughing, and I felt myself smile.

"No, you're a baker. I need something baked, obviously," she said, crossing her arms. She had some sort of designer bag on her elbow, bangles adorning both arms. "Gordon Ramsey, who's a personal friend of my father, you know, the founder and mayor of Cartersville, made the ceremony cake. But now we need a pre-wedding wedding cake and you have to make that!"

"I don't," Mo said, moving around the corner to escort her to the door. "Congratulations though. Must be exciting to get two cakes."

Amber stomped her foot and dug in her heels like a toddler.

"But you have to! I need a cake!" she wailed, and Mo looked to me for help. "Reverend Tim said he needed a Mary's cake to properly celebrate, so you have to!"

"Costco sells sheet cakes. Maybe Gordon Ramsey could... I don't know, improvise or something? Just pretend Mary made it? Though they're probably closed now and lying to a reverend might be a sin. Maybe tomorrow? You weren't going to eat the cake for breakfast, were you?"

"Uugh!" she screamed. "You don't understand, I *need* it!"

"I know, they should totally stay open past nine," I said. I didn't even want to address the whole Reverend Tim is dead thing. Let someone else tell her that. Mo made eyes at me, she wasn't telling her either.

"You will help me!" she shouted, pointing a finger threateningly. "I am the daughter of the Cartersville town founder and you will help me! I want the Reverend to be happy!"

Mo and I snickered, and her eyes flashed something dark.

"Help me or…" her voice was low and menacing. All humanity lost from her face.

"Or what?" I said, stepping between her and Mo, signaling Winnie to my side. All joy had left my face at the look in her eyes. It was an unhinged desperation I'd seen in the eyes of terrorists and people about to get bit.

It was a look I didn't trust.

"Or… I'll…" she stuttered as Winnie let out a growl. It was like watching a switch flip. She went from crazy to normal to… well, Amber. A bully… but a bully who'd get her hands dirty.

"You'll go home," a man said, and I felt my heart start to race. Ian Cruz was in the doorway- jeans, T-Shirt and leather jacket looking like a very inappropriate dream come true. All he needed was a cowboy hat and then…

"Excuse…" Amber started and turned. One look and her face went to doe-eyed innocence. "Hi."

He nodded.

"I need a cake for…for… my…" she said, moving closer to him. Winnie seized her opportunity and leapt forward, catching Amber squarely between the shoulder blades. With a scream, she fell into Cruz and he somehow caught her before her body touched his.

"Have a good night, ma'am," he said, helping her upright and out of the door before she could register more. He locked the door and turned back to us with a brow raise. Definitely would have been hotter with a hat, but not bad as it was.

"So... she still exists. How is she crazier and who's gonna tell her about the reverend?" I said, to no one in particular. At the silence, I looked at Mo nodding like a bobble head. But she was still staring at the masculine perfection in the doorway. Oh boy, he'd rendered her dumbstruck.

"Cruz, Mo, Mo, Cruz," I said by way of introduction.

He held out a hand and she went redder than her hair, accepting his hand. He shook it very slowly and deliberately with WAY too much eye contact. Cruz smiled and Mo... ran away.

"Dishes!" she squeaked and was gone.

"Deserter!" I shouted after her and I heard metal pans clatter to the ground. I turned back to Cruz and he was smiling with his wide, crooked smile. "You're an ass. You know that, right?"

"She got overwhelmed before even seeing my ass. Maybe I should back-in next time," he joked.

Four more loud crashes came from the kitchen and I rolled my eyes.

"Great, now you owe her new cookware," I said, sitting on a stool and setting down my broom. "What's up?"

"Reverend Tim's pen-" he started, and I slapped my hands over my ears but I could still hear him laughing.

"Why couldn't you have gotten blown-up in Afghanistan?" I said bitterly, and I felt him invade my airspace. "Or at the very least lost an appendage. You wouldn't be so cocky without an appendage- like an arm or a leg or...."

"Glad to hear you have been thinking about my appendages," he whispered against my ear and I felt the same thrill run through my body and warm up every good spot I had. Ian ran his hand up my arm and lifted my chin to face him. Our eyes met and I forgot that breathing was essential to life. "We have unfinished..."

Another crash from the kitchen and I shook off the trance.

"Didn't Winnie's head-butt to your-" he covered my mouth with his hand, eyes serious.

"Cyn, we..." he started, but his phone started ringing. He froze, fighting responsibility with... whatever this was. It rang a second time and he exhaled long and slow. Letting go of my face, he answered it. "Cruz."

He listened, made a few non-descript noises and hung-up.

"I have to go," he said, face etched in regret. I felt mine wash over in relief. "This isn't over."

He pulled me against him, kissed my neck just below my ear with a tiny nip of his teeth. My toes curled and he was gone before my brain caught up to my body. Panting, shaking, and bright red, I just sat on the stool and stared.

"Holy crap, Cyn!" Mo said and all I could do was nod. "This conversation needs chocolate, ice cream, and wine."

I nodded again.

"Anything but vodka."

Coffee clutched in my hand, I walked into the barn with a sense of dread. Mo and I had had too much wine and it was far too early to think about my late-night confessions. Winnie was dragging tail beside me, her mood consistent with every morning and not a wine hangover.

"Long night?" Larry said from behind me, and I looked at him. He was clean shaven, dressed in his lab coat over a button-down and slacks. He extended a hand to Winnie and she gave a half-hearted sniff before falling over onto the ground and refusing to move.

"What's with the outfit?" I said, trying not to let the drool slide out of my mouth. The boy had grown into a man that cleaned up well. If he and Ian kept this up, I was going into early menopause with hot flashes.

"We have a field trip," he said, looking at my jeans and hoodie. "Joseph didn't tell you?"

"He-" I started but the man himself boomed from behind me.

"Well, Cyn, you aren't dead," he spoke coming over. I squeezed my eyes shut. He was so very, very loud.

"Why would I be dead?" I asked, taking in more coffee like an addict at the needle.

"Why aren't you answering your phone?" he asked, and I stared at him. Then I pulled the device in question out of my pocket. I tapped the screen, nothing. I poked the button at the bottom, nothing. I pressed the power button, red box of death.

"It died," I said, and put it back in my pocket. The best part about having the cast was that my permanent upright thumb balanced my coffee, so my right hand was free to do whatever it wanted... such as drinking more coffee. "Where are we going?"

"Sweet Pea Unified," Larry answered with a smile and I narrowed my eyes at him.

"That's not funny," I said and watched his eyes light up.

"That's not a joke, Cyn. I need someone to mind the sheep and the goat. My field hands aren't allowed after the whole 'what is meat?' incident, so you're up," Joseph said and all the life drained from my face.

"I can't go there!" I said in a horrified whisper. "There are children there. I'll tell them where babies, baby cows and sausage come from! I mean it!"

"If you do that, you'll need a new job. I don't need insubordinate children on my farm," he said, and I gaped at him. "I mean it, Miss Sharp. I've tolerated enough from you."

"Children are... mean!" I said and he crossed his arms. "Look, I know I was in a war zone, and Florida, but I can't be near children. Do you know what they say? Godzilla, Destructor, Dr. Diminutive used sarcastically. I graduated for a reason, Joseph! You've tolerated far less from me than I did in my thirteen years at that place!"

"Well, I guess if they're mean to you, pretend they're too short for you to hear them. Grab the truck," he said and walked away. Fired had to be better than going back to school.

"I quit!" I shouted after him, but he just waved.

"Keys are on the hook by Betty," he shouted, and I sighed. "Also, Betty is going with Mary and Berry."

"Buck up, Little Cyn. If you're good I'll buy you an ice cream after," Larry said next to me and I narrowed my eyes at him. He raised his hands in surrender. "Fine, ice cream and Chips

Ahoy? I'll even throw in a package of Double Stuf Oreos and a lollipop."

"I'm going to need a down payment and a barf bag."

He extended a lollipop from a mysterious pocket and I conceded. He handed me a snack bag of Oreos and when I just stared at him, he put them in my cargo pants pocket. We were very close and I wanted him closer. New... confusing... I turned around to not have to think about it.

"Fine." I nudged Winnie with my toe when I got back to her. "You get to see my second least favorite place in the world today, girl."

"What's your first?" Larry asked and I shrugged.

"My mom's house on date night," I said and shuddered.

Laughing, we walked out to the horse trailer and prepared to go to school.

Chapter Eleven:
Back to School

S weet Pea Unified was roughly the size of a small city block. The community, in all its wisdom, decided a K-12 would be perfectly sufficient for the number of students in the community. Which meant if you were born here, you went to the same building nearly every day for thirteen years. Then you went on to work with those same people, most likely until you died without ever meeting anyone new.

For at least thirteen years, though, there was no escape.

It was the same building, same kids, same cafeteria... for thirteen years.

There were technically three buildings, each the size of a small apartment complex. One for K-6, one for junior high and one that served as a high school. The rest of the space, however, was shared. Which meant when I got to a new grade to try out for basketball for a new coach, the previous grade's coach was right there. Watching, flinching, waiting to cover their heads with their arms when the ball flew across the room.

The ball always flew across the room.

Any cafeteria disasters? Spilled food slip, dribble or ostracized seating arrangement- all of it was witnessed by every child in the community. No one could hide, there was no spared embarrassment or shame, everything happened with a complete and captive audience, looking to report on literally anything when they got home.

Nope, between the accidents, the incidents and Amber Carter, nothing good had come from this building. Without any athletic prowess, artistic talent or exceptional smarts, my only options for friendship came from my fellow outcasts, nerds and animal lovers. Most of us had taken to eating lunch out by the corral, but none of us were spared the taunting when our respective bullies found us.

Staring out of the window at the building, I felt a strong urge to run.

"Cyn, you're an adult," Larry said from next to me. I couldn't tear my eyes away from the building.

"So they keep telling me," I said quietly. I had distinct memories of "accidentally" getting hit in the back with various sport balls walking up the front steps. My shoes getting stolen during P.E. to dress up the clown scarecrow. One too many lunch hours came, and all of my cookies were either crushed to dust or stolen.

Nothing good at all had happened here... except leaving.

We drove past the three-building complex toward the far end of the fields. "The fields" was used to describe the sports complex fields and the agriculture arena. While the school did not have a rodeo team, there was an FFA class and a few electives that necessitated an arena for animal related activities. When the losers got tired of being bullied, we went out here. Just looking at the stadium and empty bleachers, I could almost picture the lot of us sitting with headphones, paperbacks and sketch pads.

There's something to be said for being alone without having to be alone.

"Do you want to hold my hand?" Larry asked from next to me and I forced a smile. Winnie bumped her head against my hand, and I managed a real one for her.

Definitely not alone. If Winnie could get me through war and two years in Florida, she could probably get me through a two-hour presentation. I met Larry's gaze and saw the sincerity in his, sincerity and something that made me squirm on the inside. Like any reasonable woman, I decided to run away.

"Let's get this over with," I said, popping the door handle and climbing out of the truck. Winnie leapt out behind me and we walked around to the drop gate on the back of the trailer. Inside we had Mary the Lamb, who was named by the school class at the farm for a field trip when she was born, Berry the goat, named after fruit, and Betty who was looking better after her short break from rotation.

"Cyn, are you going to be OK?" Larry asked and I shrugged.

"If I survive this, I would like first dibs on the field trip to the prison. I'd feel much safer at the prison," I said, taking Berry's lead and walking him down the ramp. A warm hand landed on my shoulder and I turned, finding myself inches from Larry.

"Hey, I was here too, Cyn. I had you then and I have you now," he said, running his hand up and down my arm.

"It was different for you. Your brother was Daniel Kirby, high school god. No one would dare piss him off to mess with you. No one put pudding on the back of your gym shorts, so it looked like you had diarrhea," I said, walking Berry a short ways and tying off the rope on the corral. I bumped into Larry on the way back and he wrapped me in a tight hug.

"You know he woulda kicked ass for you too, right?" he said and I laughed dryly.

"He was tapping every ass he'd have had to kick," I muttered. The squishy feeling was back so I squeezed once and shoved him away. "Like I said, let's get this over with. I had to leave all my military issued weapons in Florida and this fur missile is the only defense I've got."

I gestured at Winnie, and my mouth fell open. She had managed to get into the trailer and was using Betty as a bed and a pillow. The cow, for her part, looked completely comfortable with her weighted blanket. Mary the lamb was looking like she'd rather stand next to Berry.

"You can't go soft on me, too!" I scolded her as I walked over to Mary.

Granting her wish, I took Mary's lead and tied her off next to Berry. The classes were filing into the bleachers and I stared at how small they all looked. Most barely reached my hip, but they all managed to look dangerous with their bright colors, sticky hands and lack of verbal filter. It had been a while since

I was in the arena and it looked smaller than it had in high school. Bleachers that felt impossible to run suddenly looked manageable and thousands of students looked like nothing all lined up in neat rows.

"What time does this start?" I asked Larry, not daring to look at him. I could still feel his arms around me, still smell the delicious scent of man mixed with hay and dirt.

"Not for another half-hour. They like us to be here early," he said and I nodded.

"I'm going to go to the bathroom then," I said, walking back to the truck and pulling my phone off the charger.

"Cyn-" he said, but I waved my phone in the air.

"Nature calls, Larry," I lied, and walked away as quickly as possible. If there was one place you could go to hide from your thoughts, it was the women's bathroom. The women's bathroom in a school is even better because you can hear gossip, read the latest slang graffiti written on the stalls, and feel like Godzilla on the child-sized toilets.

I trekked across the campus, passing high school and junior high for the administrative offices at the front of the elementary. I opened the door and blinked against the sudden dimness.

"Cynthia Sharp how are you?" a booming voice called out and I turned to see Mr. Meden. The man had on khaki cargo shorts, a rainbow tie-dye shirt, and big rubber boots.

"Mr. Meden!" I said, noting that in the 11 years since I'd graduated, he hadn't changed much from large, gay, hippie. He still had a long ponytail, a few more grey hairs than black and his bald crown a little balder. His paunchy tummy was just a little wider, his eyes just a little redder and waterier. "I finally know what that smell is. Seriously, Mr. Meden, every day?"

His face broke out into a wide smile and he looked around conspiratorially.

"I have some extra if you're interested?" he wagged his brows and I laughed. Despite the herbal enhancements, he was one of the kindest, most energetic people at this school. More than one of my peer mishaps was due to defending him. Apparently, it is not ok to like adults that other people mock.

Also, never eat a banana at school after sixth grade.

"I'm good, thanks. I was just looking for the bathrooms for non-miniature people. Haven't been in this place since they forcibly required such things," I said, looking around the office. Each wall held pictures of school functions, classes and awards ceremonies at community and sports competitions.

"You're still up there," he said, and my head snapped back.

"For what?" I asked, eyes wide. I hadn't achieved anything in my many years here. My grades had been slightly above average, my sports skills non-existent, and no one considered reading and singing at the same time an actual talent. I scoured the wall, determined to confirm he was lying while he laughed in the background.

"Did you forget?" he asked as my eyes landed on the horrifying image in question.

It didn't even have the decency of being a school image or a snapshot. It was a clipping from the newspaper where I received an award from town council in 8th grade. The mayor's cat had climbed a tree and I was walking by. At my height, I towered six inches over him and rescued the cat from the tree. In this image

I was wearing a pink shirt and jeans, huge shoes and my hair was going through its Britney 2006 phase. The mayor was smiling up at me, shaking my hand and the cat was clawing the crap out of my arm.

I was literally immortalized on the school wall for being freakishly tall and attacked by a cat.

"Can't we take it down?" I asked, my eyes pleading. "No one would notice!"

"Girl, that is not the picture I was referring to. I actually forgot about that one. I meant that one," he said, gesturing toward the top right. My gaze followed his hands, and I held my breath. No good could come from looking and yet it was impossible not to look.

"Oh my dog," I said, staring. It was so much worse than the newspaper picture.

We were at the Dayton zoo on a class field trip and I was covered in goo from head to toe. This snapshot had to have been provided by my fourth-grade teacher. It featured the whole class, two feet away from me, and a man holding a freshly birthed baby giraffe. The birth of which was the reason I was coated in goo. Standing nearest to me was little Larry. The only one who would sit next to me on the way home. It led to a few too many rounds of Cyn and Larry sitting in a tree, and he wouldn't sit near me for a week after. Some of my earlier squishy feelings dissolved into resentment. That wasn't the first or the last time he got peer-pressured into abandoning me.

A reminder that no matter what he said, he really hadn't been there. Not when it counted.

"I'll pay you!" I begged Mr. Meden, not taking my eyes off the picture. "Whatever you want. I know people!"

"Not a chance, Cynthia. Not a chance. That picture is the best part of working in this office," he said. "That and the one of Katie Spirula winning the National Spelling Bee."

He gestured to a picture a few rows over and I shook my head. Katie was an African American girl with cornrows ending in plastic beads looking like a Victorian era princess in her picture. It didn't hurt that she was absolutely beaming with pride in the picture, but she'd been adorable no matter what. As she got older, she went from adorable to beautiful, but still managed to be incredibly smart and kind. Most of us had gone from kind-of cute to super awkward and stayed there.

Or, at least I did.

"How is she?" I asked, scanning the wall. There were a lot of awkward puberty faces and missing tooth shots. Clothes ranged from grunge to preppy and everywhere between. If the world imploded and this wall was the only that survived, the aliens were going to celebrate. Midwest middle of nowhere was definitely no Paris during fashion week.

"Good. She's invented some sort of DNA sequencing scanner to check for variants in the junk DNA to determine if they're related to some underlying expression of irregular traits," Mr. Meden answered, and I nodded.

Literally nothing after "invented" registered, but my heart beamed with pride for her.

"That's really cool," I said, taking one last scan of the wall when my eyes caught something on the far end. I went over and saw the same kid in the image next to it. He had fine brown hair, dark brooding eyes and hunger pains.

"Who is this?" I asked, hoping the early 80s wasn't too old for Mr. Meden to know.

"That... is Mitchell Scott. Called himself Mickey in high school when he fell in with *that* crowd," he said with a disapproving tut. "He was going places. There was no piece of technology he couldn't fix or improve. This was in the days of backpack cell phones and fax machines. He could have invented the first computer or founded the internet. Instead, he..."

The phone rang and Mr. Meden picked it up while I fumbled for my cell phone. My finger was hovering over Ian's name in my call log when the device vibrated continuously from an unknown number.

"Sharp," I said instinctively and then smacked myself in the forehead. "I mean hello?"

"Cyn," Ian's voice said, and my stomach did a little flip.

"I was just about to call you," I said. "I found the fake Captain Jacks."

"Cyn, they arrested Mo," he said quietly.

"What?" I shouted and could hear the phone yanked from his ear. He was messing with me. Mo wouldn't so much as jay-walk. There was no reason for her to be arrested.

"Chica, you need to get down here. They think she killed the Reverend," Ian said.

"Who is they? Are *they* being drug tested? How would she... I mean he was... what?" I stammered and the phone shut off in my hand. Staring at it, I noticed that it was once again dead.

My eyes shifted between the wall, the device and the ground. Thinking... worrying...

"Is there a problem, Cynthia?" Mr. Meden said from behind me and I stared at him for a moment. I was farther from him than I remembered, and I decided I must have been pacing. I went back to the picture and plucked it from the wall.

"I need to borrow this," I said and ran out of the building toward the field. Larry was in the middle of his pre-presentation opener and he signaled me to bring out Berry. I shook my head no, whistled for Winnie, and climbed in the driver's seat.

He had a pained look in his eye and I wanted to remind him what it felt like to be abandoned. My job was to help with the livestock, they were here. Maybe I was supposed to stay since Larry didn't work for the dairy and they were just "on loan" but I was past caring about my job.

"Cyn!" Larry shouted, keeping up with Winnie while she ran to the car. "What the hell Cyn?"

"They arrested Mo. I need to go," I said, pulling the door out of his hand when Winnie was in. "We'll be back. If I kill your brother, maybe call a taxi?"

"Cyn, you can't just..." he started, but Winnie and I were pulling away.

"I'll try not to make you an only child!" I shouted as he disappeared into a cloud of dust behind the trailer.

Chapter Twelve: Dotted Lines and DNA

If the school could be compared to a small city block, the police station was a hotel annex. Despite having been in existence as long as the town, the police station had never managed to become permanent. It was still set up as a series of portable trailers in a dirt lot off the main highway to nowhere. The one concession to a stable structure was the bunker of brick and mortar that served as a jail.

"Ma'am, you can't!" a young blonde boy called out as I pushed into the first portable trailer at the complex entrance, but one snap from Winnie and he decided his job wasn't worth it. We stormed through the exterior door and started reading signs on trailers. One trailer was marked "interview", so I elected to storm blindly into that building.

I marched up the ramp and gripped the door handle. Deep breath, turn and... locked.

"Kirby, you jerk, open this door!" I shouted, pounding on the poorly constructed material. "You have ten seconds or Winnie opens the door!"

It was obviously a bluff. If Winnie could take down doors like the K-9s on America's Next Top Dog, I wouldn't have had to drive a truck through the wall in Afghanistan.

It was fun though.

"Last warning!" I shouted, hearing the hollow floor creak as someone moved closer to the door. For show, I signaled Winnie to alert. Growl face, snarl, capable- words not usually associated with her, but she could play the part.

"Three, two..." the door wrenched open, and a haggard looking Daniel Kirby stood there, ready for a fight. His neat appearance from Roger's house the other day had slipped to disheveled. He had half a day's growth of beard, his shirt half untucked, and I wasn't sure when he spoke if he had brushed his teeth.

"I swear to God..." he started, but I moved within an inch of his face. Then I backed up an inch because he definitely had not brushed his teeth.

"Where is she, you grown up Ken doll?" I snarled and his eyes registered resignation. Always best to show a married man your mad woman side. Easier to convince them you will, in fact, remove appendages. With a long-suffering sigh, he moved to the side and I walked into a room that reminded me of a principal's office. It had one chair on one side of the table and two on the other. Seated alone was Mo, looking mildly calm for an arrested person.

"Hey, Cyn," she said smiling.

"Hey, Mo. What the hell?" I said, sitting beside her and pulling Larry's Oreos out of my pocket. Winnie tried to steal one, but I moved them closer to Mo and tossed her a treat from my other pocket.

"What are you? Mary freaking Poppins?" Daniel said and I narrowed my eyes at him.

"I might no longer have my weapons, Kirby, but I can still kill you," I said and he held up his hands in surrender. Dropping to his chair, he snaked an Oreo from the bag and popped it into his mouth. His eyes were dark and sunken, and he hadn't slept.

"Since you're here, maybe you can explain the mysterious 'wise guys'," he said, chewing his cookie and reclining in his seat. He was trying to look relaxed and in charge, but he looked two seconds away from collapsing. Which would soften me if he hadn't arrested my friend. Also, he could have been missing sleep engaging in activities that would overpopulate the elementary school and he should suffer for that.

"Maybe, since I'm here," I said, trying to keep my anger in check, "...you can explain why Mo is in custody!"

"Who the hell is 'Mo'?" he asked, and Mary nervously raised her arm. "I thought your name is Mary."

"It is," she said, shrugging and taking an Oreo for herself. She chewed it delicately, always the reserved one when nervous.

"OK..." he said, dragging out the letters. Mo blinked, Winnie blinked, I crossed my arms and he held up his hands in surrender again. "Mo is here because the last contents of the deceased reverend's stomach were muffins and a cocktail of Viagra and liquefied amphetamines. When we went to ask Ms. O'Connor about the muffins, we found this in her trash can."

He tipped a paper evidence bag onto the table. An empty plastic blister pack landed on the scarred wood and I stared.

"You found a pill pop thing, so what?" I said, looking at him with indifference.

"It's for Viagra," he said, flipping it over with his pen.

"Did you have a warrant to get it?" I asked, following his lines of thought to the most obvious conclusion. He was wrong, but it was the shortest path to answers. Answers that meant he could be home making another baby by five.

"Don't need one, it was in plain sight," he said, looking smug.

"Plain sight in a restricted employee area?" I countered; his smile faltered.

"No, the trashcan by the pastry counter," he said.

"One that anyone could have accessed, including the reverend's new suited delivery men?" I asked and his face fell a little further.

"It doesn't matter. She had access to the drugs, the muffins and the reverend. She's the top suspect," he said, deciding denial was the best way to go.

"Then where is her liquid Adderall?" I said, cocking my head to the side.

"Why would you say Adderall?" he asked, eyes shifting uncomfortably.

"Because liquid meth wouldn't have the same effect as an amphetamine-based medication suspended in a solution. It's already designed to be absorbed through the gut," I said, watching him carefully.

"I... uh..." he stammered, and Mo gaped at me.

"So, you have circumstantial evidence in a maybe murder, you leapt to the easiest possible conclusion and you didn't even bother to find out how your alleged murder happened. Am I missing something?" I said, giving Winnie a scratch on the head. She'd moved between me and Mo, offering the woman her paw as comfort.

"What do you mean 'maybe murder'? He's dead with a boner!" Kirby snapped. Men hate when you point out the flaws in their logic.

"Yes, and... what? He wasn't upset to have the boner. As I recall, when he came in he was very enthusiastic about it, the muffins and Mo's delivery men. His exact words were 'Little Mary makes magic muffins, her and those delivery men.' So how do you know he was a fan of the muffins because of the boner or a fan of the muffins unrelated to the boner?"

"Will you stop saying boner?" he asked, red in the face.

"Would you prefer erection?" I countered.

"I'd prefer not to discuss the man's penis at all," Mo interjected, and Kirby nodded.

"Fine," I said. Not sure where to go, I crossed my arms under my chest and leaned back. Winnie moved her head to my lap and started nosing her way closer and closer to the table. "Leave it."

With a long-suffering sigh, she flopped onto the floor.

Kirby's eyes bounced between the three women sitting opposite him, and I reveled in watching him squirm. Mo was daintily eating the same Oreo, Winnie just let out an impressive yawn, and my eyes were aiming to drill holes into his skull. The moments stretched on in silence.

"What's really going on, Daniel?" I asked, and he gave an impressive yawn of his own.

"What do you mean?" he said, and I glared at him.

"You haven't slept... maybe not since I saw you at Roger's house. The reverend died yesterday afternoon. Sucks, but it's not the crime of the century. Now you have Mo in here, looking like you are seconds from death, smelling worse. What the hell is going on?"

"This a police matter, Cyn-" he said, and I held up a hand.

"Save it. I've been investigating for longer than you. Tell me what's happening so I can call you an idiot, take my friend home and go pick up your brother."

"Roger is missing. Later that day, people were complaining about chickens. Chickens on their driveways, in the road, just... everywhere. So, we called Roger and nothing. We went in and he's gone. The place looks trashed, but we think it could always look like that. There's no one to ask. Then the petty thefts are getting pettier, there's church ladies after me about their money, and now you. You are here and being a pain. All I wanted was to clear up one freaking case, one case. You know it is possible to convict based solely on circumstantial evidence. Not hearsay, but circumstantial is fine," he said, coming back to arrogant and always right. The effect lost some steam when he let out a massive yawn and drool rolled down his chin.

"Circumstantial is like circumcision, it only works when the victim is too young to object," I shouted back. The turn of phrase had the desired effect, he flinched.

A loud knock sounded throughout the room and he leapt up. Like a drowning man offered a rope, he practically ran to fling open the door. On the other side was the same blonde boy I'd walked past in the lobby.

"S-sir?" he stammered, eyes on Winnie.

"What, Cadet Chandler?" Kirby responded, positioning himself between the Cadet's line of sight and Winnie. I stuck my tongue out at his back and watched the cadet get red and start to sweat.

"Sir, I have a message," he said. His voice was shaking nearly as much as the paper in his hand.

"Go on," Kirby said, but he wasn't very encouraging. The boy started shaking and I rolled my eyes. In the Army, kids like that would get eaten for breakfast in Basic. As it was, Winnie was licking her chops. He was a sucker who smelled like snacks.

"Sir, it's from the clergy," he said, hand extending forward. Interested, Kirby grabbed the paper, thanked the boy and shut the door squarely in his face.

Daniel Kirby's eyes ran back and forth across the paper. Once, twice, three times, but his face never changed. He just stood there, mouth hanging open with his hands on his hips staring at the paper in disbelief.

"Problem with your conclusions, Deputy?" I asked with a bit more attitude than the curiosity I really felt. His eyes flashed up to us, back to the paper and then back to me. I suddenly really wanted to look at that paper.

"He… isn't a reverend," Kirby said, and I creased my brow.

"He's not a reverend because…?" I asked and he looked back down at the paper.

"There's no record of a Timothy Church, or Reverend Tim, or Pastor Church. The whole identity was fake. The man who married half the people in this town… wasn't a reverend."

Kirby looked like he was about to throw up. Taking pity on the man, I stood up and guided him back to his chair. Relieving him of the paper, I stared down at the information scrawled in loopy childish writing. No record, not collecting the body, some kind of joke… not a happy note.

"How old is that kid?" I asked, trying to distinguish the jumbled print and cursive scrawls on the note.

"I… don't know. He's a cousin's kid of some town council whatever," Kirby said. "Do I have to tell the town that a man with no training or ties to the church baptized their kids? Married them? Blessed their… blessing things?"

He was staring off into space and I rolled my eyes.

"His name was Tim Church. If his name was any faker, he'd be your wife's…"

"Enough," came the smooth voice of Ian Cruz as he strode into the room. He looked at the pale deputy, the dumb-struck Mo and me. His eyes lingered on me and I felt suddenly naked. I crossed my arms like it would help and he gave me a crooked smile.

"What? I'm just saying. If people cared about the legitimacy of their cult activities, they'd have questioned a reverend named Tim Church," I said, hands in the air. "But what do I know,

I just stopped a bombing, munitions thefts and had a man arrested for sexual harassment."

"You never questioned it," he said, moving closer. My heart rate climbed into my throat.

"I never went to church... or considered him as anything other than a boring old white guy," I said, trying to move away from him to get air back into my lungs. I was losing steam for my anger. Now I just wanted to know where the angry chicken farmer is... and why Cruz smells so good.

"Old, white and not a member of the monastery is accurate. Boring he was not... at least he wasn't until he came here in the 1980s," Ian said, ignoring my bids for freedom and leaning against the wall right next to me, an arm draped around my shoulders. "His name is Antonio Scott. He went into the wind when he was paroled after committing armed robbery, embezzlement and narcotics sales."

"Scott?" I asked, suddenly making connections. "Did he have a son?"

"Why, chica?" Ian asked, somehow making chica the dirtiest word I'd ever heard. He also was moving slowly closer. I felt like he was either trying to distract me or...

"The fake captain, the one pretending to be Jacks," I said, grabbing the picture out of the same cargo pocket I keep Winnie's treats in. Cruz took the picture, looking from it to me.

"His name is Scott?" Ian prompted and I nodded.

"Mitchell Scott, he went to Sweet Pea about ten years before me in the 1990s. He was apparently very into technology. They thought he'd go places... but then there was something about falling in with a wrong crowd," I said, and Kirby seemed to shake himself free.

"What does that have to do with..." Kirby started, but Ian silenced him with a look. In the awkward silence, Ian motioned for me to continue, but I was still trying to connect all the dots. The dead man was the father of the man in debt to gorillas in suits. Was he leverage?

"When did the reverend get here? Was he married?" I asked and everyone looked to Kirby who shrugged.

"How would I know?" he said, and Mo rolled her eyes.

"Your mom is president of the church committee. Call her!" Mo said.

"Oh... right," he said, getting up and walking out of the trailer to make the call. That or he was giving up and taking a nap, but I hoped he was calling.

"What are you thinking, Cyn?" Cruz asked, but it came as more accusation than question.

"Antonio Scott might be... probably is, Mitchell's father. Mitchell is fake Captain Jacks. He brought him here when he was released, posed as a reverend and made a life somehow? Then his son gets into some bad stuff, wise-guy stuff, and his dad is... what? Taken hostage by those dudes to leverage the return of Mitchell. But then he died... so now what?" I said, speculating out loud. Kirby came back in, pale and fidgety. "When did the reverend get here? Where is Mitchell's mother? What did your mom say, Kirby?"

He stared off. Maybe he hadn't called her.

"My mom... said Reverend Tim showed up in 1985 with a small boy and a young woman. He took over the local church when Reverend Skip transferred without notice," he said, swallowing hard.

"So... Antonio Scott, fake reverend Tim, got rid of Reverend Skip, took over his job and raised Mitchell... what happened to the woman?" I asked, staring at Kirby.

"She..." he said, staring into space.

"She what?" I prompted and he seemed to shake himself free.

"She moved out just when the boy was in junior high. She married my dad's brother," he said, looking a little far away again.

"Did she ever mention Tim/Antonio? Mention Mitchell? Mention why Skip transferred out of nowhere?" I asked and he just kept shaking his head no. Beside me I could feel Ian try and radiate calm, but he was just as annoyed as I was.

"Do you talk to your family, Kirby?" I asked.

"You didn't even visit yours, Miss High and Mighty!" he came back accusingly.

"My mom buys chia seeds in bulk from the internet and thinks her house is the set of Fifty Shades. You wouldn't visit either. They live here, you live here, I was in another country, in the service of this one. What the hell is your excuse?" I asked, punching Cruz when he burst into laughter.

"She's... boring," he said, and I growled. "Seriously, are you the dog, or is she?"

Winnie and I growled in unison and he took a step back.

"No, I haven't talked to her in a while. She didn't have kids and she wasn't big on being near them," he said. "I was a kid, now I have kids and she lives an hour away."

"Didn't have kids except this one, maybe!" I said, shaking the picture and he made a face. "An hour away where?"

"You don't know that. Maybe she's his sister," he said, cutting me off when his phone rang and he answered. After a brief exclamation, he handed me the phone. "It's for you."

"What?" I said, taking the device. "Hello?"

"Cyn, I have a goat, a lamb and a cow. Where the hell are you?" Larry asked and I winced.

"You know because... you called..." I stammered.

"Rhetorical question. Get your ass back here!" he shouted and hung up.

"I... gotta go. Mo, wanna see a cow, a goat and a lamb?" I said and she nodded. Standing, she brushed cookie crumbs off her shirt and extended her hand to Kirby.

"Good to see you again, Daniel," she said, and he stared.

"You can't leave!" he shouted, and I grabbed Mo's hand.

"She can, she will, she is. After I get your brother, I'm going to visit your aunt. Maybe you should be nicer to your family," I said, tugging Mo out of the trailer with Cruz right behind us.

"Cyn, I swear to God-" he started, but Winnie turned and barked at him. "Fine. Whatever. I know where to find all of you! I'm telling my brother you suck!"

Holding up my middle finger I shouted over my shoulder, "Have a great day!"

Chapter Thirteen: Family Ties

F our hours later, Larry still hadn't spoken to me.

When I pulled up at the school with Mo, he had three ropes attached to three animals and a very angry face.

"Larry, I-" but he'd held up a hand, gave me ropes, and got into the truck. He sat in the driver's seat, staring straight ahead, gripping the wheel. Mo helped me load the animals in the trailer and we dropped her off first. Back at the farm, Larry left and I closed out my day. Technically, he didn't work there, and it was borderline creepy that he was always around. I was relieved he left. It would be much easier to go interrogate his aunt if I didn't have to tell him I was going.

After saying goodbye to Joseph, Betty and Berry (Mary had run off faster than Winnie in the chow hall), I headed to the dirt lot I'd left my car in.

Winnie let out a low bark as I entered the address I'd gotten for Larry's aunt into my phone.

"What girl?" I asked, looking up.

Larry was sitting in my Jeep.

"Get..." he'd cut me off again. I stared, he stared back.

"Whatever," I got in.

After a long, silent drive, we were now sitting in front of her house. It was an older structure with faded paint, a large wraparound porch and signs of water damage on the wood. A fence composed of wooden posts in both a perpendicular and parallel fashion marked the boundary, but it still felt open and airy. Like it was just part of the land. Fields of something were to one side, a small coop of chickens to the other. Nothing was new, but it wasn't neglected. It had that lived in feeling that countryside homes emanated.

"What's her name?" I asked, forgetting for a moment Larry wasn't speaking to me. I hoped her name would match the place.

"Maggie," he answered, and I jumped. "She's from Louisiana and didn't finish school beyond 7th grade."

"Maggie... Kirby from Louisiana?" I asked and he nodded. "You see her a lot?"

He shrugged and stared out the window.

"Are you guys close?" I tried again and he shrugged again. The speaking portion of the trip was as short as my patience at this point.

"Why are you here?" I said, exasperated and over his immature roller coaster.

He gave me his best death glare. Not even my bunny slippers ran for cover and I considered booping his nose to remind him he was adorable.

His death glare got angrier.

"What? You wouldn't let me apologize, you didn't speak to me, and you were just in my car when I got off work. Why are you here? Obviously, you don't want to talk to me and I can do this without you!" I ranted and he rolled his eyes. Apparently, I was being an idiot, which was fine because he was the second person in his family I wanted to flip-off today. Without any more comments, I climbed out of my Jeep, whistled for Winnie and slammed the door as hard as I could. My casted arm throbbed and I just wanted a nap. We went to the front door of the plantation style home, carefully moving around puddles and signs of animal inhabitants. Before I could knock, the door swung open and a small, feisty dark-haired woman stared at me down the double barrels of a shotgun.

"Git out," she said, and I raised a brow.

"No? I'm trying to find Mitchell Scott," I said, hoping the name would get me in.

Maggie racked the shotgun.

"Ain't had nothin' to do wit him or our good for nothin father in o'er a decade. Get out!" she said and jabbed the gun toward me. Winnie growled and took a step forward. The gun swung toward Winnie and I snapped. I could tolerate guns and bombs aimed at me, but no one, no one, points guns at my dog. I launched myself forward, grabbed the gun, pushed it up and she squeezed one of the triggers. The scattershot erupted and a massive hole appeared in the canopy over us as wood and dust rained down. Ears ringing, hand now burned, I yanked it away and flung it across the yard.

"Enough! I have had enough of you and all of the other stupid-ass Kirby family members. You don't want to tell me about your stupid brother or your dead father, fine. But point a gun at my dog again and I will rip leaves from your family tree one branch at a time!" I screamed and Winnie crouched low beside me and whimpered. I looked down at her and back at the woman. Maggie's face was no longer angry or indignant.

"He's... he's dead?" she stammered, and her eyes misted.

Crap.

"It's OK, Aunt Maggie, it's OK," Larry said, smoothly coming up beside me and placing an arm around the much shorter woman. He had to nearly fold himself in half to do it, but he managed to gracefully comfort her and lead her to the porch swing without doing any permanent damage to his spine.

"How.. How?" she squeaked out and I started to back away. Her tears spilled over and she released a shuddering wail. Like any reasonable person confronted with extreme emotion, I took my dog and ran back to the car. We climbed in and I stared at the house and the woman and Larry on the bench from the safety of its confines.

"Wh- what kind of person..." she stammered, gesturing toward me and I shrank into the seat.

"She's had a bad day," I heard Larry say, calmly and clearly. "My brother arrested her best friend."

"F-for what?" she stammered thickly, and I watched him shift uncomfortably.

"Maybe... it's probably best we skip that for now," he said, face suddenly beet red. It was nearly 6PM and the sun was setting, washing his discomfort in a glow that looked to be the picture of pain and regret. Mitchell Scott was her brother; Reverend Tim/Antonio Scott was her father. How had I come up with him being her ex-husband? In person, she was much younger than I imagined. If Mitchell had been in junior high in the 1990s, she was probably early 20s when she got married. More, it sounded like she hadn't enjoyed her family. But... but did she know what happened to Skip? Is she a material witness to a murder? Her crying was creepy. It had a rhythm, a steady pace, as if guided by a metronome. Sob on the downbeat, sniffle on the up.

The crying stopped as suddenly as it started, and I decided I wanted answers more than I wanted to hide. With a long inhale and exhale, I got back out of the car. Going for casual, I retrieved the gun while I could still see it and carried it back to the porch. I propped it beside the front door and went to lean against the porch railing across from the swing.

"Maggie... I'm sorry," I said, but I was mostly looking at her shoes. She had on rain boots caked in farm goo, faded well-worn jeans and a flannel button down. Her dark hair was held in a simple ponytail and her face held more laugh lines and sun damage than anything else. Aside from my neon green glowing arm, I was completely shadowed in the faded light.

"Why are you here?" she said, voice coming together. Her posture was rigid and she hadn't liked me seeing her cry. That I respected. I was also relieved it meant I probably wouldn't have to see her cry a second time.

"Skip," I said with a shrug. "Larry's mom told Daniel that he mysteriously and suddenly transferred flocks after your father came in as Tim. I'd thought... maybe..." I said, but her eyes took on a shifty panic. I watched her look all directions, her feet jiggling in her boots.

"Maggie... is he dead?" I asked quietly and she let loose a bark of laughter that sent my skin crawling.

"Dunno," she said and shook her head. "He wasn't a reverend any more than my dad was. Far as I can tell, he was another liar workin' the folks down in Sweet Pea. I didn't know until the suit men showed up, but a few things made sense when people started asking about him when they hadn' for some time. My dad was trained by Skip then, he left. We didn't talk 'bout it. Probably don't matter now that he's dead."

"Skip?" I asked, eyes wide.

"No, ma dad. Though prob'ly Skip's too. That bone bag was ancient," she said, coming into herself. "Look, I'm sorry a'out the gun and all that business with the waterworks. Jus' caught me off guard. He wasn' a man people miss, bu' he was ma father."

I nodded and looked at Larry. It was possible this woman needed psychiatric help and he was the only doctor present. Larry rolled his eyes and rose to his feet.

"I'll go get us some iced tea. You want to talk to Cyn, Maggie?" he gestured toward the open door with his thumb.

She nodded and he nodded back, leaving us standing on the porch. Maggie was staring at her boots and I was staring at

Winnie. I had so many questions, but I wasn't sure where to start.

"Ya gonna speak or should I ask the dog?" she said, and I snapped out of my thoughts. Her eyes were on me now, fierce and determined. It was such a dramatic shift that I had to do a double take. Maybe I was the one being interrogated instead of her.

"Ye- yeah. You said Skip was a fake reverend. Did anyone guess that? Poor Mrs. Kirby, failing to notice two frauds while she sat on the church board," I said, not feeling sorry at all.

"Wasn't her then, though. Some lady named Margot was in charge of the church board in those days. She an' Skip was pretty close. Don' wanna speak out of school, but it wasn' jus' your church leader board member relationship ya know what I mean," she said, pausing as Larry came back holding 3 plastic cups of iced tea. He gave Maggie one first, then held one out for me.

"Mrs. Margot and Skip? But she was- is- was married. Also she's like a million," I said, holding the cup but not drinking. I had aversion to iced tea as it was not coffee. It did, however, have caffeine which was sometimes worth sucking up the weak leaf water. It was no bean water, but it *was* theoretically better than nothing.

"Dunno if her husband was still 'round then. She left the board 'bout when he transferred. That's when their mom took her spot," she said after a long drink of tea. "Only know because I was in charge of cookies. Dyslexic, couldn't do school but I could bake."

"Mrs. Margot and... Skip? She never mentioned..." I said, trying to piece together in my mind why Mrs. Margot wouldn't mention Skip. Did she know he wasn't a real reverend? Did she know Tim wasn't? Was there actually missing Bingo money?

The last was definitely yes because I watched it disappear... didn't I?

I clutched my skull as my brain gave in and drank the tea. It needed the hit and I needed an idea.

"Was she mad when he left?" I asked and Maggie shrugged.

"I wasn' really old enough to be part of those talks," she said and I nodded as a rooster crowed beside me.

"Do you know Roger?" I asked, not sure if raising chickens was a community activity like running or quilting.

"Roger what?" she asked, and I frowned.

"I... don't know. His brother is Joe's Towing, and he has chickens and a red Firebird," I said, wondering why I had asked. Just because he was missing and his chickens were running amuck, it wasn't my business. It was just weird and there were chickens and his were the first chickens I'd ever... terrified.

"Oh... yeah, everyone knows Roger. He's nearly as big a liar as my father. Egg thieving is his big thing. Heard he has debts," she said and took another drink. She wasn't making eye contact, but some of those debts could be with her and I wasn't one to question collections.

"If your brother had debts, who would they be to and what for?" I asked, eyes bouncing to the road. A single headlamp appeared at the top of the hill. The hill only led to this house and those just beyond it with no outlet. Not an unusual place for people to travel, but it was rutted and uneven, not the place for a motorcycle.

Especially one that had turned off its engine.

"My guess? He made more promises than he could deliver on," she said, and I glanced back before returning to staring at the silent motorcycle. I set the cup down on the porch railing.

"Promises about what?" I asked and she shrugged.

"Always tryin' ta make a get rich quick scheme. Good with computers, bad with just about e'erything else," she said, not paying any attention to the bike on the hill.

"What was he trying to do with technology?" I asked, knowing Mr. Meden had said it was the reason for his award and picture on the wall.

"Summin about the brain bein' an electronic switchboard. Said e'erything could be re-wired and repro'rammed with an electrical redirection," she shrugged. The motorcycle still hadn't moved. It was sitting silently at the top of the hill.

"Do any motorcycles come out here?" I asked, moving closer to the shotgun. All of Winnie's hairs were on end and the air felt charged. Someone was watching and they had a bad idea.

"Can' make it down the road any way," Maggie said, standing and scanning the hill. "It ain't even."

I picked up the shotgun and leveled it at the figure on the hill, wishing for my scope. Despite my thumbs up cast position, my shooting wasn't impaired. The V created by my fingers kept the gun steady. On the exhale my finger balanced on the trigger.

I watched the rider, holding my breath even and steady. The engine roared to life and after a wheel spin, the motorcycle zoomed off in the other direction.

"Any ideas on who might have a motorcycle and might want to come down here?" I asked, not lowering the shotgun.

"Not a one," she answered and I waited. No engine, no headlights, just chicken sounds and crickets. I lowered the gun and handed it to her.

"Keep that handy. If you see Roger, call Kirby... I mean Daniel. He's apparently gone missing and his chickens are flailing about," I said. She nodded and checked the gun, precise and well-versed. "I'll come back in a week to fix that."

I gestured up at the awning and she shrugged it off.

"No need. Husband's had to patch that spot more than once. He'll have it done before supper," she said and I smiled. Extending my hand, she shook it and we shared an understanding. An understanding and something else, something sinister as her hand squeezed just a little too tight.

"Have a good night and be safe. Call me if you need something shot," I said and she let out a pleasant bark of laughter. Larry went in for a hug and Winnie led the way down the porch. I had her leash draped off the four fingers of my non-casted arm and there was just enough moonlight to see the walkway. All was going well until a chicken darted across the path.

A fat white chicken that decided two inches from Winnie's many teeth was the perfect place to be.

She lunged, the chicken flapped and I ended up face down in the muddy water puddle.

"Winnie, leave it!" I shouted, sputtering mud and slime but holding tight to her leash. No more chicken deaths will be on her paws. Also, Larry's aunt was still armed. A warm set of arms looped under my arms and I was returned to standing, leash still clenched.

Larry was smiling.

"Feeling better?" I said through gritted teeth.

He smiled.

"Ride to the hospital in Yellow Springs before we head home?" he asked, gesturing to my side.

"Wha-," I said, but I could see. My cast had cracked and was taking on mud and water like a beached ship. "Damn-it! Why dog? What did I do to deserve this?"

I was looking at Winnie and the sky alternately, but both were strangely quiet.

"I hate you all," I muttered and opened the door for Winnie.

Larry laughed and put me in the passenger seat of my own Jeep. Wide smile on his face, he leaned in close and whispered in my ear.

"Wait until you see your ass."

Chapter Fourteen: Revelations

"**Y**ou don't have to wait," I said to Larry as we were on our second hour in Emergency. "You can take Winnie and the car, go home. I'll get home another way. Like Uber or whatever."

Nurse Sean was on duty. He'd walked past me three times tutting and I'm fairly certain he was skipping me on purpose. It was Friday night and there was a reasonable amount of stupid and intoxicated needing medical attention, but not two hours' worth. This was punishment, my penance for destroying all of those other casts.

He was making me pay for his labor in agony.

If it hadn't been nearly nine when we got to Yellow Springs, I'd have tried to go to the clinic in Sweet Pea to avoid the Married Nurses Grimm. No such luck at this hour, everything in Sweet

Pea closes at six. Muddy, in pain and tired through and through, I'd had enough of childish men. I was ready to start throwing things at Nurse Sean every time he walked by and it would be easier without witnesses who knew where I lived.

"No way," he said, slinging an arm over my shoulders and leaning my head into him. "You are wearing your *bad decision imminent* face and if I leave, I'll just have to come back and pick you up from jail."

"No," I protested. Ready to be done fighting, I gave in and relaxed into his shoulder. "I'd call someone else so you can watch Winnie. What color do you think they'll give me next?"

"You don't get a choice?" he said, skeptical.

"Not since the pink one," I said with a shrug.

"I never saw the pink one," he smiled into the top of my head. "But Daniel said it was very cute covered in mud and chicken droppings."

"I hate your whole family," I said with a wide yawn and he pulled me in closer. Kissing the top of my head he said quietly.

"Take a nap, cranky pants. I'll wake you up when it's your turn."

I woke up warm, comfortable and not in the basement of my parents' house. Sun was streaming through the windows, there were actually windows and it smelled... like a man.

"I died," I muttered. "I've died and this is my happy place."

"No," came a gruff male voice beside me. "But I'm glad you think this is your happy place."

Instant panic.

I threw an elbow, raked my nails in the direction of the voice and summoned Winnie. She was on the floor beside the bed in an over-stuffed dog spaceship bed and a lid flutter is all I got. I whipped my head around and tried to see everything at once as someone sat up beside me, hands raised.

"What-" I said, panic growing and clogging my throat. In bed with a man and no memory of anything, hello worst nightmare. I checked myself, I was wearing clothes. Nothing was in pain, arm was... still in a cast. My eyes flashed to the man next to me... Larry.

"You OK?" he asked, trying to sit up and find his glasses with fresh scrapes down his arm.

"H-how did I get here?" I stammered. I wasn't wearing my clothes. The T-shirt and shorts were clearly his, my cast was new, and I had no recollection of any of it.

"I knew you wouldn't remember," he said, scrubbing his face with his hands. "They had to re-break your arm to set it. There were some drugs and then even more drugs. I tried to take you to your parents' house, but you started screaming about... I'd rather not repeat it. You woke up the neighbors though, so I brought you here. I was going to sleep on the couch, but you insisted that I needed to monitor you for fire-breathing stone qualities and ensure that the talking fairy squirrel didn't get you. You put a pillow wall between us, claiming to be building a castle like the aliens built the pyramids."

I was now just staring at him with my mouth open.

"Don't look at me like that. I was worried about you enough to let you sleep here, but I was more scared *of* you than *for* you."

"I was on drugs!" I hissed and he laughed. "I thought I was going to die or murder people, probably!"

"Both of those things are always true, drugs or no. But are you feeling better now?" he asked, and I nodded. "Do you have plans for the day?"

"I need to talk to Mrs. Margot," I said, and he gave me a Winnie style head tilt. "She was in charge of the board when Pastor Skip 'transferred' and she's also the one who wanted all this looked into. I think she knows more than she's letting on and I want to know what it is."

"We could call my brother?" Larry suggested, but he held up his hands when I snarled at him. "Fine, fine, we won't tell my brother. But if he finds out we didn't tell him something about his case, I'm throwing you under the bus."

I shrugged. It seemed fair.

"Where do you think she'll be today?" I asked, looking around the room. Larry had a house; it was a single-story unit and this was clearly the master with an attached bath.

"Probably the same place everyone else in town will be: Amber's Wedding," he said and then laughed at my curled lip. "Everyone wants to see if she actually managed to marry a prince."

"I'm guessing it's a frog and she's hoping he'll turn into one after. Poor little guy must be so grossed out to be stuck with something so slimy," I said, and Larry shook his head. "OK, ok, I'll get all of my frog jokes out now and then we'll go find Mrs.

Margot. No idea how this wedding is going to happen if the reverend is dead."

"I'll go get you coffee before anyone else turns up dead," he ambled toward the door.

"I'm not going to-" I started and then stopped. Looking down at Winnie, I had a saner thought. "Maybe get Winnie some food?"

"Already on it," he waved me off. At the doorway, he froze.

"What?" I asked, looking around. I didn't have coffee yet, but there were no Lego's on the floor and I hadn't hit him with anything.

"The reverend is dead," he said, eyes getting wider as he turned around to look at me.

"Oh em gee, did they give you drugs too?" I said in my best valley girl impersonation. "Now please, the coffee, Larry!"

"No... it's just... crap," he muttered, and I walked over to feel his forehead. He swatted my hand away and shook his head. "I'm not sick, but I might be. I have to marry them."

"Ew, why? Both of them? Can you opt to just marry the prince and leave Amber high and dry?" I asked and his horrified look turned into one of just pale-faced horror.

"Because I got ordained for my brother's wedding and I'm the only other person in town who can," he muttered. I blinked at him and then burst into laughter. Full-bellied, body racking laughter that stole my breath. Winnie came over to check on me, my eyes watered, but I wouldn't stop laughing.

"This is not funny!" he said, kicking clothes that were laying on the floor.

"It is from where I'm standing," I said and he turned a glare my way.

"Where you'll be standing naked when I take my clothes back if you don't stop laughing!" he threatened, but there was no conviction. "Are you safe to drive? I have to go find a suit."

"Safe as I usually am. I'd be safer with coffee," I said with a shrug and Winnie let out a grumble. "I promise not to drive through another wall."

"You... never mind. Keys are on the counter. I'll meet you in the square in an hour. Dress nice!" he warned with a threatening finger.

"Why? I'm not going to that wedding," I said, looking around for my mud stained and gross clothing.

"Yeah, you are. Because I need to go see Mrs. Margot and you aren't allowed to talk to her unless you agree to be my date," he said, hands on hips.

"What?" I protested but my stomach fluttered. He wanted to be my date? That was new from the lie he told me to get out of being my prom date.

"I need a solid buffer between me and her bridesmaids. Handsy, Footsy and Lashes," he said, and my heart sank an inch. I'm just something solid between him and something he doesn't like. What else is new. Might as well be covered in giraffe birthing liquid, again.

"Fine," I said, grabbing Winnie's leash and heading out of the room.

"Cyn-" he said, but I waved him off.

I had to go shopping.

An hour later, I was standing in the square wearing a new dress, new shoes and a freshly washed Winnie. She was sporting the best leather collar available at the local pet shop and a bow. My dress was dark green, mid-calf in length with a vintage vibe. It looked good, but I was mostly excited because it had pockets. Just in case, I'd slung a shoulder bag on with Winnie supplies: water, snacks, gas masks... the usual. We were fidgeting in place when a small hand tapped my shoulder.

I turned to look down at Mrs. Margot.

"Hi, Mrs. Margot," I said, extending a hand, taking it back and then putting it out again.

"Lawrence said you wanted to see me," she said, supporting herself on her walker.

"Yes, can we... sit?" I asked, gesturing over to a table just some ways off. She followed and we took seats at a picnic table just next to the square.

"Glad to see you own non-soiled clothing," she said with a sniff and Winnie made a grumble.

"Mrs. Margot, why didn't you tell me about Reverend Skip?" I asked, cutting through all pretense.

"Why... what?" she said, leaning back.

"Please, don't lie. I heard you ran the church board before Mrs. Kirby. You gave up your position when Reverend Tim came on. He'd arrived with two children you never mentioned, one of whom reappears conveniently after you report Tim getting COVID. Shady men popped up around the time Tim got 'COVID' and you're talking about missing bingo money no one saw move. So... let's start with Skip. You were friends?" I asked, pulling a notebook out of my bag. Writing things down wasn't necessary but I needed to do something with my hands.

Mrs. Margot worked her jaw, stretching the denture adhesive and letting it snap back into place. With a nod of approval, she began.

"Fine. I probably should have assumed you were smarter than the Kirby men. Skip was the reverend, but he was also my soul mate. My husband didn't talk to me, not like Skip did. We never crossed any lines, but he was there. When he left, he just left without a word. A month or so ago, I was doing my estate planning and I wanted him to be the man who performed my final service if he was still around. I called the church and they had no record of a Skip. No record of a Skip or a Tim, or any place called Sweet Pea."

"So you went to Tim?" I asked and she nodded.

"He said that he was as good a man as any to have the job. Thought I shouldn't be so bothersome this close to joining the lord," she said with a scowl. "I then went to the school and saw that old photograph of the boy, his boy and the name. So I looked up the name... well, my niece looked up the name. She's what one would call a hacky sack? Or maybe a cracker..."

"Hacker?" I asked, and she shrugged.

"She found out he was on the run. I went to Daniel then, but he wasn't on the run from the law so Daniel wouldn't hear it. I switched to claiming there was missing money to get his attention, but he brushed that off, too. So I asked my niece if it was possible to leave something behind for whoever wanted the reverend. She said that she could leave some crumbs behind, probably why they're called crackers. I don't understand what being an untidy housekeeper has to do with it, but it worked. The gorillas showed up and... but... it got a little out of control. I couldn't go back to Daniel and I heard you were coming home so I... asked you," she said wringing her hands. Respectfully, she never lowered her head. I admired a woman who could admit she needs help with pride, even if I personally couldn't.

I studied her face, Mrs. Margot was exhausted. Her eyes were a little sunken, her hair not quite as flawless as usual. Her decision to right wrongs had cost a man his life and it weighed on her.

"You think Tim died because you tried to get justice?" I said quietly and a small tear slid down her cheek. "It's not your fault. You just wanted..."

I stopped because I wasn't sure what she wanted. She let out a sigh.

"I don't know what I wanted either. I needed to make this right, but I also didn't want to admit what a fool I'd been. What a fool the whole town had been to never once notice these men were not real," she said, another tear following the first.

"Did you take the money?" I asked and she nodded.

"It's at home, locked up safe and tight. Not a cent is missing, though with those crooks on the loose... The ladies know I have it, we're all in the loop, but I don't know how to get us all out," she said to the handkerchief in her hand. "I never thought the people looking for Tim would kill people. Especially not Tim himself."

"You knew the Fake Captain, Mitchell, was his son?" I asked and she nodded.

"Brother made it seem like I knew less."

I nodded at her response.

We looked out at Main and I saw the two gorillas in question. Each was wearing an upgraded suit, a small flower in the buttonhole of each. Strange they would dress up for such an occasion, but maybe they were hoping to blend. As if sensing an audience, their eyes caught on us and the Mediterranean man smirked, making a fake gun gesture at me and pulling the trigger.

"Crap," I said, dropping my head into my hands.

"What is that man who stole Phil's glass tree stump doing making gun fingers at you?" she said, extreme disapproval laced in her voice.

"Long story. Glass tree stump? At Phil's?" I asked, trying not to be too obvious. Phil's was the local novelty and specialty shop. He dabbled in glass work, leatherwork and woodwork. None of it is designed to do work of any kind. At least not paid work, but they were bound to make an appearance in my old bedroom at some point.

I shuddered.

"Yes. Phil always kept an assortment of glass stumps in front of his shop. I watched that man scoop one into his pocket the other day. When I called him on it, he denied it and shoved me into a wall. Phil said it was fine, he'd make more stumps, but it burned my chaps," she said and my face flamed red.

Mediterranean man, Henry if you're to believe the boss, had stolen a glass dildo while a little old lady watched.

"Hey, Cyn," said a familiar voice beside me and I turned to look at... Larry? He was clad in a three-piece suit, clean shaven, his hair styled in an upright side part. He looked like an anatomically correct Ken doll and my eyes widened into saucers.

"He... hey," I stammered and felt Mrs. Margot poke me in the side.

"Stand up," she said sharply and I complied. My dress floated down and brushed my knees, Winnie wagging her tail at the new arrival.

"Wow," he said and I nodded, but I'm not sure we were talking about the same thing. Winnie let out a soft bark and he jostled her ears. "You look fabulous too, girl."

Winnie preened in approval.

Larry reached out for my hand and I took it. My mind had suddenly gone foggy and kind of blank and the squishy feeling was back as soon as his hand touched mine. I was here to help him, but... maybe I could get some help of my own.

He escorted me to the ceremony area, finding me a chair near the edge. He checked with the people and no one had claimed it. He helped me into it and made sure I knew where the exits were... I think. I was too busy staring to hear.

Larry Kirby, suddenly manly and not the goofy kid I'd been friends with. He'd made me squishy then too, but this felt different.

"Is this... OK?" he said and I nodded lamely. "Good... I have to go check in with the bride and groom."

I nodded again but he didn't move.

"Cyn?" he asked, and I stared at him. "You look beautiful."

"Uh... you too," I said, gently punching his arm. He squirmed and walked toward a man in a suit that must be the groom. He wasn't very tall for a prince. His hair was dark, a little oily, and his eyes wouldn't stop shifting. The tuxedo he had on looked rented, an insult to Amber if she spotted it. A breeze came from that direction and carried his voice.

"He can't..." I started when a shriek filled the square.

"What are you doing you filthy, disgusting, foul...." another scream and I looked around. Not one to miss a good wedding disaster, I wanted to get Winnie and see what I could find. My hands were empty, the ground was empty, the whole aisle was empty.

There was no Winnie.

I jumped to my feet and started running. Past Larry and the groom, past the two gorillas in suits and straight into... Amber Carter. She was in her wedding dress, but she didn't look like a bride. Her hair was coming out of its flawless chignon, her curls going flat, and her dress... was ruined. It was smeared in brown mud, and something that looked a lot like frosting. Beside her, on the ground, was a mound of dismembered and regurgitated... cake?

The cake must have been 6 layers. White frosting, mud mingled with some sort of yellow cake, and the tiny couple who had once sat atop it were completely demolished. The bride had been decapitated, the groom had no legs and whatever ornate decoration they'd stood under was gone. The whole mess was sitting on Amber's thirty-inch train, just below a perfect imprint of a paw print on her ass.

Beside her sat the source of the paw print, Winnie, devouring the demolished cake with the bride's head hanging out of the side of her mouth.

"Why? Why is this happening?" she wailed and the voice I heard answer sent chills up my spine.

"It's OK, baby, it's OK," the groom said, but it was the same voice that threatened Mickey in the movie theater.

Chapter Fifteen: The Dooms Men

B ack at the police department in less than 24 hours, and I was grinning from ear to ear.

Sure, my dog and I could be charged with vandalism or mischief. Sure the creepy man threatening non-Army captains was the groom. Sure, Larry was more than a little annoyed by my attitude but who cared when you ruined the meanest girl in high school's wedding.

"You have to stop smiling like that if you want people to think you are innocent, chica," Cruz said. He'd materialized next to me without warning, but I was too elated to be startled. "Or sane for that matter."

"I don't care. This is the best day ever!" I squealed and he laughed with his crooked smile.

"You look amazing, by the way. Green really is your color," he said, brushing some hair off of my shoulder. The skin underneath tingled and radiated warmth throughout my body. "Why is there an angry woman trying to get our friend executed?"

"She ate her wedding cake, dismembered the cake topper people, covered her dress in muddy paw prints and then peed on the groom," I said, smiling so wide I felt manic. Cruz pressed a thumb to my chin, his index finger on my cheek. He moved his thumb back and forth up my jaw line.

"If you needed someone to put a smile on your face like that, you didn't have to ruin a wedding. You could have just called me," he said, and I was suddenly a little warm and lightheaded. He leaned in and our lips were about to touch when a man cleared his throat beside us.

I jumped to my feet and stood at attention. Cruz laughed in his seat on the bench and looked at the intruder.

"Amber wants to press charges," Daniel said, eyes bouncing between me and my former training sergeant. "She did research, a lot of research, but none of the laws apply. You are free to go... or at least you were."

Daniel paused, staring at both of us. His eyes held concern, hesitation, and something like uncertainty.

"Spit it out, Kirby," I said and he shook his head, his usual confidence returning.

"Don't break my brother, Cyn," Daniel said and walked away.

"He broke me first!" I started after him, but I felt the guilt creep into my face. He had been trying to tell me something, calling me beautiful, letting me sleep in his bed...

"I can see you, chica," Cruz said, beside me again. He snaked an arm around my waist and gave me a quick hug before letting go.

"Your brain is on fire. Let's grab some dinner," he said and took my hand. His hand was warm, welcoming, and mine was clammy and one step above overcooked pasta. "Do I make you nervous, Cyn?"

He'd whispered it directly against my ear and I shuddered.

"N-no," I lied and he smiled against my cheek.

"Liar."

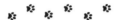

We slid into a corner booth at Suzanna's Diner. It was a small-town affair with food that was comforting, filling and more than a little fattening. The owner and proprietor was Suzanna Williams, and she still wore the collared shift dress from the 1950's and walked around with a coffee pot offering top-offs. Everyone called her Suzie, age indeterminate and time-less, her long hair in a ponytail changed colors every week and no one could beat her cat eye lining skills.

"Every time I go somewhere new in this town, I think I've stepped into a time machine," he said, and I smiled.

"A time machine to a land where gay men sell glass dildos on the sidewalk," I said and he rolled his eyes.

"That man tried to offer me a tree stump," he said and I let out a laugh.

"He offers everyone a tree stump, you aren't special," I said casually, and his leg brushed mine.

"I'm a little special," he countered, but I moved my leg away to avoid answering.

"Did you hear the whole church in Sweet Pea is basically fake?" I asked, getting my iced coffee from Suzie and ordering a burger and a milkshake.

"I heard some of it. I know Mrs. Margot suspected the reverend of being a fake after trying to get the contact info of the reverend before. He was also not a man of the cloth?" Cruz confirmed and I nodded.

"Con men, it would seem. I'm not sure how Skip ended up here, or how Tim knew he could hide out here. The daughter is... armed. I think the man on the motorcycle last night was Henry," I said, popping a French fry in my mouth from the newly appeared plate.

"Because he gave you the guns before you destroyed his boss's wedding?" Cruz asked, and snagged a fry for himself.

"That and... wait, what?" I said, stopping mid chew.

"I assume the gorillas in suits are the same, but today they were groomsmen. Groomsmen gorillas standing up for their boss," Cruz said, and I chewed slowly, thinking.

"Who is their boss?" I asked, not expecting an answer. A wedding program landed beside my plate and I stared. Ryan Bordeaux, Count of Manheim, to marry Amber Carter, Heir of Carterville graced the heading above a picture that looked photo shopped to within an inch of its life.

"What is Manheim?" I asked and Cruz shrugged. "Also, I think count would make her a countess."

"I sent it to some people, but they haven't gotten back to me yet. You'd know better than me on the second. How long has he been in town? Is this some sort of a shotgun wedding?" he asked, and I grinned.

"That would be so perfect! But no, I think Amber just wants to be a princess besides in her head. If she made it to adulthood child free, she knows what she's doing," I said, and he gave me a thoughtful look. "Yes, I have a petty and slightly vindictive streak. This should not be new to you and the peanut butter in your pocket business..."

"That was you?" he asked, mouth gaping slightly.

"N-not if you didn't know it was," I said, taking a huge bite of burger to keep from saying more.

"I'm going to get you back for that," he said, mischief dancing in his eyes.

"Get up," a gruff man grumbled beside me, and I turned into a discreetly pointed handgun. "Boss wants to see you."

I looked up into the eyes of Henry, the Mediterranean member of the goon squad. Beside him was the second man who had yet to be named and besides the gun, his pockets were spilling out with what must have been stolen things. I swallowed my bite of burger and smiled sweetly.

"No. He can come here though," I said and his eyes bulged. "There's plenty of space in our booth."

"You can't say no, lady. I've got a gun!" he said, voice a loud whisper and some people at nearby tables looked over. "If you won't come, I'm going to shoot other people."

He said the second more quietly and I felt the first tickles of fear run down my spine. In the corner booth was a small boy celebrating his birthday with his family. Beside them was an older couple, holding hands across the table while having a dinner special.

Crap.

"Yeah, OK," I said, starting to stand. Cruz followed me, but the goon stuck his hand squarely into his chest. "You stay here."

The second half of the doofus duo appeared beside the first. Henry grabbed my arm and goon two took my seat.

"Leo will keep you company," he said with a sneer. Cruz gave me a look, looked back at Henry and sat back. The picture of calm indifference. My life meant nothing to him.

"Can I have her keys, at least?" he said and my mouth fell open.

"Suit yourself," he said and started to put his hand in my pocket. I stomped on his foot in my flats and got the key myself.

"Thanks," Cruz said when I tossed them to him. "Just in case I need back-up."

"Whatever, chicken. Just like Afghanistan," I said and turned to lead the way out.

"Hey, Cyn," Cruz shouted, and I spared him a glance. "Exactly like Afghanistan, yeah?"

"Just watch out for The Doomsman," I said with a shrug. "If they'll stand for their boss, they'll fall for him too."

We exchanged a nod and I opened the door to walk out on the street.

A chill had set in and I wished I'd thought to put on my sweater. Then I remembered I didn't own a sweater because I had lived in Florida. I didn't buy one when I bought this dress because I thought I'd be home in sweats by now. Thinking about all of this helped me to avoid thinking about the man with a gun behind me.

"Stolen anything good today?" I asked as we walked up Main Street to Mary's Muffins and More.

"Shut up," he muttered as I felt his hand brush my arm to grasp something off the table in front of the knitting shop. Instinctively, I pushed my elbow out and caught him in the diaphragm. He dropped the object with an *oof* and clutched his arms to his stomach.

"Oops," I said, with absolutely zero sincerity. He rewarded me with a gun muzzle shoved into my kidney and I felt like we were even. He disagreed and thought he'd also like to shove me into a light pole as we finished crossing Main to the front of Mo's. His plan backfired when I anticipated his move, changed the angle and he went headfirst into the pole instead staggering back with his hand cradling his skull.

"You should really watch where you're walking," I said sweetly. Henry righted himself and started to lumber forward.

"You should watch all of your talking," he growled, and I got in a low crouch, beckoning him.

"I should watch my *talking*? That doesn't even..."

"Enough," came the accent from the movie theater. The same man from the wedding ceremony stepped out from between Mary's Muffins and the appliance repair shop. "This way."

Henry opened his mouth to protest but the man silenced him with a look that wasn't altogether steady. Silently, Henry and I followed him between the buildings to the back of the bakery.

While the alley smelled as charming as most, her open back door emitted the scents of cinnamon, sugar and...

"Bacon?" I asked her as I walked in and she was seated in a chair beside a third, previously unseen goon. Hard to imagine how, given his size, anyone could not see that man from miles away, but here he stood. A new face and a new threat level to assess.

"Maple bacon cupcakes. People like them," she said with a shrug when I made a face. Her eyes were trying to widen and convey messages of distress, but we were in the same boat now and I was officially useless until I knew the depth of the water.

"I had to leave my burger, got any extra bacon?" I asked, eyes wide and meaningful.

"No," she said, discreet eye roll. "I used all of my bacon yesterday."

I nodded. Daniel Kirby wouldn't be helping us after I sprung Mo yesterday. Though part of me had, in fact, wanted bacon. If Kirby was steering clear of her, we couldn't count on him looking into her shop closing early, either.

I also couldn't eat any bacon if I found it since she said she didn't have any.

"Have a seat," the man known as Count Ryan Bordeaux said. He was roughly two inches shorter than me and six inches shorter than his muscle. Henry towered behind him, a red spot on his head from the pole and a face that read revenge. Forgetting that I was technically a hostage, I pointed to my forehead.

"Walk much," I mocked. He lurched forward but his boss stopped him.

"Enough! I said sit!" he barked, and I took a step back gesturing.

"There's nowhere to sit," I said and his eyes flashed annoyance.

"There is a floor," he answered but I shook my head.

"This dress is new," I said, eyes filled with fake horror but mostly 'go screw yourself'.

"It won't be new when it's covered in blood," he said, gesturing to the gun in Henry's pants which Henry pulled out with a delighted flourish.

"If I'm going to die in this dress, it's going to be clean except for that blood. Find me a chair, shoot me, or let me stand. There's no option where I sit on the floor," I declared and I saw a vein in his temple throb. Henry fondled the trigger in anticipation and Mo let out a small squeak.

Probably I should have conveyed my plan to be a pain and maintain the high ground. Maybe next time we were hostages.

"Is every woman in this town a pain in the ass?" he hissed, the European accent slipping. I detected a whiff of the Garden State.

"Yeah, basically. There's nothing else to be here," I said, walking to a counter covered in cookies. I popped one in my mouth and leaned against it. "Good enough?"

"For now, yes," he said, accent back. "Let's talk."

"Sure. It's cold as hell outside-" I started, and he held up his hand.

"This isn't a social visit, tell me what I want to know," his voice deadpan and fake accented.

"What do you want to know?" I asked casually, sampling another cookie.

"Where is Mitchell Scott, my money, and my program?" he asked and I raised a brow.

"Like a weight training program?" I asked, cocking my head to the side. "I guess you could use some toning, but why not ask these guys to help?"

I gestured to the two men while I scoped out the area. Two ways in and out: through the back door and through the shop.

"No," he answered.

"Program to the VCR?" I asked, trying to figure out which would be better. Mo was dead center. Her captor was bigger, but the boss and Henry were by the back door. Felt kind of even.

"I am tired, Ms. Sharp," he gestured for Henry to point his gun at Mo. "I want what I was promised."

"What were you promised?" I asked, not taking my eyes off the gun. Exits wouldn't matter if he shot her. None of them were surviving if he fired that weapon.

"I was promised power, Ms. Sharp. Power I will use to become whole and fulfill my goals," he said.

Chapter Sixteen:
Toxic Technology

"I ... what?" I asked, looking away from the gun and back at the man. Is he nuts?

"I want control, Ms. Sharp. I want control over the things people think beyond control. Life, death, who takes it and who gives it," he said, and I felt the hairs on the back of my neck stand up. Yup, officially nuts.

"Control anyone, like... the Princess of Pain you were going to marry?" I asked, noting that on a prep table to the left was a massive knife by a pile of nuts. Knives are good. I'm better with guns, but I could work with a knife. I kept my eyes on Ryan Bordeaux, Count of Lies, as I slowly started sliding along the counter. Each step I took, I rocked back and forth in a shuffle to look like I was fidgeting nervously. My stomach turned over—there was still a gun pointed at Mo.

I needed the gun down and to get at least one side of the goons to clear a damn exit. So, I ate another cookie, because that would probably help. Not as much as the ice coffee I had to leave behind.

Focus, Sharp! Right, bad men with guns.

"No..." he said, eyes and feet shifting as well. He couldn't stop blinking and it was unnerving. "That was... a longer-term endeavor. I must thank you for helping me end that ceremony. Louis had a bigger distraction planned, but your disruption turned out to be equally efficient. Quieter except for the crying and drastically less fire."

The bigger man nodded and now I knew the meat wall behind Mo has a name. If Leo and Henry were the Doomsmen, Louis was the Henchman of Honor. He had a completely shaved head, equal parts tall and wide, casting most of the room in his shadow when he turned from left to right. His eyes were steady, but he was sweating excessively, and I was starting to get nervous.

"Not using mind control on Amber, got it. She's not much of a mind anyway. How was Mitchell going to control other brains for you?" I asked, walking around the table pretending to look at cookies. I saw something that looked like it had pistachios in it and I ate it. Like everything else, it was amazing.

Like everything else, I wanted to throw it right back up when I looked at Henry's gun.

"Using technology... what are you doing?" he demanded, looking back at Henry. "Put the gun down."

Henry shifted and his boss fisted the lapels of his tux.

"I told you..." he said and I bumped a spatula so it clattered to the floor. Both men turned and the gun was safely aimed at the ground.

"Technology as mind control is not that original. I think cell phones already did that, Count Bordeaux. Ever been to a public place? Just a bunch of zombies walking around looking down," I said, slowly moving closer to the knife. Mo looked calm, a little glassy eyed, but she would be ok now that nothing was pointed at her with the intention of death. Her red hair was spilling from its hair tie, her clothes were spattered in baking powders, but a few cookies and she'd survive this. Probably I would owe her money for the cookies I was eating and a bottle of wine.

Maybe also some new undergarments, but we could go shopping for those together.

The Henchman of Honor was really sweating. His hands were clasped in front of him, and they were empty. No weapon on him, but his body probably counted. Near him were a number of options, cookie sheets and heavy metal pots. A rack of bread was cooling beside him, in addition to the oven and on his opposite side was a dishwasher.

Nothing threatening, but lots of potential weapons. I just needed everyone to stay calm until I could get to something.

"The mindless techno-philes are not the same thing! It's an algorithm that mimics brain waves and patterns of behavior so you can make people do things they think are their idea!" Boss Man hissed in annoyance and I stopped my advance toward the knife.

"People like... who?" I asked, trying to move slowly but not wanting to miss anything that would reveal the endgame. If you know the endgame, you know how far someone will go for it.

And who's essential to keep alive to see it happen.

"Anyone and everyone. No one with a brain is impervious to this program. That is what makes it genius. People will do literally anything with the right programming," he said, eyes darting around the room. He was antsy, couldn't settle.

"Like The Cha Cha Slide or the YMCA?" I joked, but I wasn't feeling funny.

"Strangely, yes. But instead of persuading people with the approval of their peers at mastering fancy footwork, they are persuaded by their own brain. It will not give someone an idea they've never had, only encourage them to act on it without a sense of control," he said, looking both pleased and confused. He started to reach for a cookie, pulled his hand back, reached again and then punched a wall. "There is too much control. People need to let go of their control."

"Let's agree to disagree on that. You want an electronic motivator to... what? Poison people's conscience or eliminate it altogether?" I asked, back to only half listening, but very aware this man should probably be evaluated. It didn't sound impossible, there were drugs that did that. If someone could use technology as hypnosis, there would be no end to what terrifying acts people would commit believing themselves to have thought of it. It was the plot of an animated movie sequel, but it didn't seem impossible with the advances in AI and neural studies.

The man also looked like a painted-face character of B-level supervillain movies and nightmares. I could handle people making crap decisions on their own, but violating freewill, taking away their morality, that was Charles Manson level messed up. Why would someone want you to do something that both of you knew was wrong?

"Yes, we called it Toxic Technology and prolonged exposure will make it permanent. Like the apple in the Garden of Eden, it will lower from grace those who do the will of man with the righteousness of gods!"

The Count Ryan Bordeaux flung his hands in the air at his exclamation and smacked Henry. He jumped, took a step back, folded his hands and stared at the floor. His eyes were flashing a mix of anger and fear. Mo and I needed to get out of here fast.

"That's... biblical. What do you want people to do?" I asked, nearly at the counter with the knife. No one really noticed me moving. No one was working hard at noticing much of anything. A smell of fear was filling the room and it wasn't mine. The men were nervous, their boss was deteriorating, and they had two different reactions. Louis held perfectly still, and Henry fidgeted.

"It doesn't matter! Once I have the program and the money, they'll do it!" he shouted, and I took two steps closer to the knife. "My will be done, Ms. Sharp!"

"Right... How did you end up here in Sweet Pea? Engaged to Ms. Carter? Is your name even Ryan?" I asked, changing the subject three times over. His face went from anger to the confused look of utter bliss. The henchmen relaxed their shoulders. Whatever the bigger picture, they weren't onboard with the rant.

"No, my name is Steve Karchowski," he said and his voice was all Jersey. "I found Amber's blog and thought it would be a killer mark for easy money and I only had to pretend to be a prince. If I'd met her first, I might have reconsidered. Then... then I found Mitchell and I knew I could get something better than the fortune of a town founder."

"Yeah... that fortune is grossly overstated. The town of Cartersville has one veterinarian and one doctor and they are the same person," I said but his eyes were bouncing all over the place. "So what? You were going to marry her and kill her originally?"

"No... I needed an heir. Genetic heir. I really am a count," he said, no longer sounding European or Jersey. He was robotic and panicking as his eyes flashed emotions and thoughts like a movie on fast forward. Every word was alternately too loud or too quiet and every sentence was punctuated with a limb jerk toward nothing. "In the eyes of God, I count and it is His will that I continue."

"Continue to be a count?" I asked, but he was muttering and heard nothing. He was back to pacing and flinging his hands. Wisely, Henry moved out of the way.

"Where's Mitchell?" he screamed, arms bouncing at his sides. I wasn't sure if he reminded me of a chicken trying to fly or a rhino preparing to charge. "I need the program and I need my money. I'll pay, they know I'll pay, they just need to say yes. They want to say yes. They all *want* to say yes. They're just too *afraid* to let go. I can fix that. I can fix everything."

All of his limbs were moving different directions. Mo shrank into herself and Henry took a small step farther from the man. Louis was a wall. He didn't move, but his eyes were screaming.

"No idea where Mitchell is," I said truthfully. I was in front of the nut table and I slid the knife off, holding it behind my back. "But if you let Mo and I go, we'll go find him. Let him know you'd like a chat."

"You know where he is! Tell me!" he screamed and then pressed hands to either side of his face. He howled and both men remained perfectly still while Steve looked to be having a brain implosion. "I don't have a lot of time! Where is he?"

"I really don't know. You killed his dad," I said, indifferent and working my way toward Mo. From the back I could see she wasn't tied to the chair. Useful for when I pushed her onto the ground and stabbed a complete stranger.

"You were at his sister's house! You know him! You know where he is! Tell me or I'll dispose of you like the chicken man," Steve screamed, his hands still wrapped tightly around his head.

"The chicken man?" I froze. He couldn't mean...

"The man with the chickens. I thought the gun was real. It was so loud. He needed to be quiet. I just wanted the chicken man to be quiet!" Steve was screaming and I watched Louis sway on the spot from the heat. Steve had killed... for quiet?

"You killed Roger?" I whispered.

"He had a gun!" Steve screamed and a loud bark resonated from the front of the room. Something heavy fell to the ground and I heard the sound of feet shuffling on the clean linoleum floor.

"Louis!" The leader called out. "Louis, stop... make it stop!"

"Stop what?" he asked, but another thunk came from just behind the kitchen door. Steve was curled in a ball, Henry staring at him. Louis took a step toward his boss, froze and waited while the sounds of people fighting continued to carry.

"Louis!" Steve wailed. "Go stop them!"

Having received his answer, the oversized man went to the door and tried to push it open quietly. After a last glance back and a look of concern, he slipped through the door and entered the front room. His arrival was greeted with a metal display crashing to the floor and another bark.

"Henry, help him!" Steve shouted, watching the other man disappear. Just as the door swung shut, I threw my knife at Henry who still hadn't moved to help Louis. The knife pierced his thigh and he howled as I dumped Mo out of the chair onto the ground. I hovered above her, hoping Steve did not have a gun. He was unsteady and unpredictable. When no gunshots erupted, I pushed up to see what was happening.

Henry was gripping his thigh. Steve had his hands against his head, holding his ears and watching Henry bleed. The goon pulled the knife out, and blood surged out of the wound, splattering Steve. At the sight, Steve screamed, the sound dulled as what must have been a glass display case shattered in the other room. Trying to run, Steve got to his feet and slipped in the blood. Flat on his back, he called for Louis while Henry looked relieved to bleed on the ground for a while.

I could hear barks and snarls. A man grunted, screamed and the door between rooms flew open as Louis staggered in with Winnie clamped on his arm. Steve latched onto the man, trying to get back up, but Louis had no hands to offer as he fought to loosen Winnie's teeth.

"Shoot it! Shoot it!" Louis screamed. Henry tried to take aim from the floor, but I grabbed a piece of cookware from the counter and smashed it against Louis's head. He staggered into the line of fire and Henry lost his shot. Steve fumbled his way toward the door, and I needed someone to chase him.

"Out girl!" I said, and she released Louis's arm to stand at the ready beside me. I crouched low and watched as Leo, sporting a broken nose, fell through the door with Ian Cruz on top of him. His hair was tousled, a small sheen of sweat across his brow, but he was otherwise spotless. Struck by the sight, I missed it when Steve pushed open the back door. "Cruz, he's getting away!"

"Sharp!" he said, throwing an object at me. I caught the heavy metal gun and aimed it at where Steve had been standing, but he was gone and somehow so was Louis.

"Henry!" Leo called out and I watched the bleeding man lift his gun hand once more. His eyes were unsteady, and he couldn't quite focus, but there was too much metal in the kitchen. A bullet could ricochet any direction, could hit anyone.

"Drop it, Henry!" I said, but he continued to sight down the gun as his arm shook with blood loss. His hand was unsteady, trembling on and off target. His eyes were sliding closed and snapping back open. "I'm serious, Henry. Drop it and you can limp out of here."

He looked at me, at the gun in his hand, and back at me. As if thinking through all options, he swung it around to point dead center at my chest and two shots rang out through the bakery before absolute silence fell.

Chapter Seventeen: One Step at a Time

"L et's start from the beginning," Daniel Kirby said.

"I shot off a man's hand!" I shouted and clapped my hands over my mouth. Kirby let out a long sigh, his 6th of this conversation, and patted my shoulder.

"We'll get back to you... again," he said and walked toward Cruz. The two men stared at me from where they were leaning against a prep table and I tried to look away but every other direction had blood. There was nowhere to look besides at Daniel and Ian, but I had nothing to say to either.

Henry was on his way to Yellow Springs hospital in Daniel's pick-up truck with a doctor in the bed with him. They'd left about ten minutes ago, and the room was still awash in red and blue emergency lights from the 21 speed bicycle Daniel had ridden here. The town's one police cruiser was being driven by Officer Fife (no relation, according to him), following Henry to the hospital with Leo in the back seat. He'd taken the only other labeled vehicle with lights just for the outward show.

He was also wearing shorts and looked ridiculous.

Mo, Cruz and I had been separated to give our statements. Kirby had started with Cruz, his statement the calmest and most concise. Mo had been mildly catatonic but had managed to answer and get cleared. A volunteer firefighter walked her home, and I was fairly certain his medical training was not what she wanted. Everyone had been questioned, their statements documented, and released into the wild.

Everyone except me.

"Cyn, you have to tell them what happened," Cruz said beside me and I jumped. I was sitting on the floor, no longer concerned with tactical advantages and cleanliness. The cutting board that once held nuts was now covered in cookies and I was using it as a plate.

"Poof... no more hand," I said, glassy eyed. Cruz tried to take my cutting board and I growled at him. "Mine."

"Empty," he said. I looked down. All of the cookies were gone. I strained my neck to look at the counter, no more cookies. I searched all of the counters... no cookies.

"More?" I asked and he shook his head.

"In an hour you're going to throw up all the cookies and then you can eat a vegetable," he said, crouching to the balls of his feet and gracefully sitting next to me. He slung an arm around my shoulder and pulled my head to him, kissing the crown and smelling deliciously like bacon burgers and pie.

"What kind of vegetable?" I asked suspiciously.

He cocked a dirty smile, and I rolled my eyes.

"Whatever," I said. Daniel was now in front of us and he sat down with a notebook.

"From the top?" he asked.

"Make it drop-" Cruz clamped his hand over my mouth, but he was smiling. Daniel was also smiling, but it looked more like a ritual baring of teeth.

"Fine." I muttered and he removed his hand. "Henry, the newly one-handed man, came into the diner and said his boss wanted a meeting. We got here, Mo was being held and the boss was here. His name is Steve Karchowski. At least, that's what he said but honestly who knows. It sounds as fake as Ryan Bordeaux."

"The Count?" Daniel asked and I stared at him.

"How far behind are you? I thought we told you he was a criminal after we demolished the wedding cake. At the very least Mo told you he admitted to not being a count and using Amber. Did you even listen to her?" I ranted and he responded with a smirk.

"Just checking you hadn't suddenly become a robot or were suffering shock," he said, and Cruz gave him a fist bump.

"I hate both of you. This whole thing started when Mrs. Margot was trying to find Reverend Skip, or Pastor Skip. I know so very little about church-y titles. The church hadn't heard of him and said there was no one from the church in our town. Could not, in fact, find Sweet Pea on a map. So she made up the stolen money to get you interested. When that failed, she found out Tim was an ex-felon named Antonio Scott and alerted the people who were looking for him because of... Except..."

I trailed off. Steve was already working over Amber when he arrived in Sweet Pea. He'd found out about the Scott's by accident. Who had Mrs. Margot's niece contacted? Where were the people here solely for Antonio?

"Speak, Cyn, speak!" Daniel said and Winnie let out a bark.

"I think there's more people than we know about," I said, ruffling Winnie's ears. I'd given her all of the oatmeal cookies after verifying they were oatmeal blueberry and not raisin. She was content, her muzzle covered in crumbs, but I needed her comfort. "Steve and his crew were leveraging the senior Scott for Mitchell. Who was here for Antonio Scott/ Reverend Tim? We know Mrs. Margot was trying to have Daniel look into the reverend but then he didn't. She called someone who had beef with the fake reverend. Who are those people? Who haven't we seen?"

I looked between the two men and neither was blinking. Kirby looked ready to call over a medic, but Cruz was thinking so hard he was chewing on his lip. It would have been hot, but I'm not a rich man who's into vulnerability, so mostly I was annoyed he was ignoring me, and I started humming. His face relaxed, but he still hadn't moved.

"Did you die?" I asked, poking Cruz in the ribs.

He grabbed my hand, squeezed it and kissed my knuckles.

"I have to go," he said, rolling to the balls of his feet and standing.

"What? I mutilated a man! You have to stay and..." I started, but he was already on his feet.

"Why did you lie?" I asked him and he looked down at me.

"About what, chica?" his eyes shifted.

"Nice to know there's more than one. Toxic Technology. You said it was just a typo," my brain finally moving past the whole shot off a hand thing. "You said it was a typo and you meant toxicology, but Count Steve said Toxic Technology is the name of an algorithm designed to lower people's inhibitions. Is that why you're here? The Army wants it? Did you know who he was from the beginning?"

"It-" he started, but he wouldn't meet my eyes.

"Don't lie. If you can't be honest, then just leave."

"Cyn, it really was a typo," he said quietly.

"Yeah, but a typo about something real. You knew someone was making an algorithm to electronically lower inhibitions. Phones don't come up with Toxic Technology on their own. What is it to you?"

"Just an assignment," he answered, and left. He'd managed to carefully avoid the red smears and leave without so much as a shoe print.

"Just like Afghanistan," I muttered and stared at Winnie. "He's using us again."

"Winnie is pretty useful," Larry said behind me and I threw a spatula at his head. He caught it and placed it on the counter. "You should be nicer to me; you need a place to sleep tonight."

"What's that supposed to mean?" I asked and he looked a little uncomfortable.

"I uhh... drove past your parents' house to see about getting your clothes so you could be comfortable and..." he trailed off, eyes unfocused.

"Oh my dog, what did you hear?" I asked, then pressed my palms against my ears. "No! Don't tell me! I'm sorry!"

He turned red and his brother laughed. The Kirby brothers, freakishly good looking, nothing like each other. Daniel was all self-assured confidence, his body a gift he liked to show off. Larry had muscles like a nerd who accidentally walked into a gym and was too embarrassed to leave without giving it a try. Their smiles were the same, but their eyes told different stories. Daniel had lived the life of those privileged with good looks and charm. Larry had lived a life hiding from his bullies and trying to climb out of his brother's shadow.

Yet still, they were friends. If only I could forgive Heidi for giving our mom those damn E. L. James books. It was bad enough they were riddled with repetitive language and errors, but now they were a "healthy past time for my parents".

I shuddered.

"Can I sleep on your couch?" I asked him and he smiled wide.

"Just my couch tonight? You don't want to go back to your happy place?" he said with an eyebrow wiggle and his brother's jaw fell open. Despite the blood and carnage, I laughed out loud. It had been a great morning in his bed before I scratched him. Between the attack and the drugs, he was probably relieved by my suggestion.

"Did you two..." Daniel was looking between us and I was suddenly feeling much better.

"I was on drugs. It wouldn't be fair to comment," I said, standing up and kissing Daniel's forehead. "Have a good night, officer."

Larry was still laughing and not saying a word. Daniel was red-faced watching us as Larry took my hand and led me out of the back door. Ian had parked back here or moved the vehicle before he left and somehow Larry had known. Winnie immediately went to the Jeep and Larry followed, pulling keys from his pocket.

"Where's your car?" I asked and he gave me a look, putting my own keys in my hand. "What?"

"It's at my house," he said as though I was thick.

"You walked here?" I asked, closing the Jeep door with Winnie inside. "Isn't it..."

Larry grabbed my shoulders, turned me to the left and pointed. There, on the corner of a cross street was his house. It looked innocent enough, but its presence was mildly alarming. He'd have seen the man with the gun.

"You... live there... Did you see..." I said, staring at the house. Somehow in my haste to leave that morning, I hadn't really paid attention to how close it was to Mo's bakery. He probably saw everyone who went in and out the back door. She'd probably give him free muffins if he was a good neighbor. The house wasn't grand, just a front stoop, modest house and a reasonable-sized backyard. Nothing like his aunt's house, I thought as a motorcycle rode by and I had an epiphany.

"You asshole!" I said, turning and punching him in the arm.

"Ow! What the f-" he started but then looked between the house, me and the motorcycle. His face fell and he turned bashful. "Look, I can explain."

"I shot off a man's hand, Larry! His dominant hand! He's going to prison and he doesn't have his dominant hand! What is he going to do there? Crochet? He can't knit! He'd need two hands!"

"He was going to shoot you! You should be glad he can't do *that* anymore," he said, eyes still darting around the area nervously.

"If you'd been honest yesterday, Amber would be married, that man would have all of his hands and... and... " I punched him again because I ran out of words.

"He's my cousin! He helped me through med school! If you'd told me you thought someone would murder people to find him, I'd have asked him to come outside and talk yesterday," Larry said but I was glaring at him. "OK, I probably wouldn't have because you shot an awning, threw a gun and sometimes you're terrifying. But I'd have told him to text you at the very least."

"Now we have to go all the way back there!" I said, walking to the driver's side door. "Get your lying ass in the car."

"Cyn, it's almost nine. It's an hour drive and it's dark! Can't we go tomorrow after you've slept, had pain pills, eaten something, and hate me less?" he asked, looking more than a little scared.

"No! I shot off a man's hand Larry!" I said and Winnie barked her agreement.

"You were in the army," he said as though he assumed this was normal.

"I've never dismembered anyone in my service. I did indirectly cause a man to lose some fingers and there's a man missing part of his butt cheek, but I have never fired my weapon in my service to this country. Less than a week home and I have shot off a man's hand! We are going to go see Mitchell Scott at your aunt's house and you're coming with me so I can keep yelling at you!"

"At least let me drive," he said, walking around and nudging me to the other side of the car stealing back my keys.

"I'm not going to drive us off the road!" I said but conceded that my arm hurt too much to drive and opened the passenger side door.

"Mostly I just don't want you to hit me again," he said, rubbing his arm as I climbed in.

"Oh, you being the driver won't stop me," I said, and punched his arm again.

Chapter Eighteen:
Mitchell Scott

T he house looked exactly the same tonight as it had last
night. It was still tired and lived in, the hole was patched,
and tonight the porch light was already on.

"You told them we were coming?" I asked and Larry turned
to protect his arm.

"Yes, but…" I raised my hand and he cowered.

"Just kidding. So he'll talk to me?" I asked, checking the front
door. The shotgun was propped outside, an invitation to come
in without getting shot.

"Does he have a choice?" Larry asked, massaging his arm. I'd
fallen asleep five minutes into the drive and hadn't punched him
once during this car ride.

"You are such a baby. He doesn't have a choice, but it's
nice that he's participating willingly," I said. I opened the door

and Winnie followed. The moon was brighter, somehow bigger though it had looked full last night. For just a moment I stood and took a long inhale of the night air. It smelled like sweet grass and there was a buzz of insects playing the night's soundtrack.

"It's nice out here," Larry said, wrapping an arm around me when I shivered.

"It is," I said, leaning into the hug. He tilted my chin, our faces got closer and... I punched him in the arm. "I'm still mad at you, Romeo. Between you and Cruz, I'm not going to need a gym. I'm just going to punch you both until my arms get tired."

Instead of looking like he was in pain, he laughed. Before anyone could speak, the front door opened, and Maggie called out.

"Get in here, you two. I'm itchy with this thing ou'side," she said and picked up the gun for good measure. I hesitated, but she walked in with it pointed to the ground, so I followed with Larry coming up behind me. Through the door, I was met with modern furnishings and a clean design that betrayed the outward age.

"What-" I started but seated on the couch was the fake Captain Jacks. He was still small, but his slight frame was somehow smaller, his eyes bigger in the sunken face. His facial hair was still non-existent, but his hair had grown out into a limp shag and he clearly hadn't been eating.

"Mickey," I said, and he held up his hands when Winnie growled.

"I don't have any cookies!"

Larry, Maggie and a man who could be Daniel's twin all turned to look at me. I opened my mouth to explain about the

NutterButters in court and the chocolate chip cookies in the chow hall, but I stopped. It was so absurd that just repeating it would be a nightmare.

Also mentioning cookies made me queasy after the four dozen I'd eaten tonight.

"Does Daniel know he's here?" I asked Maggie instead and she shook her head.

"You'd fill three encyclopedias with the things that man don' know," she said, and I smiled.

"Sounds accurate," I said and stared at the sad man on the couch. "Do you want to start?"

He shook his head *no* but at a low growl from Winnie, he changed his mind.

"Can you put a muzzle on that beast?" he snapped at me but before I could move, his sister had smacked the back of his head sending him folding forward.

"I ain' raise you ta puberty for you to be given' sass when you' wrong," she said, and he nodded.

"Sorry," he said to his shoes and Maggie sat down. I smiled wide.

"Can we be besties?"

"No!" Larry and Mitchell said at once. Also at once I punched Larry in the arm while Mitchell got another smack to the back of the head. Both men yelped and closed their mouths.

"Now... Mitchell, why does the scary man want to relieve people of their inhibitions with technology?" I asked and he winced. "And who else knows about it?"

"Can I start by saying I didn't know he was crazy? The program wasn't a secret, I guess lots of people know the basic premise." he took in the room as a whole, but no one looked understanding. "Great. In school, I met Chase and Emery and they had cousins in the city."

"Dayton?" I asked to clarify, and he shook his head.

"Trenton."

One piece fell into place. I gestured for him to continue.

"So, the cousins were trying to find a buyer for a predictive program based on outdated neural output research. With actual money, I could get up to date research and it could work, but the cousins marketed it as mind control and then Steve happened. He's sick, something in his brain that they won't operate on. He's convinced it can be fixed, but the doctors are just too cautious, and no one wants to get sued. They sold him on the idea that of course the doctors want to, and my program will encourage them to because they want to and they can."

"What does it actually do?" I asked and he shrugged.

"It doesn't do anything. It was an idea with a fake prototype," he said and I cocked my head to the side.

"So you had an idea, that you sold, to a crazy man using a fake prototype?" he nodded at my question. "But other people knew the concept and believe it's real?"

Another nod. This explained Cruz and the Army. It explained the crazy man in the bakery. It did not explain why Reverend Tim was dead.

I stared at the boy in front of me. He was both older and so much younger than me.

"How old were you?" I asked and he started counting on fingers. I massaged my temples. Anyone who believed this man is a genius had to be mad.

"I was 20 when Steve bought it, but the concept started in ninth grade. It would revolutionize the world if I could make a device to reduce inhibitions without diminishing motivation and motor skills," he was pleading his case and the jury had already reached a verdict.

"Who knows about Toxic Technology? The actual thing you sold?" I asked and he stared at his shoes.

"No one," he was lying.

"No one being... the US Government?" I poked harder but he just stared at the floor and I sighed. "I don't want to rain on your parade, sunshine, but that type of technology would be abused by more than just desperate patients. I mean it does the same thing as alcohol, but you have no say in your exposure to it. You think some bad guys aren't going to use that for criminal enterprises?"

"But it could also help a lot of people! Overcome fear and nerves, make the pitch and kiss the girl..." he was staring at his shoes again. Mitchell, for better or worse, was just a nerd. He wanted a confidence boost and got a maniac. I could both relate and still dislike him for it. "What everyone else wanted it for... that's why I never made it. I mean that and... you know, financing."

"Alright, so you sold a man something that doesn't exist. You were 20, it's been what? Fifteen or Sixteen years? He's still alive, you're still alive, it doesn't exist... how did we end up here?" I asked and he shifted.

"I used the money to go to school, and I worked hard to make it a reality. It's just the neural scanners couldn't create a common frequency," he said in despair. "The brain was too varied in signaling. A new miracle cure came about and he pushed my plan to the back seat. It was a reprieve, but when he ran out of money and was running low on time, he started looking for me to collect. I'd moved around some, but the only sure way to be safe was to hide out under a fake name. I bribed a guy, sent him to Mexico and just... became him."

More lies and half-truths, but I got the gist. He took on someone else's name, someone he knew, and the Army let him do it.

"Until Steve saw your dad?" I asked and he shook his head.

"He never saw my dad, he wouldn't have known my dad," he said and I raised my brows. "I swear; he didn't even know what I looked like until someone sent him a picture."

"Who sent him a picture?" I asked, trying to reconcile his statement with the ramblings of a mad man. Steve had said he found Mitchell. The good reverend had been missing for at least a month when I got home and Mitchell got back here at the same time I did.

"I... I guess he found it in my dad's things?" Mitchell said and I shook my head.

"If Steve didn't know your dad how did he find your dad? You said he didn't even know you. Who told him?" I asked and Mitchell's beady eyes were getting wider in panic.

"I just thought when he went to the church for his... wedding," Mitchell paused, "but it wouldn't make any sense if he'd never known. I guess I thought maybe someone had mentioned my name near a picture. I never thought I'd be able to hide forever or anything..."

"Mrs. Margot said she put out breadcrumbs to find who your dad was running from. Who was he running from? What was he in prison for?" I asked, looking at everyone in the room. No one seemed to know or have an answer.

"The charges were armed robbery, embezzlement and narcotics sales. Was he working with the mob? With the... drug people?" I asked.

"Cartels," Larry said, and I pointed at him.

"Yeah, that. Was he working with them?" I asked but Maggie and Mitchell were both looking struck by the stupid stick. Mitchell's mouth opened and his eyes glassy. Maggie... looked more confused than caught off guard. Something to think about.

"You... knew your dad was arrested, right?" I asked and they shook their heads, Maggie only after seeing Mitchell. "But... you called him a good for nothing and a liar, same as Skip?"

"He cheated on our mom," she said, crossing her arms. Confident and no hesitation in her voice. "He was a cheat and a lay about, claiming disability after he left the Army. That's where he said he'd been when he moved us. Our mom got sick and passed and he was let out of the Army, so he brought us here. Said he knew a man of the cloth who would train him in the ministry."

"Skip, right? You said your dad was a liar and Skip was just another liar. Did you hear anything?" I asked, trying to match yesterday's story with today's information. This would be so much easier if people would just tell the truth. Even now, she was shifting. Either she was trying to remember a lie or come up with a new one.

"I was quoting a bible verse I'd heard and was trying to understand, and he said it was hogwash. The only thing I needed to know about life was that someone would always want to stab me in the back so I should never turn around," she said staring at her shoes. "Dad had said they met in the Army."

I dropped my forehead into my hands. He was either in the Army, prison or both.

"Why did you pretend to be in the Army? How did you come to bribe that guy?" I asked Mitchell.

"My dad knew him," he admitted, and I chewed my cheek in frustration. OK, so actual retired Captain Jacks knew Antonio Scott and... maybe they both knew Skip. Now I wish I'd asked someone if Skip was a nickname or his given name, but I was not in a room full of answers. I was in a room full of half-truths and family drama.

"So... who are the goons? How does Steve afford goons?" I asked, trying to change the subject while I processed the first bit. "He said he needed your program and the money he gave you, one or the other would be fine but he wanted both. How does he pay hench people and need money?"

No one answered.

"Has he always had them?" I tried again and Mitchell shrugged. Maggie answered.

"No... I don't think so. When Steve first showed up to court what's her name, it was just him. Those men arrived at least a month after."

"So... who sent them and why were they listening to Steve?"

"Because someone told them to," Daniel Kirby said from the doorway and everyone jumped. Maggie pointed the shotgun before Daniel had so much as inhaled for another sentence. "Hey, Aunt Maggie."

"Well, if it ain't the law," she said, casually lowering the gun but not letting it go. She was somehow even less enthusiastic to see him than she had been to see me.

The delights of family.

"Maggie, for the last time, I had to cite you for egging the Mayor's house! He saw you do it and it is vandalism!" he said and I stuffed my fist in my mouth to muffle my laugh.

"He cheated!" she shouted, gun inching up.

"Probably, but it's still illegal to egg someone's house!" Daniel replied and I noticed his uncle had left the room at some point. This was not a new argument.

"They was his own eggs!" she shouted back and the gun got a little higher.

"Woah, hold up!" I said, taking the shot gun from her hand. "Much as I'm not against him getting shot, I don't want to be a witness or go back to the hospital. What are you doing here? Finally believe there's something going on?"

"I... I need your help. The rumor mill is churning out stories and speculations. Mo's place is trashed, and people think the former reverend was murdered. I need answers, but no one wants to talk to me," he said, and I smirked. "Yeah, yeah, I know."

"Fine, I'll help. Beats another night at the hospital. Where are we going?" I asked and he smirked back.

"I need you to come with me to the hospital," he said and I stared at him. "Leo wants to talk, but only to you."

Chapter Nineteen: Marked Men

I sat in the hospital waiting room with my arms crossed, pouting. I had seen both Nurse Sean and Nurse Denny who had made a point to applaud when my green camouflage cast was still whole, dry and clean. I wanted to flip them off, but my arm was in a permanent thumbs-up and I was too tired to move my other fingers.

"The doctor said we can go in soon," Daniel said, standing beside me. He was still in the same jeans and T-shirt he'd shown up at Maggie's house in, but his face was looking like a sad clown on a drama poster.

"Woo freaking whoo," I replied with a little finger circle. I'd already seen the Hench-people tonight, talked to them, knew they were idiots and I didn't like them. I'd rather go sleep in

Larry's bed than get answers. Preferably with Larry, but only because he was warm.

Also the sky was green and my Jeep was really a unicorn named Fred. As long as he didn't know, it would probably be fine.

"You could be more pleasant."

"You could have listened to Mrs. Margot and avoided this whole situation. I say my frustration is warranted," I snapped back, and he shook his head.

"She calls 9-1-1 about kids riding their bikes in the street by her house because she thinks they're going to get injured," Daniel was crossing his own arms. I was personally glad because it emphasized that he'd been letting his pecs go now that he was old and married.

Larry walked back up to us and threw a candy bar in each of our directions.

"Shut up and eat, you're both annoying the crap out of me."

I looked down at the Reese's he'd gotten me and my eyes watered.

"Oh god, what?" Larry panicked searching the room for a man with a blow gun or a taser who had discreetly attacked me.

"I just..." sniff. Wiping my nose, I tried again. "I just really love Reese's."

Daniel and Larry were giving me a wide berth and I decided that while I must look nuts, it was nice to see them alarmed. They were both looking way too calm and confident for the level of crazy revelations we'd had in one night. Two bad guys had come to town for two different Scotts, and no one knew who the secondary players were... or primary players since Steve was crazy and only participating at someone else's urging.

With another sniff and a few tear wipes, I shoved a peanut butter cup in my mouth. It tasted perfect and I tried to draw my legs up and sit in a little ball, but the hospital chairs were tiny, and I had too much leg. The hem of my dress skirt caught on my big toe and I lost my balance. The whole chair tipped, and I fell sideways, landing face up with my skirt bunched in front of Larry.

"Did I drop my candy?" I asked, new tears welling. He was not looking for my candy. His face was red and staring directly at my skirt. His sudden shifting reminded me that my underwear were... not full coverage. "Oh geez!"

Daniel was the first to offer me a hand. Upright, my skirt floated back into place and Larry suddenly needed his hands clasped in front of him. Daniel, bright red, could at least make eye contact. Without a word, he handed me the second Twix in his pouch and I stuffed it in my mouth.

"The doctor said you can go in, Officer," Nurse Sean said to Daniel and he nodded, motioning for me to go first. "Two is the limit though so your brother might want to get some air."

With a sneer and a full body scan I could feel blindfolded, Larry made a mad dash outside.

"Gonna check on Winnie!" he said, voice a few octaves too high. With one more smirk from the nurse, he was gone.

"You got good taste, Cyn the Determined. Between him and Mr. Suave, I'm surprised you have time to go outside and ruin casts."

"Mr. Suave?" Daniel asked and Nurse Sean gave a wink.

"There's a whole host of men interested in your victims. But he still only wants her," he sashayed up the walk and through the swinging doors, knowing we would follow. A uniformed security guard stood outside the door to a room that appeared bigger than any other in the area. Kirby gave his ID and we were cleared through the door. On the other side was a buffet for the eyes.

Sgt. Ian Cruz in full dress greens, a tall dark-skinned suited man I knew but couldn't name and...

"Commander Allen?" I asked, head tilting to the side like Winnie.

"Sharp."

That was all he said. Just Sharp with a look of panic and searching for the exits. Probably I deserved that, but it still stung a bit. My eyes scanned the room, but no one explained Allen's presence.

"Are you here for the Toxic Technology that doesn't exist?" I asked him. He shot a look at Cruz, but remained silent. My eyes bounced back and forth between them.

No one spoke.

"Cyn the Determined, you look good," the suited man said and my mouth fell open.

"Rodney? Holy cow did you grow up!" I reached out to give him a hug and he nearly crushed me.

"FBI has pretty good fitness trainers," he answered, and I shook my head.

"No, you always had fitness, I'm talking about this," I tugged on the bottom of his suit jacket. "I didn't think you knew how to put on anything besides jeans and gym shorts. Even the football coach had to force you to put on slacks for the MVP awards ceremony and you still refused to wear a collared shirt. I think even your mom gave up after the Yo Gabba Gabba senior school picture incident."

"Yeah, well..." he shrugged, and I smiled. "My wife has more influence than my mom."

"Can we get this over with?" a man wheezed in the corner and I turned to look at Leo. Cruz had done a number on his face, a number that was probably repeated by the medical staff to correct. His arm was in a sling, some smears indicated oozing stitches various places and his jaw was either wired shut or too painful to move.

"Yup. What do you have to say to me?" I said with a smile.

"Fu-" he started but Cruz accidentally leaned on his leg and the swear turned into a scream.

"Sorry, my bad," Cruz said moving his hand but he shot me a wink and I grinned.

"You're all sick," he slurred and I decided his jaw was definitely wired shut.

"No, I was vaccinated," I said and Leo opened his mouth. Cruz gave him a warning and he shut it again. "Let's start over. What is your real name?"

"Leonard Straub," he gurgled around spit.

"Unfortunate name to have when your jaw is wired shut. Who do you work for, Leonard? Besides Louis and Henry, who else is on your team?"

"Dunno."

"You... don't know? Do you get a paycheck?"

"Yesh," spit flew out when he answered me and I tried not to gag.

"Who signs it? Whose name is at the top?"

"Cass" he said, and I looked to the guys for help. None of them had any.

"A person named Cass? Cass what?" I asked.

"No, Cass! I was pay cass!"

"Cash... in an envelope? Did someone hand it to you? Where were you when you got word of this lucrative cash offer to be an asshole?" I was waving my hands as I spoke and a look at Cruz sparked an urge to look down. I was not still fully contained in the dress.

"Military. I wanted to be military, but I couldn't pass the test," he said and Cruz and I rolled our eyes together. Commander Allen tried not to laugh out loud. "Ish true!"

"The ASVAB? You couldn't pass the ASVAB? The minimum score to pass for the Army, National Guard and Marine Corps is 31. Most middle school students can get a 31," I was standing hands on hips after fixing my wardrobe and Cruz looked more than a little disappointed. I was too, a little bit, that bra was cute and deserved a night out.

"Got twenty-two," he said. "Third time, got a letter to join a side service for immeasurable skills."

With the slurs and number of times he needed the letter s, I was fighting tiredness and frustration. Obviously, he lacked a lot of mental aptitude, but who would believe an under the table military side gig letter? That was as bad as believing someone named Tim Church was actually a reverend.

"Were Henry and Louis also sent this letter?" he nodded in response and tried to yawn. It led to a stifled scream and a nurse bringing him water. "Where did you first meet the others?"

"For-da."

"For da... love of dog?" I asked and he thrashed in annoyance again.

"Forida! We wen ta FORIDA!"

"Florida?" I confirmed and he nodded. "Anyone besides Louis and Henry in Florida?"

He shook his head no.

"No one? Not even a looming shadow figure giving instructions in a robot voice?" I asked, trying to imagine a scenario that wasn't too advanced for these guys to operate. If they couldn't pass the ASVAB, they probably couldn't use more advanced technology.

"Pho," he said and held an index finger and thumb to his ear. I blinked and looked around. I was out of ideas and questions, someone else had to have something.

Cruz and Rodney were making notes, looking very official. Kirby was off to the side, holding up a wall. Commander Allen had stepped out to make a call. They were all silent, no one offering questions, suggestions or offers of insight. All we had was a bunch of men who weren't smart enough to join the military meeting in Florida to be specialty soldiers...

"Were you asked to do anything illegal?" a sudden inspiration struck, and the words popped out of my mouth.

He shrugged and his eyes shifted to the law enforcement in the room. Sweat popped up on his forehead and he started wrinkling and smoothing the top edge of the sheet. Every time he shifted; the sheet rose a little higher. First a big toe, then the rest of the toes.

"Too late to care about anything else you might have done, man. Kidnapping, attacking a man, destruction of private property and manslaughter. Might as well give us the complete resume."

"Ish just... da pho man fretten..."

He shifted nervously, tugging faster at the edge of the blanket on top of him. It rose to reveal his instep, his heel and a very pale ankle. The ankle was free of hair, but it wasn't free of markings. Moving closer the mark became an image. It was a tattoo and I'd seen it before.

"No freaking way," I said, looking at his ankle. Just in case I was tired and hallucinating, I poked the flesh with my casted arm. Definitely real, definitely there. The image was simple, a hunting knife piercing a stack of cash emblazoned *American Capitalist*. I'd seen better artwork on prison tattoos, but this one ... This one wasn't prison ink, but it did remind me of some of the worst years of my life. This one was identical to one I'd seen on my first day in Florida. "Where's Henry?"

"What is it, chica?" Cruz asked but I looked to Nurse Sean.

"The one-handed bandit? He's passed out up the hall," he gestured with his thumb and I went out of the door. At a fork I turned and saw Nurse Sean behind me. He gestured to the right and we followed a little tape line and the rhythmic sound of an equipment beep. Room 407 had the door standing open and I peeked inside to see a woman, dripping sweat with her legs in the air.

Not that room.

Next door that stood open was room 414 and a pale lump was in the bed. At first I thought it was a dead body under a sheet, but the gentle rise and fall showed the skin was just very, very pale and the sheet had a head. It wasn't moving but the monitor showed the lump to be alive so I crept closer and leaned in.

Definitely Henry.

He looked less terrible than I thought he would, a minor relief. He still looked one step away from buying the farm, so to speak, but less close than I thought. His hand stump was bandaged, and they'd managed to clean him up pretty well. His head lump was starting to bruise, and his leg may have been in some sort of stabilizing cast, but he would probably live. He might need a hook hand and he'd have a limp, but he did try to shoot me so basically, we were even.

I tugged free the lower left corner of the blanket. With a twitch of the sheet, I revealed a tanner ankle with the same tattoo I had just seen. A dagger through a stack of money, on the outside of the left ankle just like the other two.

"Mean something to you?" Rodney asked, while Cruz snapped a picture. He'd gotten some of the first man on his phone and he'd now be only a few shy of a complete set.

"Yup. Means I should get a new court martial hearing," I answered, crossing my arms and looking more annoyed than angry. Winnie was always the best judge of character and the Army should have looked into him the day she peed on his leg and I'd seen a random tattoo on his ankle. Also, I should have mentioned the weird tattoo to someone or suggested someone look into him. "They are working for Colonel Ross."

Chapter Twenty: Dead Men Walking

F inally, we pulled up in front of Larry's house and I fell onto his shoulder.

"Carry me, I'm dying!" I whined and he laughed.

"No way. Not after you puked chocolate and cookies all over that hospital bed," he joked, but Winnie was still keeping her head out of the window to avoid the smell. The dog would eat literally anything, but chocolate and cookie vomit were where she drew a line. I had expected to have to fight her off, but she got as far away from me in the car and stayed there the whole ride. Not only was my dress ruined, but not even my dog wanted to be near me.

Larry opened the rear passenger door and she shot out, leash free, to stand on his front step. Next, he opened my door, and refused to breathe through his nose. I considered punching him in the gut so he wouldn't have a choice, but I could smell me and it wasn't great.

Still though, he could be nicer.

"You gave me the Reese's!" I complained, sliding out of the passenger side of my own Jeep. He was holding the door, keeping his face tilted away.

"I didn't know about the cookies," he said, taking my hand but keeping me a fair distance from his personal space. Winnie jumped on the front door, paw pushing the lever handle and opening the door. With a tail wag, she trotted inside.

"You should have assumed the cookies. I was in a bakery! You don't lock your front door?"

Alarm bells were sounding in my brain. My dog could open doors, but doors should be locked. Why wasn't this door locked? Winnie wouldn't try a door handle if she didn't smell something.

Please be food, I thought.

"Not when I leave the house to cross the street. Did not know I would be beaten into driving to middle of nowhere Ohio," Ohio was said on a wide yawn and he raised his arms over his head, showing off some smooth, firm abs and I licked my lips... which reminded me the last thing I did was throw up all over a hospital room.

"Someone was maimed across the street! You should lock your door."

"Maimed by you and I'm sleeping with you," he answered, and my heart fluttered in my chest making my brain go hazy and my body hummed with approval. "I mean... not *with* you with you... but I'm there..."

He was turning red and shifting awkwardly. My stomach plummeted and I considered throwing up again. Something heavy crashed in the house and I screamed.

"Winnie!" I ran inside, wishing I'd kept one of the guns I'd had tonight. I cleared the threshold, staying low and hoping Larry would follow suit. My eyes adjusted and Winnie was sprawled on the floor snacking on something that had been in a glass jar.

"What's that?" Larry asked from behind me and I kept inching closer.

"It looks like... a..." I finally got close enough and my stomach turned. "Winnie out!"

"Cyn, what is it?" he asked again as I scooped the object off the floor and dropped it on the counter. We both stared, a little pale and a lot nauseous. "I should call Daniel."

I nodded agreement and then the spinning started.

"I'm... going to lay down..." I said, watching the finger on the counter multiply by a million while I crashed gracelessly to the floor.

A rhythmic beep sounded beside me and I growled.

"I better not be in the hospital," the beeping stopped, and someone laughed.

"No, chica, that's the ambulance backing out to go to a real emergency and take your finger to the morgue," Cruz answered, and I blinked up at his face.

"You're pretty," I whispered, and he pushed my hair off my face.

"You are sweaty, pale and smell like vomit," he said back and scooped me off the floor. Without discussion, he carried me down a hall and into a bright lit room. Flinching, I let out a small scream that echoed.

"Pain?"

"Bright!" I squealed and he laughed. I was dropped onto the counter and the door closed behind us. "What-"

He was pulling his shirt off over his head and kicking off his shoes. My dress was tugged over my head and my shoes disappeared. Without moving away, Cruz turned on the shower and warmed the water. My throat closed and I just stared, mouth filling with water at the chiseled perfection on display. A hand went to his zipper and I clapped my hands over my eyes.

Well, one hand covered my other, the other smacked myself in the head with a cast and my vision swam.

"Relax, chica. You need a shower and I need to keep you from drowning," he said, tugging me against him. His body was smooth and warm, his scent an intoxicating mix of salt and sea. Involuntarily I moved my face into the curve of his neck and licked a long line up to his jaw.

"Stop," he said, capturing my face and turning my head away from him. "Not here, not like this, Cyn."

After pulling a trash bag from under the sin and covering the cast, Ian Cruz pulled me into the warm shower and I shivered.

He shifted me, my whole back pressed against his front as the warm water beat a steady rhythm against my front. He held tight, passing me a washcloth and soap. A quick glance and I was still wearing my bra and undies. I went to unhook the bra and he stopped me.

"Insurance policy. I only have so much self-control and you're a little handsy," he said against my cheek and my whole body shuddered. He reacted and I grabbed for the one part of him I hadn't yet seen through the now soaked boxers. "No."

He took my hands and moved them back to me, keeping my back pressed tight against him.

"Why?" I asked, rubbing my back against him. My brain was filled with the hum of bees, severed fingers and vomit-covered victims of gun shots. He was the solution to my problem and I made a grab for him again.

He responded with a growl.

Shifting both of my hands into one of his, he took the soap and washcloth. First my arms, then my back, he was washing with the efficiency of a soldier. No motion was wasted, no movement was extra, I was clean and wrapped in a towel with a toothbrush in my hand minutes later.

Worse, my mind was still filled with the horrors I'd seen. It was impossible to hide from them out of the shower, standing in the light of the sink, staring at the lemon-yellow toothbrush.

"Brush," he said, and I nodded. "What's wrong?"

"N- nothing. I'm not going to drown. Can I be alone?" I asked, not meeting his gaze.

"Cyn," he reached a hand toward me, but I stepped back.

"Just... alone," I turned away from him and stared at the wall until I heard the door open behind me. One long whistle, the tap of claws on tile, and Winnie was in the bathroom with me. A pile of clothes was placed on the sink counter, and he ruffled Winnie's ears but I wouldn't look at him. Cruz closed the door and I dropped to the floor beside the only person I could depend on, Winnie. With my arms wrapped tightly around her, I cried until there weren't any tears left.

Dressed in the sweats from the counter, I went into the living room. The new green dress was stuffed into the trash, along with the wet underclothes. There was no need to keep any physical reminders of this day.

And at this point in the evening, there was no longer any need for a bra and underwear.

At the end of the hall, I heard the beginnings of the speculations and I stopped to listen.

"So the finger was probably put in the jar on your counter while you were out," Rodney said.

"Yeah, but why and whose is it?" Larry answered.

"We think it belongs to Henry, but we'll have to... compare," Cruz.

"Who would leave a finger in my kitchen?"

"We don't think it was for you. Who knew Cyn was here last night?" Daniel this time but I heard someone clear their throat that may have been Cruz.

"I don't know. Anyone could have known. We left the hospital, drove by her house and came here. Despite the drugs she came quietly without causing a disturbance. It wasn't a secret she was here," Larry again.

"How did someone get Henry's finger?" I asked, walking into the room with Winnie. "Didn't all of his parts go to the hospital with him?"

All of the men stared at me and I refused to look anything but calm, even and neutral. Rodney was by the front door, leaning against the wall. Presumably not to wrinkle his suit but who knew for sure. Maybe he remembered that time Larry broke an ant farm in elementary school and was afraid the hobby had followed to adulthood.

Daniel and Larry were on the couch, both in lounge clothes. Cruz was beside the door frame leading to the kitchen, he had some damp spots on his clothes and wet hair but was otherwise completely the same as he had been minutes ago.

Except the concern in his eyes.

"I got sick; I'm not broken. How did someone get the finger?" I repeated, looking at anyone who wasn't Cruz.

"We don't know," Daniel answered. Everyone shuffled, but no one offered an alternative.

"Did you find Colonel Ross?" I directed my question at Ian's shoes to avoid the pity in his face.

"No," he replied, and the silence stretched on as I stared blankly at the counter that had once held a finger. The broken glass had been cleaned up from the floor, but there was something under the table. Ignoring the stares, I walked over, dropped to my knees and shimmied under the table. It was a piece of paper, a small smear of blood in the bottom corner.

Switching to a cross-legged position, Winnie joined me and bumped her head against mine. We shared a look, and I knew she was telling me the smell matched. This note had come with the finger. My hands shook, but I took a deep breath and kept going. Cruz dropped to the balls of his feet in front of me and looked at my shaking hands.

"Do you want me-"

My eyes flashed fury and he promptly shut his mouth. I unfolded and stared at the words. Except it wasn't so much words as a picture. The symbol from the tattoo was stamped on a computer printout of a map. My eyes were tired, and I had to squint, but the symbol was placed on top of... my parent's house.

"I think..." I said, turning my head both ways and passing the paper to Cruz to lay flat on my back. Winnie licked my face and I held her close while Cruz processed, and Daniel worked at mobilizing the town's two officers while Rodney contacted actual professionals.

"Cyn," Larry said and my head flopped to the side. "It says seek. Seek what?"

"I... I don't know," I stared blankly at his face as I tried to process this and Cruz appeared beside him.

"Where is Ross stationed out of?"

Cruz grimaced and I stared.

"Let me guess, he also doesn't exist?"

"No, chica, he does. It's just... he's technically been dead for four years," Cruz said, eyes filled with something like alarm. It was the first time tonight he'd looked genuinely fearful of something and I felt my heartrate go up. "We're trying to ID him now."

"Start with the real Captain Jacks, Antonio Scott and Skip," I said, trying to imagine some sort of criminal walking in on my parents having date night. May their mental scarring drastically surpass that of my parents. May they lose a limb for making me think about my parent's date night. "I think Scott really was in the Army. I think all of them were, and they had business in Florida or near it."

"Why do you think that?" Cruz said and I stared at his beautiful mouth. Strange that he wanted to know why but didn't seem concerned on this front.

"Because there is literally no other reason to go back to Florida," I said and went back to staring at the bottom of the table. "I'm guessing none of this is new to you, Mr. Toxic Technology."

He stared at his shoes, still not confirming my suspicions. The Army had known Captain Jacks was a fake. Had they let him stay because they wanted the program? Meaning Cruz was here to either get the program or make sure no one else did.

"They're going to be pissed when they learn the program never existed," I said to no one in particular. Cruz shifted but held his silence. No one spoke again until a throat cleared by the door and I turned to see Daniel.

"Cyn... your parents' house is empty.

Chapter Twenty-One: Hide and Seek

D aniel, Ian and Larry tried, but they couldn't stop me.

I was in my Jeep, Cruz just managing to climb in with Winnie before I threw it in reverse and pulled out. I blew through four stop signs and scared the crap out of a deer, but I was at my house in under three minutes. Cruz looked like he might throw up, but I didn't have time to worry about him.

"Winnie, seek!" I ordered and we went inside.

The house was dark and quiet. She led me upstairs to my parent's empty bedroom, to the door of their empty playroom, to Seth's old room which is now a library. There wasn't a sound, no sense of life, but Winnie's nose kept working. Down in the basement, I found all of my clothes clean and folded on top of the freshly made bed, but still no humans.

Winnie led me back up the stairs and pawed at the back door to the kitchen. I grasped the handle and went out into the backyard. Winnie circled the house and moved toward the storage shed on the far-left corner of the backyard. I ran toward the structure, seeing a light coming from underneath the double door. A small window was set about eight feet off the ground.

"Here," Cruz laced his fingers together and I put my right foot into the step. He lifted me and I grasped the ledge of the window. It took a minute to see through the dust and fight my revulsion at the cobwebs. When I could finally focus, my heart stopped.

In the middle of the floor was my dad. His pants were gone, his arms were bound behind him and a scarf was wrapped around his eyes.

"Dad!" I shouted, pounding on the window. But he didn't move.

I jumped out of Cruz's hands, ran to the door and looked down at my feet. I was only wearing socks. I looked at Cruz's feet, he was wearing boots.

"Open!" I shouted and he stared at me. "You have shoes!"

"Is it locked?"

I grabbed the handle and turned. It was not locked. Throwing open the door, I ran into the room screaming.

"Dad!"

Then I froze.

The air was heavy with incense and music of the rhythmic variety. Behind my dad in the corner was my mom in all leather, holding a flogger.

"Oh my god!" I screamed and ran back out of the barn. Behind me, I heard the sexy laugh of Ian Cruz, mocking me.

"Chica, your family is..."

"Shut it!" I pointed a finger in warning at him, but he would not stop laughing. So I did what any woman who just saw her parents date night up close and personal would do. I stomped on his foot.

"You still aren't wearing shoes," he said, snaking his hands around my waist. "How much like your family are you? Do I need a safe word?"

"Geez!" I said, shoving his chest. He held me tighter and inhaled at the nape of my neck. My heart was still racing, and my breathing was shallow. I took a long inhale and tried to settle myself but instead I caught his scent, and my pulse went back up.

"You OK?" he whispered and I nodded. His warmth was comforting, his hands a solid weight on either side of me. My parents were fine, so whatever the map had meant, it didn't concern me. "Are we OK?"

"We-" Winnie let out two sharp barks and I stopped talking. She was at the far-right corner of the house and I went to her, stooping at the sight of another jar. My heart skipped a beat and I hesitated. If there was another dismembered finger in there, I was going to need another shower.

A smooth arm reached beneath the house, praised Winnie and unscrewed the lid.

"No fingers," Cruz said, passing me the note. There were no blood smears or droplets. It was a promising sign that accompanied the wedding program for Amber and Steve, aka Ryan the Count. Beneath the location was a handwritten note beside the same stack of cash being stabbed symbol:

Til death

"Cyn, what are you doing here? I thought you were having a sleepover at Larry's!" my mom had come from the shed wrapped in a robe, her mouth fell open at the sight of Cruz. "That's not Larry!"

"Ma, Sgt. Ian Cruz, Ian Cruz, my ma," I said, staring at the note. "Til death" on a wedding brochure for a wedding that didn't happen?

"Are you and my daughter..." she started and I felt him smile so I stomped on his foot.

"No, ma. He was my K-9 training Sgt and though he still claims to be that I think he's CIC. Also, he gave me a shower earlier and did nothing, so he's just a friend. He might even have a condition," I said in revenge for the laughter. He looped a finger into my pants and pulled me flush against him. "I'm really great at just being a friend. Ask Mo, I got her out of jail."

"We're going to talk about that," he said against my ear and it became somewhat hard to stand.

"Cyn! What happened to Larry?" my mom insisted, and I shook my head.

"He's fine, ma," I said, returning to stare at the paper. The faces looked the same as they had on the copy from earlier. Amber's fake smile grated my teeth, but it wasn't unusual. Names were the same, date was today, time was earlier.

"Cynthia! I asked you a question!"

"What, ma?"

"If he's fine, why are you with this man?" she was being rather accusatory for a woman who was just wearing leather holding a riding crop.

"He runs faster than Larry, ma. We thought you were in danger and…" the address was wrong. The wedding had been in the center of town. This address was on the outer edges of town.

"Ma, where is Tourney?" I asked, interrupting whatever rant she was on about Larry. Cruz was strangely quiet but not retreating from his place flush against me.

"Tourney? There's nothing out that way except the cemetery," she answered, just as puzzled. Taking the paper, she stared at the address. "Did little Amber get married in a cemetery?"

"No, but I'd like to put her there permanently," a hand flew out and smacked the back of my head as the words left. "Ow!"

"That's poor manners, Cynthia. We did not raise you to speak death to the living or ill of the dead," she raised her hand again and I conceded.

"I'm sorry, I'm sorry," Cruz was laughing his ass off next to me and I gave him my best death stare and an elbow to the gut. "We gotta go now, ma."

"Cynthia, you can't just go running around with strange men in the middle of the night…" she started, but I was through the back door and traveling toward the front.

"Bye, ma! Have a good night! Don't forget to let dad have air!" I hollered and we were back in the car.

"Cyn, your family..." Cruz began.

"Don't start or I'll murder you at the cemetery," I answered, but before I could drop the car into reverse, he hauled me across the front seat into his lap and kissed me. His mouth was warm, needy, exploring every inch of mine until I was warm everywhere and my body was trembling with anticipation.

"I didn't say I didn't want to Cyn, I said it wasn't the right time," his voice warmed my temple, and a small quiver went through my lower parts. He might be a liar who was trying to steal a program to control people for the government, but he was a sexy liar and my body had no qualms.

"Is... Is now the time?" my voice was way too breathy, and I wanted to punch myself. I also wanted to be much, much closer.

"No. We have to go to a cemetery," he said, kissing me again and pushing me back into the driver's seat.

"Is that where you want..." I stammered and he burst out laughing.

"No, chica. That's where the man who left you a finger is. Nice to know you have an open mind, though," he took my hand, squeezed it, and put it on the gear shift. I nodded and shifted into reverse, backing out of the driveway with his hand still on top of mine.

Not only was the cemetery outside the boundaries of the town, it was apparently outside the boundaries of electricity and pavement. The bumpy dirt road threw Winnie against the window, me into Cruz and vice versa. There was no way to avoid the ruts and trenches, because there were no streetlights and I nearly crashed into the gate when we arrived.

"Who gave you a license?" Cruz mumbled as the seatbelt braced him from going through the windshield. The black metal wrought-iron gate was topped with ominous looking winged creatures that may have been intended to start life as angels. In reality, they looked like vultures with fingers, and I shuddered.

"State of Ohio," I opened the door. Winnie gratefully jumped out and sniffed at the fence. She too looked concerned about the winged things on top, but she decided to put her nose to the ground rather than dwell.

"They should take it back," he said and I shrugged. "You drove through a wall in Afghanistan, you ignore speed limits and stop signs..."

"But did you die?" I asked, following Winnie along the wall. The gate was locked, but based on Winnie's nose, we didn't need to open it. I followed the fuzzy green, ancient brick wall toward the farthest end of the road. Ian Cruz followed, but he was keeping a safe distance in case I fell... or maybe just making sure he was first back to the car for driving privileges.

About fifteen yards before the wall ended at a meeting point, Winnie stopped. She buried her nose into a shrub, sniffed long and hard before digging. Her paws worked furiously, and I stood clear to avoid the sand. After a minute, she stopped, looked at me and barked. Cautiously I walked over and looked into the hole she'd dug.

"What..." I pulled out a plastic bag and inside was a feather. The logo was drawn on the plastic; this is what we were meant to find. Just... why?

"A feather?" Cruz questioned from behind me, and I nodded. It was short, white and coated in some sort of film. I turned it one way and then another, but it was just a feather. My phone went off and Cruz stuck his hand in my pocket to grab it out.

"Yes?" he waited for a beat. "No, she's here and her parents are fine."

Another beat and he shuffled his feet.

"Any idea where?"

I poked him in the ribs, and he held up a finger. At a pause on the other end, he explained.

"Mitchell Scott is gone, and his sister doesn't know where he is. He'd gone out to check on the chickens and never returned," Cruz explained, and I stared at the feather.

"Chickens?" I said and he stared at the feather.

"Where else are there chickens in this town?" Cruz asked and Daniel answered through the phone at the same time I did.

"Roger's house."

"Is it far from here?" he asked and we both answered no again.

"Alright, we will meet you there," Cruz said and hung up my phone. He put it back in my pocket and rested his hand on my hip. "Is this the dead chicken man?"

I nodded and kept staring at the feather. The light from my cell had caught something shiny, and I held it up to the moonlight.

The feather glinted again. Pushing the feather between my fingers, there was a grainy texture through the plastic, which managed to be thicker than the traditional freezer bag. Instead of having a zipper seal, heat had been used to contain the object inside.

It glinted again.

"Do you have your knife?" I asked, shifting the feather toward the moonlight.

"Are you going to stab me in the leg?"

He flipped open the knife and handed it to me.

"No, but only because it would ruin my plans for later," I said, inserting the knife into the top of the heat-sealed bag. I slid it carefully across the top, surprised by the vacuum seal effect. It was almost as though the goal was to keep air from touching the feather.

Which was proven when the whole thing burst into flame.

Chapter Twenty-Two: All the Colonel's Men

"**I**s it bad?" I asked again.

I was in the passenger seat of my own car being driven by a man to a medical facility for the second time that night.

"Just keep the ice pack on it," Cruz replied, holding my hand. He wouldn't let me use a mirror, but my face was definitely burned. The cold pack had been in the First Aid kit in my trunk, as was the gel he smeared on my face and hands. I'm not sure who'd stocked that first aid kit, but I probably owed them a sandwich.

My cast was toast.

The arm underneath was un-injured by comparison to its counterpart, but I could see the bruising from where they had to break it again the other night. There was a small lump and I squinted.

"Are we... going to the hospital?" I asked and he nodded.

"Yes, chica. You need a new cast and better burn dressing."

"Then what happens?" I asked, trying to sound seductive but he laughed.

"You go back to Larry's house and sleep," he said, placing a hand on my leg and squeezing my thigh.

"Not allowed with you?" I asked, leaning my head against the window, hurt mingled with relief. He was so hot and cold... or maybe just regular hot. I closed my eyes. Freaking men.

"You are always allowed with me," he picked up my injured arm, touching it gently and placing a small kiss on the lump. "I just don't have anywhere to take you."

"What do you mean?" I asked, but he remained quiet so I let it go.

Grudgingly, I had to admit Cruz was a better driver. He avoided the potholes and the ruts in the dirt road, navigated around wildlife, and re-entered the highway at a safe but accelerated speed that kept the back end of the car in line with the front. I leaned my head back, the cold pack pressed tight, and the feel of Ian running his thumb in small circles on my thigh lulled me to sleep.

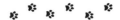

"Not who I expected to show up," Nurse Sean said, and I blinked at him.

"What do you mean?" Nurse Tina was wrapping my arm in a new cast. I hadn't asked what color it was, nor had I cared. I just wanted the dumb thing on my arm, a lifetime supply of whatever they put on my face, and a pillow. It was almost one in the morning and no one could explain to me why I had stayed awake for this. The nurse pinched my arm, and I got a momentary head rush.

"I called Daniel when I learned, but he wasn't available, so I left a message. I figured he'd be the one to get back to me," Sean said and I stared at his mouth but the words were beyond me.

"What's going on?" Ian asked and I switched to staring at his mouth. It was such a nice mouth... Now there were two mouths, and it somehow was not creepy.

"The men are missing," Sean responded, and Ian motioned for him to elaborate. "The one who lost a hand and the one whose jaw we wired shut, they're gone."

"Gone... how are they gone?" Ian asked.

"Someone came in, wanted to see them. The officer knew her, said it was OK and she went into the room. Then the officer was out cold, the men were gone, and no one could identify the woman," he was speaking in a conspiratorial whisper and my eyes were suddenly very heavy.

"Drugs?" I asked, swaying around in a circle.

"No... we didn't give you..." Nurse Sean snapped around and then put the blood pressure cuff on my arm. "Crap, push the blue button on the wall!"

Cruz pushed the button, and the room was swimming in blue light. I had the urge to sing Under the Sea, but it probably wasn't the best time. My eyelids fluttered and I saw the flash of a needle go into Nurse Tina's pocket.

"Hey," Cruz shouted but there were a few of him. None of them were in focus.

"Nurse. Nurse has needle, needle bad," I rambled. As the overhead lights danced and blended.

"Which nurse?" he asked quietly.

"Lady nurse. Nurse lady," a large pool of drool was forming at the corners of my mouth and Nurse Sean came in.

"Go, ask questions, we got her," he gave Ian a shove as doctors and medical professionals rushed into the room. Machines appeared, they made noise and people rushed around. Someone shouted about blood and it went dark.

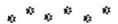

"Rise and shine, Cyn the Determined," a farm hand from the dairy said and I blinked up at him. His name was Jim, or Joe... maybe Peter? It was dark and smelled like grass. Everything was spinning and out of focus. Throwing up again seemed like a good idea.

"You help?" the words were slurred, and spit dripped down my face.

"No," a female outline appeared behind him. "We not help."

My brain told my head to nod but it was hard to tell for sure if it cooperated. It wouldn't turn left or right, but the lack of ambient light said we'd left Yellow Springs. As did the complete absence of sound beyond the chirp of insects and the rustle of grass and leaves. It sounded peaceful, like home. Home and... chickens.

"Inside," a new voice. It was deep, masculine. Much older than the two in front of me. The farm hand put his hands under my arms, Tina took the feet, and my ass was dragged along the ground. Nothing was focused, but it was familiar. Like everything else around me, I knew the sounds and the space, but had no idea where I was.

A door creaked open, and the air shifted. We were inside now, and a small amount of light drifted in from a neighboring room.

Kitchen maybe.

"Put her with the others, there's still one more," he said and I blinked. The older man sounded like a villain from an old timey movie. It was impossible not to hear the jaunty piano music and picture a handlebar moustache. My head bumped against a doorframe, I was thrown to the ground and the door slammed shut behind me.

"Wude," I muttered, my voice sounding like I'd become a victim of the Weasley twins. Holding perfectly still, I listened to the room. There were at least three people breathing, not in sync. Someone to my left was shifting and something to my right hadn't moved.

Carefully, I extended a hand to feel the mass. It was rigid, but squishy. The temperature was cool but not cold. My fingers probed and found a damp spot. It was fabric, covered in something sticky. Without thinking of all the options, I put my fingers to my nose and sniffed. Metallic, sticky... blood.

"He's dead, Cyn," Maggie said from directly in front of me. I couldn't make out her shape, but I also wasn't certain my eyes were open.

"Who?" I croaked and then choked on the spit that had pooled in my mouth. I sputtered and hacked, but Maggie stayed away and no one else appeared.

"Dunno who he is. You OK?" her voice was concerned. "I'm tied up. Daniel and Larry are tied up and gagged, not sure completely why... "

I nodded and tried to lift my shoulders. Success. Next up was my legs, a second success. I dropped my head forward into my hands to stop the spinning and felt the dead man's blood smear across my forehead. When the urge to vomit passed, I opened my eyes and could see a stream of moonlight filter in through a window about seven feet up. It was a narrow rectangle; frosted glass window and I checked my assumption.

We were all in a bathroom. I tapped the floor. We were all in a bathroom in a manufactured building. I inhaled the air, unclean. I checked the toilet seat, it was up. Unclean man, manufactured home, sound of chickens.

"Roger's house?"

"Dunno," Maggie said, but her voice was strange.

"Mitchell?"

"Dunno that either," now she was concerned again. "I was hoping you did."

I patted the pockets of my sweats and felt a hard solid box. With an unsteady hand I pulled out my cell phone. With a quick battery check, I flipped on the flashlight app. Daniel and Larry were tied back-to-back in the shower, eyes bugging out. Maggie was bound to a pole above the toilet. The dead man was... Steve.

"Ugh..." I groaned, knowing Steve's blood was on my forehead was more gross than being on the floor of a bathroom. The Kirby brothers were closest, so I crawled along to them and removed the cloth in Larry's mouth. I freed him from his brother, and he took over while I collapsed.

"You OK, Cyn?" he asked, checking my pulse.

"Yup," I answered, but I closed my eyes again.

"Are you going to call for help?" he whispered, and I stared at the flashlight in my hand. It was also a phone. Since my mouth was still filled with spit, I elected to text Ian Cruz instead of call. The happy chime dinged from just outside the house and I held perfectly still. A flurry of movement came from the other room and a herd of footsteps stampeded out of the open door while another set smashed through the one to the bathroom.

"Get up," it was Louis the Brutus. Daniel surged to his feet and gave him a fist to the gut. He let out a woosh of air, grabbed Daniel by the collar of his shirt and flung him into the neighboring room. "I'm not in the mood. Get up!"

Larry helped me to my feet, and we trooped into the living room. Louis took up position by the storm door and scrutinized each of the pseudo soldiers as they trooped in. The farm hand, Nurse Tina, Leo and Colonel Ross all ambled into the room.

They formed a little circle on the outer edge, and I glared at the colonel, waiting for him to speak and reveal himself as the leader. Someone came up from behind me and yanked the phone out of my hand, shoving my head to the floor.

"Who's out there, Cyn?" she said, and I turned to look at Maggie.

"You... what?" I asked, as she tried to unlock my phone. She was waving it in front of my face, but the device wasn't locked, I'd just put it through a lot.

"Who did you call?"

"No one," it came out as more spit than words, but it wasn't a lie.

"Whose phone dinged outside, Cynthia?"

"I don't..." a swift kick connected with my chin and I tasted blood in my mouth. Maggie's face had gone red, the calm woman lovingly disciplining her brother was gone. This was Mad Maggie.

"Enough games. Who did you call and where is my brother?" Maggie repeated, stepping to the very center of the circle and looking down at us.

"Colonel," I slobbered, and she laughed.

"Just another foot soldier," she said, tapping his shoulder lightly. "It took some time to collect them all, but I have quite the team. At least I did... until you."

"Your team?" I asked, looking at the room of assembled hench people. Louis's arm was bandaged from where Winnie bit him. Leo somehow had even more bruises than I noticed in the hospital. The farm hand similarly was sporting a black eye that I couldn't place. The only people in the room without injuries were Nurse Tina, Maggie and Colonel Ross.

"My team," she confirmed with a wide smile.

"We are so not besties anymore," I slurred into the floor.

Chapter Twenty-Three: Confessions

"You killed your own father?" I asked, mouth hanging open. That was low even for a criminal.

"No… that was the dead man. My father had outlived his usefulness, but it was unfortunate," she said with a shrug.

"Steve?" It came out like "sleeve", but she understood and cocked her head to the side.

"No, Henry. Steve was just nuts," she said with a shrug. "I found him hiding here and shot him. Henry was a liability who could cost me more than he gave me."

"You broke him out of the hospital to kill him?" I asked, annoyed by the inefficiency.

"No... he's still there, just in the morgue," Nurse Tina chimed in and Maggie nodded at her. Leo shifted uncomfortably and I got the impression if I outed him as a man who runs his mouth, she'd shoot him dead on the spot.

"That was smart. My dad told my brother a secret. A secret I need to fully access my revenue streams. A secret that he didn't understand until you told him our father's history. He realized... well, that I wasn't the uneducated blubbering mess he thought I was. Poor timing for me, he was about to tell me after days of hiding out everything he'd learned from my dad's old drinking buddy in Mexico.

He went to the bathroom after you left and ran. I caught Larry and Daniel, got Leo out of the hospital, knowing he'd stay true. I was going to use the Kirby brothers to get you, but then you walked into Beverly and Tim. My good luck continued."

She gestured toward Nurse Tina and the farm hand. Beverly? Who names their kid Beverly? She looked much more like a Tina... the drugs were wearing off and I knew Cruz was outside... or at least his phone was. It can't have been a coincidence.

Hopefully he brought Winnie.

"What about my uncle?" Daniel breathed out, having recovered from Louis' retaliation and seething with anger. He apparently cared about the family name, if not the family members he'd ignored half his life.

"He's about as bright as you are," she smirked. "He thinks all the money I bring in is from chickens. Never saw a reason to tell him otherwise. He thinks my brother and I are talking to the police."

She laughed and a sharp pain seared through my skull. Eyes drooping closed, I pressed my throbbing head against the floor. Maybe the drugs were wearing off. Not a great thing, as I could suddenly feel all of my burns, bruises and aches from the past 24 plus hours.

"What happened to your face?" Maggie asked, looking down at me.

"Your stupid feather," but it sounded like baby gibberish. I swallowed and tried again.

"Did you know your brother was posing as a Captain in the Army?" I was trying to piece together why she'd send men to help capture her brother using her father. Why not just ask?

"No. He was hiding out from that Steve guy and I wasn't especially motivated to find him, but my dad would have told me if I asked. When that hacker trail appeared leading to my dad, I thought I'd need a fall guy so I saw to it Steve found my brother. Then my men leveraged my father in the guise of helping Steve, but they were supposed to get information from both men. I needed his contacts in the cartels and the location of their cache, but Henry got carried away. Henry always gets carried away. Should have retired him sooner. Then you show up. Why did you have to show up? My brother was an easy mark until you brought up logic and reason."

She half-gestured to the colonel at some point but my mind had blanked out and I wasn't sure where in the story he'd come up. I replayed what I could remember, but still nothing.

"Who's he, then?" I asked, staring at the grouchy old white dude. If I was going to die, I'd like to know who wanted me out of the Army.

"Colonel Ross, his death was just to end an investigation, but no one checks if you're dead when you walk on a base. He, my dad, the real Captain Jacks... they worked together but my dad took the fall. I took over while he was inside, but I never got the complete list of contacts. I was just a go-between. Then I pretended we were cut out to my dad. Then I quietly took over," she shrugged as though this wasn't needlessly complicated.

"What did they steal?" I asked no one in particular and Ross bared some teeth.

"Munitions. Went on for years after he left the crew," Ross filled in. "For years we'd hit base munitions bunkers stealing guns and ammo... until San Antonio. The new group was weak, but what they lacked in imagination they made up for in simplicity in design. Cartels wanted weapons, they traded drugs for weapons, and we sold the drugs to local distributors. It was flawless."

"Until... San Antonio?" I repeated, blinking. "You weren't in San Antonio. There were... six guys... the one with the jerky and the bottle explosive. He burned up. Then the one who got hit in the arm, the one whose butt was partially removed by Winnie... And the one who ran..."

"After taking a bullet to the leg. I can't wait to pay Winnie back for that kindness by the way," he growled, and I fought my way to my feet.

"Touch her and die... again!" I made it to my knees before I fell over again. "What the hell did you give me?"

"Ketamine," Beverly said with a shrug. "Gave you enough to take down a charging rhino. You should probably be dead."

"I'm hard to kill," I muttered as three sharp knocks shook the whole trailer.

"Open up, Maggie!" A man bellowed. She froze and pulled a gun from the back of her pants. With a wave of her arm, the others armed themselves and took cover, leaving the hostages in the center of the room.

"Who is it?" She asked, and the trailer shook with another knock.

"Mitchell! This has to stop, Maggie!"

She slid back the bolt and the door opened to reveal Mitchell Scott. He looked disheveled, filthy and covered in little scratches. Clutched between his hands was a cardboard box, his fingers near white with the grip.

"Well, I guess I don't need this lot anymore," she said, grabbing the box and tossing it to Louis. Mitchell flinched, but he relaxed when the large man set the box on the counter. "Sit with the rest of the idiots."

Her foot flicked out and connected with the back of his knee. He dropped to the ground beside us and took Larry's hand. The men exchanged a look, they had a plan. Mitchell looked at me, I was apparently allowed to be part of the plan.

"Alright, Mickey, how do I connect with the cartel?" Maggie said, pointing the gun at her brother.

"It's in the box," he said, shooting a look at me. "It's featherweight but the information is good."

His eyes widened at featherweight and I blinked. Feathers? What would feathers have to do with drugs? Larry stared at me with meaning and looked at my fried arm skin.

"Feathers shiny as gold."

Again, the meaningful eye raise and I stared. Shiny feathers... that sounded pretty. I'd seen a shiny feather. Just tonight actually...

"Seriously?" I hissed, grabbing Daniel by the hand while Maggie inspected the box. Daniel opened his mouth to object but I dug my nails in and bared my teeth. He fell in line and wiggled toward the door with the rest of us while the bad guys weren't looking.

"What's in the box, Mitchell?" Maggie asked, not turning to look at us. The door was still at least two yards away and if the first feather was any indicator, we needed to be moving faster.

"Dad told me that the best part about being in the Army had been following clues. That he'd made his living with treasure maps and childish games," Mitchell said, voice staying calm. We were a mere foot closer, but it was better than nothing. "Like the stories he used to tell us about the pirates."

"What pirate stories?" Maggie's eyes flashed our direction, but she didn't turn.

Unfortunately, Beverly did turn.

"What the hell are you doing?" Beverly turned her gun on us as she spoke. Her hand was steady, and she looked experienced in shooting holes in people.

"Just... giving space?" I answered but it was a crap lie. Her finger twitched and now the whole group was looking at us. Three additional guns, each of them trained on... me.

A distraction would be really great right now, I thought.

"Get back-" Louis said, as the door slammed open behind us. I jumped and dragged everyone toward the wall closest to the door. Cruz was standing there, gun extended, with Winnie.

He fired at Beverly, Winnie went after Louis who screamed and took off down the hall. Beverly went down, clutching her abdomen. Leo jumped behind Ross and then slunk behind the kitchen counter, arms above his head.

"What do I pay you people for?" She shouted, fury re-directing her gun toward her own men for a moment. Ross started raising his hands in surrender, when she hit him with her gun. "Put your hands down and open this!"

She pushed the box into Ross' chest and his hand shook as he tried to peel off the tape.

"Ian!" I said and he spared me a glance. "Just like Afghanistan but bigger!"

I took a tight grip on Daniel's arm, and he nodded. He and Mitchell had done this together. We were going to run, and they were going to burn. Larry was with Mitchell; Cruz had our backs and Winnie... Where was Winnie?

"Winnie! Here girl!" I shouted and she pranced to my side. Strips of black fabric were hanging from her teeth and her pride radiated. Her nose lifted, scenting the air, and she caught sight of Colonel Ross. She let out a low growl and just the tip of her tail wagged as she crouched low.

"Shoot it!" Ross said, eyes wide at Winnie. She crouched lower.

"Winnie!" I called at the same time Maggie shouted.

"Shut up and do what I said, grandpa!"

Ross' hands were shaking too much. He couldn't get a grip on the box and he dropped it.

"Winnie!" I called her again and with a reproachful look, she came to stand beside me as Maggie directed a kick to Ross's abdomen. He fell over in a heap on the floor, landing beside Beverly who was suspiciously unmoving.

"Useless, worthless..." she scooped the box off the floor and set her gun on the counter.

"Go!" I screamed, dragging Daniel. When he resisted, I did what Winnie would do. I sunk my teeth into his arm. With a scream, he turned toward me and I cold cocked him.

"Excessive, chica," Cruz said, grabbing his other arm and dragging him down the steps of the trailer. Mitchell and Larry hadn't made it far, the lot of us tumbling down the last step and landing in a puddle of water and chicken crap as the sun creeped up the horizon.

"Keep going!" I shouted, hauling Daniel along with Cruz while Larry and Mitchell led the way. "Faster!"

Daniel was coming to and he took over dragging his own body with Cruz's help.

"Assaulting an officer!" he started shouting. Cruz let his grip slip and the man went face first into a pile of chicken poop. Larry and Mitchell stifled laughter.

"Sorry man," Cruz said, picking him back up. We'd just cleared Roger's chicken coop when a whoosh sounded behind us and I tripped as the heat from the trailer reached us. We landed in a massive puddle as Rodney and the FBI arrived with uniformed service members.

"Crap!" I shouted and Larry looked over at the same time as Cruz. The cast was sopping wet and destroyed. Another burp of fire erupted from the trailer and the men laughed as the wail of fire trucks arrived and the assembled alphabet agencies took a step back.

"I'm going to need you to give a statement," Cruz said, reaching over to give me a hug. "Your Jeep is over there, but this time try not to get drugged and abducted from the hospital, chica."

His lips brushed my temple, and he was gone.

"Maybe I should drive," Larry said, staring at his brother. "Just so we don't crash when my brother starts hitting you."

Winnie growled in warning at Daniel, and he put his hands up.

"She hit me first!" Another growl. "Fine, but I do this under protest!"

Winnie wagged her tail and we trudged off toward the Jeep in the rising sunlight, another cast in my future.

Chapter Twenty-Four: Sharp Investigations

"I should be allowed to see the woman who saved the town!" Mrs. Margot shoved past my mom and sat beside me at the kitchen table. My head was resting on my arm on the tabletop, and I had a straw going into my coffee mug so I could drink without lifting my head. I'd gotten the silicone straws as a gag gift, but they turned out to be the best thing ever when you're basically an invalid.

"Hey, Mrs. Margot," I said. Winnie gave her a nose to the crotch in greeting and then laid back down. A week had passed, and I managed to not need my sunshine yellow cast replaced. Mostly that was attributed to the fact I was also not going to work, solving crimes or leaving the house, so it had decent odds. My week-long recovery was coming to an end and I was due back at the farm tomorrow. My cast was to be wrapped in plastic and Joseph had agreed that I could participate in birthing from the sidelines until it was removed by an actual medical professional.

"Cyn, you haven't been outside this house," she clicked her teeth in disapproval, and I shrugged.

"Wanted my eyebrows to grow back first."

My mom was standing in the kitchen at her island, watching and drinking tea. Since Ian and I had left, she'd only heard that I was at the hospital, drugged and I burned Rogers' house to the ground. Like a kid who was grounded, I didn't answer my phone, open the door, or take visitors. After two days of silence and shrugs, my mom had stopped asking questions and kindly asked me to remain in the basement like Harry Potter under the stairs until I was feeling human and reasonable.

The first day of my self-imposed quarantine, I ordered a pound of Cheez-its, a pound of Oreos, 500 K-Cups and a Keurig machine. Amazon next day is truly a godsend, because I didn't have to come upstairs once until today. Today, I had to relearn what the sun looks like in preparation for tomorrow.

Winnie and I had become vampires. We went for runs and nighttime strolls while the rest of the town was quiet and still. I'd watched Mo bake bread through the window. Larry stayed up late reading books. Joseph had a disturbing hobby of screaming at produce after dark that I only ever intended to admit I knew about if he tried to fire me.

"I need you to come with me," Mrs. Margot said and stood up.

"I'm…"

"It wasn't a request, Cynthia," she clicked with her dentures and I dragged my head off the table. From there I had to drag my body out of the chair. "Bring your partner… probably also the coffee. You look like crap."

I stared down at myself. My feet were only in socks and I had on unicorn leggings with an Army sweatshirt.

"So… change?" I asked, hands wrapped around the coffee mug like it was the only reason to exist.

"You will need shoes, the rest is fine" she advised, and I shuffled to the basement, grabbed some clogs, and shuffled back up.

"Keys?" I asked and she shook her head.

"We will walk there."

"Where is there-" my mom started, but Mrs. Margot held up a finger.

"You will see soon enough. For now, the ladies and I have something as a thank-you for Cynthia and we want her to know first," she said and nudged me to the front door.

Winnie immediately stopped to pee in the front yard. She took her time and I stared absently for someone to bombard me with questions. It was nearly noon on a Sunday, and I noticed the complete lack of people on the street.

"New minister auditions," Mrs. Margot said. "I wanted no part in that after I confirmed the church was officially supplying one."

I nodded and we continued up the block to Main St.

"Did they die?" it came out as a whisper.

"Speak up, child."

"Did they die?" I asked the sky this time, shaking slightly at the thought of her answer.

"No. They are hairless and scarred, but they'll live. Except the one who, as I understand it, was already dead," she patted my hand and I stared down at Winnie. She'd stopped to sniff a giant candy cane and I took in the town for the first time. It had a bright, festive feel. Thanksgiving had just passed, the town was dressed to the nines for Christmas and no new people were dead. I had forgotten the massive tree and shiny bobbles that hung from every inch. A giant Menorah was assembled in the gazebo, the electric candles lit with each night of Chanukah that passed.

"Is Larry and Daniel's uncle OK?" I asked, stopping to pick-up a fallen over poinsettia.

"He's fine as he always was. Not that bright. Maggie didn't drug him or anything. My niece called him a prop in school. You could put him anywhere and he'd just fill in as scenery," she said, tugging me along from where I was staring at the garland coated in snowflakes. "It's cold, Cynthia. Let's move it along."

"I forgot how pretty it is at Christmas," I commented, mostly to myself. "They turn the lights off after ten."

"Well, you can't forget from here," she declared, stopping in front of the library.

"The... library?" I asked, and she handed me a small brass key.

"Next to it, dear," she replied and nudged me over. A small window to a single office was lit with gold lettering on the front.

Sharp Investigations

"We thought you could use a space to work when you're not at the farm," she pressed a silver key into my palm. "We also thought you'd like to live in the apartment above it. Mrs. Zuber's son lived there before, but we cleaned it. Your young man helped."

As though she summoned him, Cruz walked out of my office holding a rag.

"Hey," he said and I waved. "Eyebrows are looking better."

"You look..." hot, mouth-watering, edible, "well."

"Liar," he said, coming flush with me and taking my hand. "Can I take over, ma'am?"

"No you may not. Cynthia, we wanted to thank you, but we also want you to know that we appreciate the help and services you offer this town. The space is yours, so long as you never turn away someone in need."

I smiled and gave her an awkward hug.

"I won't Mrs. Margot," I said into her hair and she nudged me away.

"And you still have to work at the farm because the people in this town are cheap," she said, and I nodded.

"Yes, Mrs. Margot."

"And try not to set anything else on fire," she added.

"Yes, Mrs. Margot."

"Alright, now you may show her around," she said to Ian and he gave her a bow. "What the hell was that?"

"I... don't know," he said, turning red and I pulled out my phone to snap a picture.

"Oh, my dog, this is the best day ever!"

"Give me that," he said, grabbing for my phone and I ran into my new office space. I was certain Mrs. Margot was laughing at us, but she ambled away with a wave as he chased after me and I locked him out. He pounded on the door and I stuck my tongue out at him.

"No boys allowed!" I shouted.

"You forgot something!" he pointed toward his shoes and a very sad Sgt. Winnifred Pupperson stood there. She looked forlorn and there was no way I'd lock my best friend out. I looked from him to her and relented.

"Sorry, girl," I said, opening the door for them both to come in. Cruz lunged toward me and I danced out of reach. Winnie bumped my hand with her head, and I hid my phone in my underwear when I learned my leggings do not have pockets. Cruz watched my hand go into my pants and his eyes filled with heat. "So..."

"So..." he said, hands in pockets rocking awkwardly from heel to toe. "About the whole Captain Jacks... we knew he was fake, but we wanted to keep an eye on him. Not just for the Toxic Technology program, but we thought maybe his dad was involved in the munitions thefts. We figured if we kept him nearby, we'd know when something happens."

"So... you're CIC?"

"I'm CIC," he confirmed and I nodded, stroking the top of Winnies head. He was standing there, hands in his pocket looking nervous and sexy, weight shifting back and forth. My mouth watered and I tried to remember why any of it mattered... everything was fuzzy behind the pounding of my pulse in my ears.

"You... like it?" he'd moved closer, but it wasn't close enough.

"Maybe... I haven't seen upstairs yet," I said, giving him a wink. His face broke into a dirty smile and I gave him one back. "Is there a bed?"

"Let's go find out," he said, and took my hand to lead me upstairs.

Sneak Peek of Book 2: Chasing Empty Caskets

Chapter One: F.M.L.

Staring at the paperclip on my desk, I wondered how hard I would have to stab myself in the eye to die. I'd never been suicidal or prone to ideations of death, but an hour with this man and I was ready to throw it all away. Life, liberty, snacks, coffee...

Maybe I was going a little too far.

I should aim to scramble my frontal lobe to the point where I could no longer understand the man sitting in front of me.

Except I already didn't understand him, and my brain was perfectly intact. His voice droned on with the same thing, the same accusations...

Instead, I should poke myself in the eardrums so I could no longer hear him.

It's sad when one has to resort to self-mutilation to make it through the day.

Mr. Figs wasn't an attractive man. I'm told in his prime he looked like George Clooney, but now he just looks like The Penguin from the Michael Keaton Batman movie. He was short, round, had a nasally voice, and he smelled like rotted garlic and onions, causing me to choke on my next breath. Another wave of the stench wafted toward me, and I tried to breathe through my mouth before I lost consciousness.

The rotary fan made another pass of the room, and the scent disappeared.

I sniffed the air, nothing. My eyes dropped to the floor and stared at my partner. Sgt. Winnifred Pupperson, ex-military police K-9 just like I was her ex-military handler. She was a snack-loving German shepherd Malinois mix, and as far as the Army was concerned, we were carbon copies of the same nightmare. The two of us had made Laverne and Shirley look like put together ladies, but we'd survived quite a bit together. Despite the honorable designation in our discharge, we had been anything but during our four years of service to the United States. There was the destroyed marketplace in Afghanistan, the crushed pretzel statue in Germany, the cow in Sweden... not to mention the attempt to blow up Florida, though I personally considered that a service *to* this nation and not against it.

A small *pooft* sound escaped and the smell came again. It was stronger with every wag of her tail, and I fanned my face.

We may not survive this gas.

"That was disgusting. How can I survive years in Florida, but you raiding the trash can at 3AM for cheese wrappers is grounds for a chemical warfare treaty violation?" I said to her, and she let out a wide yawn and rolled onto her back. "Could you at least try to be professional while murdering us?"

Another *pooft*.

"Ms. Sharp, are you even listening to me?" the small man whined, and I turned back to him.

"Yes, I'm listening. I've been listening for an hour. Nothing has changed, Mr. Figs. I cannot go to your house and exorcise your wife's ghost from the premises."

"Why not?" his voice whined at the end. "Aren't you an investigator?"

"I'm not a paranormal investigator, also-" he interrupted me.

"Didn't Mrs. Margot make you promise to help? My dead wife's ghost is a problem! Help me with *my* problem, Ms. Sharp!"

He was just this side of a toddler stamping his foot and whining about how he didn't want to go to bed. I clawed at my face and hoped for a meteor or a radioactive spider. Maybe a Russian man who wanted to experiment on me in the name of science?

Nothing.

"Her ghost is not a problem," I tried again, calmly, while banging my head against the desk. "You are a problem, but her ghost is not now, nor will it ever be, haunting you because you will definitely die first."

The pot of coffee sat empty beside me. My cup beside me, declaring me a unicorn trainer, was also empty.

Mr. Figs sniffed in disdain and I found my patience was as empty as my caffeine supplies.

My office was a small room that sat beside the town's outdated public library. The wide front window, looking out onto Main street, sat beside a wooden door with an old school brass knocker. Above the office was a minimalist apartment where I lived. The apartment had a kitchen, a bathroom, and a closet. There was plenty of room for my bed, Winnie's bed and snacks for both of us. As far as closet space... I didn't have many clothes from when I was in the Army that weren't issued by the Army. After living in Florida for four years, most of the ones I had purchased were tossed due to sweat stains and weird smells. The whole building belonged to an older woman who I'd helped rid her church of imposters and crooks just over a month ago, Mrs. Glen Margot. The agreement was I wouldn't refuse help to any townsperson who asked, but I was starting to think living in my parent's basement wasn't so bad.

"She's haunting me! I can't get away from her!" he shouted again, and I stared longingly at the paperclip.

"Mr. Figs, she is not dead. She is standing right there!" I pointed at the front door. In front, leaning against an old four-door vehicle in a hideous shade of blue, was a pleasantly plump woman in a flowered dress. She had a sweater on in deference to the January air and an ice cream cone in each hand. One white and the other a shade of pink that screamed sugar rush.

"That's her ghost!" he insisted and I got up, Winnie rising beside me. "Banish her to the afterlife!"

"I am much more likely to banish you to the afterlife if you don't..."

"Ghost! Ghost!" he shouted over me and started bouncing in his chair.

"That is your wife. She is alive. And she bought you ice cream!" I marched to the door and pushed it open. Winnie scented the air and her tail went full helicopter. "Stay!"

Winnie flopped over in dismay. We both knew Mr. Figs didn't deserve his wife's ice cream, but Winnie hadn't earned it, either. The farts and the four AM alarm every Thursday when the trash men came were definitely grounds for ice cream refusal.

I glanced at the calendar; it was thankfully only Tuesday. The woman cleared her throat.

"Mrs. Figs!" I called, gesturing her in. She came closer and smiled wide, her wrinkled face pleasant and comforting.

"Good morning, Cynthia," she said, extending a hand. "Would you like this ice cream?"

"Sure," I said, taking the cone of single scoop of chocolate chip. "Thank-you."

"Of course. Why has Elmer been in here for an hour?" she asked. He was pointedly looking anywhere but at the door. At least he had stopped jumping and shouting. If he gave himself a heart-attack it would be the second time I had summoned EMS here for a client this week.

"He said you are dead and haunting him."

"He... really, Elmer? You brought Little Cynthia Sharp into this?" She was scowling at the man, and I stifled a laugh into my first bite of ice cream. At six-feet tall and a size 14, no one had ever called me little. From my blonde hair to my lavender eyes, I was much more a "Cyn" than the proper name Cynthia my mother gave me. It would seem that the older folks in town didn't believe in nicknames. They also thought everyone should be addressed by their complete name- Cynthia Sharp and Sgt. Winnifred Pupperson, K-9, was the official title added below the gold lettering naming my business Sharp Investigations.

"Banish her ghost at once!" he shouted, and Winnie tilted her head. I ate more ice cream and leaned against the door frame. This was now someone else's fight *and* I have ice cream.

The day was looking up.

"Stop it, Elmer! Just because I said the Game of Thrones books are better than the TV show does not mean I am dead!" she exclaimed, and my mouth fell open. My last suspected "haunting" had been from a woman with cataracts confusing a portrait of her with her deceased husband with a mirror. She said he was always with her in her house and wanted him with her everywhere. I pointed out that it was a painting, and when I moved it she tried to beat me with her walking cane. Apparently denial is more than just a river in Egypt.

Once the bruises healed, I made a new policy to no longer make house calls.

"This is about... books?" I asked, staring between the two. I love reading, but Game of Thrones? I had been tortured to the point of considering self-mutilation over Game of freaking Thrones? While it was my opinion that both the books and the

TV show weren't the greatest, I now had a whole new reason to hate the series.

As well as the people in this office.

"No! It's about taste, and she doesn't have any!"

Again, I had to disagree. Except, she married him so maybe that was true.

"The book is always better!" his wife countered, and I rubbed my temples with my index fingers.

"Books are stupid!" he shouted, and she fisted her hands on her hips.

"Books are not stupid, Elmer. You are dyslexic and audio-books make you feel old!" she countered and he went back to jumping.

"I'm not old! Audiobooks are for people who don't have TV!"

"Stop," I sighed into the silence. No one bothered to even lower their voice.

"STOP!"

"Do you want a divorce?" I shouted over both of them and their heads whipped around.

"No!" they shouted at the same time. I was both disappointed and relieved.

"Then work through this at home. I have to get to work; we're birthing a calf today." I walked over and took each of their shoulders, faced them toward the door and gave a little nudge.

"Which do you prefer?" Elmer asked as Winnie helped me herd them forward, hoping to score some ice cream.

"Prefer what?" I asked, taking my first bite of the cone now that I'd cleared the ice cream off the top. Winnie had them just at the threshold.

"The books or the show?" Mrs. Figs asked and they both stared at me seriously. They weren't walking out the door, and suddenly my brain wasn't the only thing frozen. Two Figs stared at me with hope while also ready for condemnation. They demanded an answer.

"I... uh...." Stuffing the cone in my mouth, I made a show of looking at my watch. "Late! Sorry!"

Full coward mode activated; I ran upstairs. Once there, I stared at the space. It was small, but comfortable. The couch was used but not old, a faded grey faux suede that Winnie loved to flop on. The same place I'd shared one of the most promising kisses of my life. I could still feel his hands under my shirt, his lips on mine...

I shook my head clear.

"Focus, Sharp. You need to get ready for work." I scolded myself out loud, and Winnie cocked her head. Just in case, I checked my cell phone. No missed notifications and I sighed.

Grabbing my backpack, I checked that it still had the work essentials of sunscreen and a hat. I stuffed snacks in my cargo pants pockets. Oreos and Cheetos for me, biscuits and doggy jerky for Winnie. Metal water bottle for each of us went into the bag, and a change of clothes, just in case. With a last look around, I sighed and checked my phone again.

Still nothing.

I listened at the top of the stairs and couldn't hear any voices. I crept lower and paused at the door that separated my space from the office. Still quiet. I pushed the door open a crack, and Winnie poked her nose into the room. She looked back at me, I looked at her and nodded.

The room was clear.

After opening the door, I checked that nothing new had entered my office and ducked at the sight of the Figs outside of the front window. They were still yelling. Mr. Figs was having a tantrum so loud, Daniel Kirby from the village police department had shown up. I fought back a snicker as I crawled along the floor to the wooden door. Back pressed to it, I reached up and rotated the deadbolt to the locked position. Satisfied with my immediate safety, I got off the floor and stood at the window a moment to see Officer Kirby take an ice cream cone to the face. I smiled wide, waving goodbye to Daniel as I closed the curtains on the front window and left through the back door.

Winnie and I arrived at the farm twenty minutes early. I fiddled with the radio, but all I could find were talk shows and smooth jazz. My CD player held a country music CD leftover from when Mo and her EMT had needed a four-wheel drive vehicle to explore the sand dunes on the coast. Mo, aka Mary O'Connor, was owner and operator of Mary's Muffins and More. She was one of my best friends, had been since elementary and the only person I'd trust with my Jeep. Despite being a "trip to the beach for four-wheeling", there was a lack of pictures and her bra was under my back seat. I expect they just needed a little more room to maneuver than her Nissan offered.

I was so proud.

I stared longingly at my silent phone.

Then I picked up the third of four iced coffees I'd purchased on the way here through a drive-up chain. I hadn't had enough cup holders for all four, but I took care of the problem in the parking lot by immediately drinking two and chucking the empty cups in the bin with Winnie's whipped cream cup. Cup three was gone as some guy sang about having dirty shoes. No idea why Mo thought this was romantic, because I'd personally prefer he take a shower and chill on the couch.

Without any good reason to stay in my car, I hopped out and made my way to the barn, killing iced coffee number four. I looked around at the cow, sheep, and goat enclosures, at a loss for where to start. Our newest calf would be born in the arena on the other side of the barn. The sheep milk was the last thing I checked yesterday, and the goats were just jerks. Speaking of jerks, I checked my phone again.

"You know how they say a watched pot never boils?" a friendly voice said behind me.

"Shut up, Larry," I grumbled, stuffing the phone back in my pocket.

"It's been a month, Cyn."

He ignored my request. I checked my pockets for duct tape to force the issue, but came up with only cookies, so I ate one.

"I don't know what you're talking about," I responded, but I was lying. Sgt. Ian Cruz, my K-9 training handler in the Army, had come to Sweet Pea to solve the mystery of a fake captain, a weapons theft contingent that had been working for decades, recover or destroy a mind control program, and set up the Sharp Investigations office. He was Cuban, hotter than the surface of the sun, and has now made out with me on two continents.

Then he promptly left to never be heard from again.

Most recently, he had shown me around my new apartment, and just as I was about to get my hands on ALL of him, in front of the very comfortable couch, he left. A phone call came in, he listened, stared at his shoes, and left. He said he'd be back, he said he'd call, he said I could have anything of his I wanted.

He was a stinking liar.

"Yeah, you do," Larry walked up and put an arm around my shoulders. He reached down and unclipped Winnie's leash, but she stayed with us as we ambled toward the open-air paddock where the cows usually gave birth. Better than goats.

Currently in labor was Pooh. They'd originally named her Winnie the Pooh, and then Winnie, but I called her Pooh because it helped me keep straight which four-legged friend we were talking about.

"Whatever." I stuck a hand in my pocket and pulled out another Oreo, stuffing it in my mouth.

"Do you wear cargo pants just so you have places to keep your snacks?" he asked and I narrowed my eyes at him. "I'm not judging."

"Yes, you are. For your information, these pants also hold Winnie's snacks, her toys, and a Taser for annoying childhood friends." I smirked at the last, but he only smiled wider.

"You don't have a Taser," he said smugly, and I bared my teeth at him.

"Are you willing to risk your neural pathways on it?"

"Yeah," he said, moving closer and stuffing a hand in each of my thigh pockets. While my cargo pants were loose fitting enough that it wasn't terribly intimate, my breath still caught at the intrusion.

"Hey!" but he was too quick and he had all my dog treats, snacks, and my cell phone. He held them above my head, taking small steps backward with Winnie trotting along beside him. He danced down the barn aisle and I gave chase. We rounded the horse stall on the end, collided with a fence, and landed in a pile of hay with Winnie jumping on each of us in turn. She licked our faces, grabbed her treats from Larry, and ran.

"Seriously! What is this? Are you six?" I demanded, completely out of breath.

"I just wanted to see you smile." He handed everything back and I touched my face. There was, in fact, a smile on it.

"You have to clean up Winnie when she poops out all those treats," I looked over at him. He was tall, muscled in a gangly way, with dark hair and light eyes that filled me with fond memories of being a kid and building mud castles in the sandbox.

"No, I don't. I'm a doctor," he said, wiggling his brows. I punched his shoulder as I remembered the not-so-fond memory of the time he took Amber Carter to the 8th Grade Dance because I wouldn't give him my string cheese.

"Exactly, an *animal* doctor. She's an animal and you just gave her three times the recommended daily amount of treats," I crossed my arms, as though it settled the matter and I won. Unfortunately, crossing your arms flat on your back just pushes your boobs into your chin and Larry smiled bigger.

"He's missing out," Larry spoke softly, his smile going from immature to serious.

"I don't…" my mouth started but he pressed his against it, warm and inviting. It was a brief kiss, and just as suddenly he was gone. On his feet, he offered me a hand up, but I was confused and processing.

He waggled his fingers and I instinctively reached out. Taking his hand, I let him pull me up. He took a small step back so we weren't pressed against each other, but if we inhaled at the same time, we'd be touching. He didn't release my hand. and I wasn't sure if I wanted it back. The feel of his lips lingered on mine and we stared at each other.

A moment passed, and then another, neither of us sure what to say or do.

Larry broke first and the moment ended.

"I know I messed up before…" he started, and I decided I did want my hand back. His face flashed a second of hurt, but he stuck the hand I emptied in his pocket. He scratched the back of his head with the other hand, lifting the bottom of his sweatshirt. It would seem his arms weren't the only part of him that had gained some muscles, and I involuntarily licked my lips. Then I remembered his most recent "mess ups".

"Messed up?" I asked and he stared at his shoes. "Messed up like when you said you couldn't go with me to the prom because someone else already asked you, but really you decided you'd rather not go than go with me, your supposed friend? Or when I asked you to hang out on summer break my first year of college, but you said you were busy and then Mo and I saw you in the drive-thru of Chicken Palace? When we waved, you drove off and spilled soda on the employee who worked there."

"I…" he opened his mouth, but I shook my head.

"No, Larry. You were a crap friend, and honestly, I don't know if you're any better of a friend now. Messed up is far too kind for what you did. Every time we got close, you slammed a door in my face. Now, after all these years, suddenly you want to kiss me in a pile of hay and act like you're somehow better than Cruz? He never promised me anything. I recall in fourth grade, you promised to always be there for me on the way home from the zoo, and then you blew me off because of the teasing."

"That's not fair! It was fourth grade!"

"Yeah, and I needed you. I needed you and you were gone. Mo was the only one there. She was the only one who made time to see me and maintain a relationship. You were too busy to even grab a bucket of chicken with us, but not too busy to get one for yourself."

"I texted you to go bowling with me during those two months after college before you went into the Army, and you never even responded!" He shot back and I stared at him, head cocked to the side. Texting? In the post 2010 world? I hadn't done much texting... because...

"You know I didn't have a phone for those two months, right?" I asked him, and he switched from indignant to confused. It was as though I had told him I was from the planet Pluto and bled green goo. "And Pluto is a planet!"

"What? No... what happened to your phone? What the hell do I care about Pluto for?"

"It fell out of the Jeep in Missouri and I ran over it," I said with a shrug and he gaped. "Also, Pluto is a planet. I just want everyone to know Pluto is a planet and deserves planet status."

Great, I was rambling about Pluto. My face was warm, and my heart was racing. I could still feel his mouth on mine, and it was warm and comforting.

"How..." he started, then changed his mind. "Or rather why?"

"Don't ask. It's like the arm casts. I couldn't keep a damn cell phone to save my life then." I brushed hay off my clothes and looked toward Pooh who needed some more water. "As far as Pluto..."

I shifted uncomfortably.

"So then... how did you get in contact with people?" he was still baffled by a woman in the second decade of the year two thousand not having a cell phone.

"Same way I did before there were cell phones," I said, noticing Pooh also looked to be panting a little harder. "Time to get to work."

I turned toward the arena, ordering Winnie to stay. She and Pooh had a history of animosity. Specifically, Winnie thought she was a really big dog who wanted her snacks and Pooh thought she was a nightmare on four legs in need of a kick to the head. Neither was wrong, but we needed the calf to be born without elevated cortisol levels, so I kept them apart on principle. Just under the fence, something caught my leg and I turned over my shoulder to stare at Larry, holding my foot.

"Problem, doctor?" I asked, grabbing the rail to keep my balance. My leg ached, and I acknowledged there was a very real possibility I needed to stretch more.

"Just give me a chance, Cyn," he said quietly, letting go of my foot and taking my hand. I shook out my hamstring and popped my hip just to watch him wince at the sound.

"A chance to do what, Larry?" I asked as I popped my other hip and stretched out my back.

"To make things between us right."

"We're fine, Larry," I said, turning my back to him again. "Go get your stethoscope or whatever."

"If we're fine, have dinner with me Friday?" he said and I turned to gape at him. "If we're fine, then there's no reason not to go, right?"

My mouth worked, opening and closing, but nothing came out and he smiled.

"I take silence as a yes," and then he walked away, showing me his very cute ass. My face burned and I tried to make myself look away, but it was hypnotic. Still, a girl has to have her pride.

"I take my grudges to the grave, Dr. Kirby!" I shouted after him, but it came out just a little breathy. He shot me a wink over his shoulder and did a little shimmy for my benefit.

Stupid cute butt.

Stupid Larry Kirby.

About the Author

A person with several dogs

Description automatically generated with low confidence

About the author

E. N. Crane is a fiction author writing humorous mysteries and thrillers with plus-sized female leads and their furry friends. She is one of two authors under the Perry Dog Publishing Imprint, a one woman, two dog operation in Idaho... for now. My dogs are Perry and Padfoot, the furry beasts shown above. They are well-loved character inspiration in all things written and business.

If you are interested in joining my newsletter, please subscribe here: https://e-n-crane_perrydogpublishing.ck.page/57 8ed9ab37or on my website, PerryDogPublishing.com

You will receive A Bite in Afghanistan, the prequel to the Sharp Investigations Series, as a thank-you for joining. The newsletter has content from both of my pen names, the other of which rights spicy romance. If it's not your jam, no worries. I only have one newsletter for mental health reasons, but you can follow Perry Dog Publishing on all socials to stay on top of the latest news... and pet pics.

Made in the USA
Las Vegas, NV
10 December 2024

13817069R00153